With a defiant gesture ... levelled it at him. A loo... the sight of it.

'If you do not move out of my way immediately, I shall shoot. I mean it!'

'You have already killed once. I've told you the second time would be easier,' Douglas replied humourlessly. He gave her the impression she did not frighten him in the least. Did he think she would not pull the trigger? She would! She must! If he detained her . . . She dared not consider the consequences. She had betrayed her mistrust to him now, and he would have no reason to keep her alive. 'I don't think you have the nerve to kill me, because deep in your heart you know your suspicions are wrong.'

'I know nothing of the kind!' she flung back. She tensed as he turned aside and thrust the torch he held into one of the wall-holders. What did he intend to do? Surely he was not mad enough to challenge her?

He moved so swiftly that she had no chance to fire. One minute he was turning back to face her again, the next he had flung himself across the space separating them. The pistol was torn from her hand. She was grasped roughly by the front of her jacket and flung backward into the stall. As she caught at a post, trying desperately to keep her balance, she caught sight of his face, and she cried out. It was the face of a devil, with blazing eyes that held murder. . . .

Valentina Luellen was born in London in 1938, and educated in Gloucestershire and London. She began writing at school—mainly because she loathed maths! It took her twelve years of writing before she had a book accepted, but she has now had over 40 stories published. Historical romances are her favourite to write, because she loves researching into so many different countries, learning about customs and costumes and the way people lived hundreds of years ago.

Valentina Luellen and her husband moved to Portugal six years ago when he became seriously ill. There his health began to improve and they now live in a renovated farmhouse on the Algarve with their 20-year-old son, 21 cats, two Portuguese dogs, and around 100 trees—almonds, olives, figs, plums, lemons and oranges —most of which they planted themselves.

Valentina Luellen has written 20 Masquerade Historical Romances. Recent titles include *Where the Heart Leads*, *The Passionate Pirate*, *The Devil of Talland* and *Black Ravenswood*.

# LOVE, THE AVENGER

## Valentina Luellen

**MILLS & BOON LIMITED**
15–16 BROOK'S MEWS
LONDON W1A 1DR

First published in Great Britain 1986
by Mills & Boon Limited

© Valentina Luellen 1986

Australian copyright 1986
Philippine copyright 1986

ISBN 0 263 75591 6

Set in 10 on 10pt Linotron Times
04–1286–83,900

Photoset by Rowland Phototypesetting Limited,
Bury St Edmunds, Suffolk
Made and printed in Great Britain by
Cox and Wyman Limited, Reading

# CHAPTER
# ONE

SOMEONE WAS touching her! Hands were moving slowly, deliberately over her limp body as she lay on the dusty ground, feeling arms, legs, thighs in turn. Fingers probed her face, examining a bruised cheek and the gash on her forehead just below the hairline, pushing away the cloud of dark hair which covered her bare shoulders before moving down to the torn bodice, savagely ripped open in the brutal attack that had rendered her insensible. Cool fingers lightly trailed across exposed breasts, and she steeled herself not to shudder in revulsion.

From the realms of unconsciousness which had given her blessed relief from fear and pain, Sian struggled to regain her faculties, sought to gather what little strength remained in her exhausted body to fight off this renewed assault. She thought the man was dead! Thought *she* had killed him in her frenzy to be free of him, but cruel hands still tore at her clothes.

Weak, dazed, terrified out of her wits, she clenched her fists and struck upwards, blindly, in an attempt to ward off this man she knew meant to rape, and then kill, her. They thudded into something as unyielding as solid rock and she heard a vehement oath close by her ear, which served only to increase her desperate pummelling. When he had finished with her, he would throw her body in some ditch and she might not be found for months. Roland would never know what had happened to her. And Timothy . . .

Her wrists were coupled in a grip that made her cry out in pain. Fingers biting like a steel claw into her shoulder effectively pinned her to the ground, and she was helpless once more.

'Be still, woman.' Sian almost fainted again with the shock of the strange voice. It was not the same man! 'By the look of it, you've had enough force. Don't make me use more.'

Her eyelids flickered open slowly, hesitantly. What new demon was she going to find bending over her? Late afternoon sunshine blinded her and she moaned, unable to bear the additional agony that clouded her vision. So late! Yet the carriage had been ambushed early in the morning! A shadow moved over her to block out the fierce red glare and she lay in silent terror, gazing at the man above her.

From beneath a thatch of thick hair, the colour of ripe corn at harvest-time, chillingly cold blue eyes stared down at her, containing not one flicker of sympathy for the pitiful condition in which he had found her. The bronzed face was that of a man old before his time. It was hard to assess his age accurately—he could have been in his early thirties, or much younger. She had seen many such faces at Versailles over the past years, mercenaries most of them, willing to sell their souls and their loyalties for money. A thin white scar seared one cheek to give him an almost menacing appearance. His clothes were well worn. Dark hide breeches and long boots reached almost to his knees. Beneath the open doublet of black leather, she glimpsed a wicked-looking knife thrust into a wide belt.

'If I let you go, will you be still while I fetch some water?' She recognised his accent now that her senses had cleared a little. He was a Scot, most likely one of the many exiles who had either enlisted in the French army after the failure of Charles Stuart to gain the English throne, or wandered Europe in penniless droves, fighting, begging, dying far from their homes. Ten years after, many of the swords that had been last used at Culloden, or in the heather as men fled before the Duke of Cumberland's troops, were still offered for sale.

Mutely she nodded, wincing as a pain shot through her aching head, and he released her and climbed to his feet. He was tall and well built, she saw as he crossed to the black and white stallion grazing peacefully a few yards away, and her suspicions as to his distasteful profession seemed to be confirmed by the huge sword suspended from a leather scabbard across his back. It looked a frightening weapon. She knew it to be a two-handed broadsword, once the most popular weapon in the Scottish Highlands. It could be wielded with any skill only by the strongest of men, the most proficient of fighters. A mercenary, without a doubt!

She had to get away. She was in as much danger from such a man as from the assassin who had sought to have his way with her before he killed her. This man had offered no reassurance that he would treat her any differently. Her vision blurred again as she hauled herself up on one elbow that was already scraped and bruised from where she had dragged herself into hiding. How long she had remained beneath sharp-thorned bushes, hardly daring to breathe lest the man she had overcome recovered from the hammering she had given him and came after her, she did not know. At last she accepted that he must be dead, and she crawled away deeper into the forest, afraid to remain near the coach lest his friends returned to find him—and found her too. Her legs had refused to support her for more than a few minutes at a time. It was little wonder she felt as if she had been dragged by a horse! But she was alive —at least for the moment. Surely someone would come looking for her soon? And then she remembered she had meant the long journey from Scotland to the family estates in France, to be a surprise for Roland's birthday. He did not even know of her coming! How excited Timothy had been. Dear God, where was her young brother now?

She came up on to her knees, swaying unsteadily, and collapsed once more. She was too weak to stand. She would have to crawl again. Desperation gave strength to a body bereft of energy, cleared a mind dulled with pain. She had managed to get half-way towards a large clump of bushes before being roughly seized and swept from the ground and imprisoned against a leather-clad chest, despite her feeble struggles.

'Let me go! Please . . . please!' Her voice was hardly audible.

Her entreaties were ignored. She was carried to the shade of some trees, deposited none too gently on the ground, and forced to drink from the water bottle held against her lips. She gulped down mouthfuls of the cool liquid as if it was nectar. Never had water tasted so refreshing!

'I shan't warn you again. Give me any more trouble, and I'll leave you here for the wolves,' the stranger threatened, and she shrank from him, back against a gnarled oak, the last fight drained from her. Whatever he intended, she was powerless to prevent it.

Sian was aware of his gaze raking over her as he went down on one knee at her side, ripped a strip of linen from her petticoat and proceeded to soak it with water. Her grey travelling dress was torn in several places, and dusty. Long black hair framed a face lost of all colour, and wide blue-grey eyes mirrored the fear inside her. There was a cut at the corner of her mouth, and blood had streaked across one cheek and dried as she lay unconscious. In silence he wiped it away. She flinched as a hand was laid against the side of her head, which felt as if it was about to split in two, so fierce was the drumming there.

'You've bled a lot. Do you feel dizzy, or weak? Can you hear what I'm saying? Do you understand me? Yes, I see you do. Answer me, then.'

'A little. My head hurts terribly. Please help me? I can pay you . . .'

'In your condition?' A humourless smile touched the lean mouth, and she gasped in horror.

'I—I didn't mean—like—that! I have money. I am the Comtesse de Saint-Rémy. Would you take me to my home? I promise you will be well paid by my brother.'

'So it's your coach I passed two miles back. I guessed it might be: coat-of-arms on the doors, fine horses and liveried servants. What a pity your money didn't save their lives or prevent you from being so roughly man-handled. I'm surprised they left you alive to tell the tale!' Sian blinked at him stupidly. Two miles! Had she come that far? She had wandered blindly, at times barely conscious, her only thought to get as far away from the wrecked coach as possible. 'It wasn't money they were after, was it?' the stranger demanded. As she stared at him, not answering, he lifted her scratched hand and she saw that her rings were still intact. Had they been missing, she doubted if she would have noticed in her present condition!

'He would have taken them afterwards.' Sian closed her eyes for a moment, to shut out the ugliness of the scene which rose in her mind. The murder of her two servants, one of them a young boy of seventeen, while she pleaded in vain for their lives. Her little brother being dragged up on a horse. Effie, her maid, screaming and kicking until she fainted away in the grasp of her abductor. And then the terrible silence after the four men had ridden off, taking them with them, and leaving her alone with the last member of the band, a burly, evil-looking man whose breath had reeked of wine and garlic. And then the sound of her screams ringing in her ears as he grabbed her to him. She opened her eyes again on the dark features hovering beside her. 'They have taken my brother. Abducted him! He is only seven years old . . . They left a man to kill me, too, but he thought first to . . .' She broke off with a shudder.

'Have a little fun? Who despatched him to the here-after—not you?' He sounded surprised. 'I saw an extra body with his face smashed to pulp, but I thought perhaps the coachman . . .'

'I did it.' Sian shuddered again as he reminded her of the scene with seeming indifference to her fragile state of mind. 'A stone . . . while we were struggling on the ground. I hit him—again and again and again.' Her voice began to rise shrilly as memory of the ghastly nightmare returned. Immediately the stranger's hands were on her shoulders, and he shook her hard.

'Enough of that! You need to rest. There's an inn of

sorts some way from here. I'll take you there. When you've recovered, you can tell me how I can find someone to come and fetch you. That's as far as my responsibility for you goes.'

Sian looked at him, unable to believe her ears. What kind of inhuman monster was he? She was still so dazed that she did not even realise she had not yet asked his name.

'Haven't you been listening to anything I said? My little brother has been abducted. I was nearly killed. I demand you take me home. My twin brother will be out of his mind with worry. I should have reached there hours ago,' she lied. It was in her mind that if he guessed that no one was expecting her, she could still vanish without a trace. For all she knew, the Forest of Ardenne was full of the bodies of unfortunates waylaid and robbed and murdered. She had played here as a child, hunted with Roland when they grew old enough, but today the forest was different—a frightening place full of shadows and ghosts of the dead, who threatened to reach out and pluck her from the land of the living. It had so nearly happened!

'Demand? You are in no position to demand anything of me, woman!' The insolent reply told her he had respect neither for her orders, nor for her authority. She recoiled from the hand outstretched to help her to her feet, and his features grew taut with anger, tightening the scar across the right cheek. 'Neither are you in any condition to travel. You are soft and useless in difficult circumstances, like all women in your position. You expect others to help you because you are incapable of helping yourself. Ordinarily I should have obliged you and returned you to your home—and expected, in return, to be well paid for my services. However, I've had more than my fair share of your kind of woman lately and I don't intend to alter my plans to please you, Madame la Comtesse,' he drawled, and managed to somehow make the title sound an insult. 'I shall say this only once, so listen carefully. In an hour it will be dark. Either I take you to the inn and we spend the night there, which may not be to your liking—but, then, it is not to mine either—or I leave you here. You do know, I suppose, that there are wolves and wild boar in this area? Not to mention more men like the one you killed. Poachers, petty thieves, and worse—all of whom would think a small miracle had come about if they happened to find a helpless woman in the woods. Neither your money nor your fancy title would save you then. And you are helpless. Without my protection, you won't last until morning. In fact you have had the devil's own luck to have remained alive as long as this.'

The words were flung at her with a quiet fury behind them. He meant what he said, Sian realised. He would leave her without a qualm of conscience. Such a man did not possess one! She forced back a rush of tears.

'And with your protection?' she whispered, her wide eyes never leaving the hard, uncompromising face. 'Why should I trust you?'

'Do you have a choice?' came the terse answer. 'Besides, if I had found you interesting, or if I were the kind of man you obviously think me to be, your state of undress would surely have prompted me into action before now?' Her back was still against the gnarled trunk of the oak, and so there was no escape from the hand laid without warning on her naked breast. She trembled as brown fingers caressed her skin, pausing for a moment on a dark bruise. Then, with a strange smile which did nothing to ease the apprehension mounting inside her, he abruptly drew back, demanding, 'Well, woman? Speak up.'

'Help me? I am so afraid,' Sian pleaded, and folded like a rag doll into his arms.

She came to in a crude bed with the sound of voices close by. One she instantly recognised as that of the Scot who had found her, but the others were unknown to her and receded swiftly as her returning senses brought with them the terrible pain in her head. Some while later she managed to open her eyes, but not until she opened them for the fifth time was everything still.

There were a table and several chairs immediately in her line of vision. A bottle of wine and a plate of cold food. Beside this, an earthenware bowl of something hot—she could see heat rising from the contents—and she remembered she had not eaten since starting out early that morning. How could she think of eating after what had happened to her?

The stranger came through the door carrying a bowl of water and clean cloths which he deposited on the stool beside the bed. He did not look at her and immediately turned away to close and lock the door behind him. Sian felt icy fingers clutch at her heart.

'What—what are you doing?' she cried, struggling to sit up, and not succeeding. She could not raise her head from the pillow for the pain which racked it.

'Ensuring that we are not disturbed. Would you like the landlord or someone else to come in while I am attempting to make you look like a clean, well-bred respectable young woman again?' he mocked, and she thrust out her hands in an attempt to ward him off as he reached for the blanket covering her.

'No! You can't! If you touch me, I will have you whipped.'

'If you continue to act like a spoilt child, I will treat you like one. Offer one shred of resistance, and I'll tie you to the bedposts and then strip you.' Light eyes with sparks of tempered steel in them flashed their warning at her, and Sian emitted a cry of horror—of shame, as she felt her torn clothes being removed. First her dress, then what was left of her petticoat and undershift. 'Pretend I am your brother,' the sarcastic voice commented in her ear. 'Would he not care for you if you were sick or hurt?'

'I have servants for that.' She closed her eyes tightly, but could not keep the hot colour from staining her cheeks as he washed the dirt from her body and administered some kind of salve to the many abrasions and cuts she had sustained during her headlong flight through the trees and bushes.

'Of course, I was forgetting who you are.' His tone

implied, if anything, that he was being deliberately
obnoxious in his dealings with her, deliberately humili-
ating her because he did not like women of her station.
What was it he had said to her earlier? She fought to
remember the bitter words. 'I've had more than my fair
share of women like you lately.' Women like her? Titled
aristocracy—was that what he had meant? 'Be easy,
woman, I'm not of a mind to jump into bed with you.
I've been travelling since last night, and I'm too damned
tired for one. Besides, I prefer an honest whore any
day. She'll only try to pick my pockets or overcharge
me, not connive to get me killed.'

At that astounding statement, Sian's eyes flew open.
Why did she suddenly have the feeling they had met
somewhere before? She was sure they had not, yet the
way he spoke, his contempt for her class, roused a
memory in her—only her head hurt too much for her
to try to concentrate on what it was. She had a vague
recollection of many people—of him standing beside a
beautiful woman . . . Had they met? Where? When?
How? She was not in the habit of mixing with men such
as him. Scotland, perhaps? No, she met few Highlanders
there. Ard Choille was not open house to those who
had fought against King George. She must say nothing
of Scotland to this man. His scorn and ridicule were
enough to bear as it was.

'Only a moment more, then you can drink some hot
broth and sleep.'

'Sleep?' she echoed. 'Do you think I shall be able to
sleep, after . . . I killed a man?'

'The first one is always the hardest. The second time
it will be easier,' he replied, and she winced at his
callousness.

'You speak as if death is second nature to you?'
she quavered, and was subjected once more to his
penetrating gaze, which lingered for a deliberately long
moment on her firm, rounded breasts and tiny waist.

He laughed shortly, and moved away from the bed,
returning with the bowl of broth and a wooden spoon.
'I've fought many a fight, under many flags, these past

few years. Perhaps it is. I've seen death, I've killed, and
I've tended my fallen comrades on the field of battle—
and some of their women, too, when there was no one
else to help them. At such times you don't stop to think
if you will embarrass or annoy. So you see, my fine
lady, you have no need to look at me with such reproach.
If you could have seen what happens to open wounds,
even scratches such as yours, when they become
infected, you would be thanking me instead of turning
up that tiny nose and telling yourself I am not good
enough to touch the hem of your skirt, let alone your
body. Ach, what's the use talking to you! It will be an
amusing story to tell your friends when you return to
Versailles.'

Sian watched him sit down at the table and open
the bottle of wine, and felt herself grow cold with
apprehension as he put it to his mouth and tipped almost
half the contents down his throat in one large swallow.
She had never seen wine drunk so before. It was horrify-
ing. Did he mean to get drunk?

'Would you care to join me?' He glanced back at her,
the satanic features alight with mocking amusement.

She shook her head and concentrated on consuming
the soup he had given her, but it was tasteless and
greasy, and she put it aside after only a mouthful,
grimacing as she did so. Instantly he was on his feet,
frowning at her action.

'Not up to your usual standards of fare, but good
enough for poor folk with empty stomachs! But I doubt
if yours has ever been empty, has it?'

'No, and I thank God for it,' Sian replied, stung by
the unjustness of the remark. Was it her fault that her
mother had been born to money and a title that she in
turn had bequeathed jointly to Sian and Roland on her
death? Shadows crept into her eyes at the thought of
how she had died, that gentle, generous woman who
had never had an ill thought for anyone. An accident
had been the general opinion, but not that of her step-
father, Phillip. Murdered, he swore, by the dour-faced
villagers who lived in their drab-stoned huts beside

Ard Choille. Stony-faced, unapproachable people who hated the English as much as did this man before her. Nothing had been proved, but the suspicion of foul play still hung over the hills. Roland had thought it, too, and soon afterwards had returned to France, leaving her alone with little Timothy and a step-father she detested. But for her frequent journeys to visit her twin, life would have been unbearable. No matter how hard she tried, she was not accepted. Neither was Timothy. But in France, he was smothered with kindness, and it did her heart good to watch him so happy. Ard Choille offered no laughter, no play, no young friends to come calling. Memories were too long, and the sight of Phillip riding the village road rekindled old resentments, to be directed at all who lived beneath its roof.

Timothy! Oh, Timothy! Sian thought, near to distraction at the idea of what might have befallen him. Where would he be taken? What ransom would be demanded? She looked at the silent figure who had returned to his bottle, and watched him drink again. In the bravest tone she could muster and with as much dignity as her present unclothed state would command, she said,

'I shall need clothes to travel in tomorrow. Will you find someone to ride out and see what damage has been done to the coach? Perhaps it can be righted. If not, I will need my trunks.'

'I have already done that. I did not imagine you wanted to ride through the forest in the state of nature,' was his dry retort, and she was silent for a moment, not having expected him to have such foresight. He had showed little so far—or consideration for her plight.

How she ached, and the pain in her head would not go away. She wanted to lie down and sleep, but the sight of the broad back in front of her kept her sitting rigidly upright, the blankets pulled securely about her shoulders. Whenever she made the slightest movement, however, they always slipped away. What would she have given for a nightgown! She was terrified even to close her eyes in his company.

'My sole interest is in finishing this bottle, woman. Go to sleep.'

It was as if he had read her mind. She felt herself colour, even though he did not turn to look at her.

'My brother—what will happen to him?'

'They took him alive, so that means a ransom. You can pay, of course?'

'Anything,' she said. 'Anything. Why him? Why not me? I don't understand.'

'No more do I. They could have taken both and earned themselves double the ransom, yet they chose only to take him and try to kill you.' He swung round, and the eyes which surveyed her were dark with suspicion. 'Perhaps they had good reason.'

'What? I know of no one who should want me dead.' Sian's voice became silent as she puzzled over his words. 'No one would benefit from my death except Roland, my twin brother, and we are very close. Would they have sent him a ransom demand already? Will they treat Timothy well? Oh, I wish I had not listened to you! I could have gone on . . . reached home . . .'

'You would not have lasted a mile, and well you know it.'

'I killed a man, didn't I?' she flashed with sudden spirit. 'I crawled two miles? Who are you to sit in judgment on me? You know nothing about me!'

'Do I not?' The devil's own mockery danced in his eyes as he rose and came to the side of the bed. He moved with the stealth of a mountain lion, she thought, as he regarded her, hands on his hips.

'You don't recall me, do you?'

'I do not know you, monsieur.' But she knew the devouring gaze of those penetrating eyes, as bottomless as a mountain loch. If only she could remember from where. Perhaps the blow on the head had affected her memory?

'I would not have expected to make any impression on you. I am only another of those Scots exiles who live off innocent women and prey on their weakness for money! Faith, that's funny. From La Pompadour down-

wards there's not an innocent woman at Versailles, and
that includes you, Madame la Comtesse. And don't give
me that wide-eyed look, pretending you don't know
what I'm talking about. You are afraid of me only
because you know if you dared to flutter your eyelashes
just once, as you do in the company of your overdressed
fops who have the gall to call themselves men, I wouldn't
kiss your hand and pay you meaningless compliments
in the hope that you would reward me with a smile.
Perhaps, to some of them, you give more? I'm not
interested. You know I would take what you offer, and
you wouldn't like that, would you? But I doubt if you
have ever had anything to do with a real man. You might
find the experience not only exciting but satisfying.'

Sian gasped, and retreated as far as was possible
across the bed. The words delivered at her with a bitter,
vengeful spite behind them were her words, spoken to
her close friend Madame de Pompadour herself at a
recent party at the Petit Trianon at Versailles. A smile
spread across her companion's face as her expression
registered absolute horror. He sketched a mocking bow
at her. 'We were never properly introduced that night.
I am Douglas MacGregor. In the undesirable part of
Paris, my friends know me as "Le Blond". I was with
Madame de Brissac.'

Now it came flooding back to her. The unforgivable
behaviour of the woman in question, married of course,
who had brought her lover to the occasion knowing full
well her husband would also be present. It had been a
deliberate attempt to shame him into giving her a div-
orce, and everyone there knew it.

'You almost killed Monsieur de Brissac,' she gasped.
'How could you?'

'He drew his sword. I fought him to save my own
skin—which happens to be very precious to me. I did
not want a fight.'

'Then you should not have gone with her.'

'At the time, I did not understand the little plan she
had devised—which was to kill her husband, leaving
her free to marry.'

'You?' Sian's disgust and loathing for this man was intensifying with each passing moment. A MacGregor! That very name made her grow cold with fear.

'Good heavens, woman. Me? Marry that whore? If I ever take a wife, she will be a simple maid and innocent. Not a well-used commodity!' MacGregor laughed, and more colour crept into Sian's cheeks. But how could she rest easily when she knew he placed her in the same category as Madame de Brissac, a twice-married woman, notorious for her affairs?

MacGregor turned away from her, beginning to whistle as he did so. Sian's eyelids drooped wearily and she pinched herself hard to ward off the sleep which threatened to take possession of her. She could not— would not—sleep in the company of this odious man. As if he were alone, he removed his knife from its sheath and placed it on the table beside him, then took the long broadsword from its scabbard and proceeded to clean it with oil and a cloth taken from his saddlebags.

Sian pushed the hard pillow up behind her head and lay watching him, noting the meticulous care he took over the weapon. How many men had he killed with it, she wondered? One, two, half a dozen? More? If he had been out in the last uprising, it had been well used. The bloodstained tool of a hired killer. He was no better than the ruffians who had waylaid the coach and killed her servants. Yet there had to be a little good in him. He could have continued where her assailant had left off, for she was too weak to prevent it, but he had brought her to this inn and bathed her wounds, as he would have done to a fallen comrade-in-arms. She did not like him, indeed she feared him, but she owed him her life and somehow she would repay him. She had no doubt that, if she offered him money again, he would not refuse it. His clothes were proof he was not a man of substance. He lived by the huge sword he handled with such loving care; and such an existence never showed great profit, for more often than not, death came before payment. She shuddered. How could anyone live so casually within the shadow of death?

She had come close to dying, and never wanted to experience the like of it again.

Men fought for so many confusing reasons. Hate, revenge, money, excitement, boredom. Why did Douglas MacGregor fight? She wished she had the courage to ask him.

'What is that tune?' she asked instead and wondered why she had chosen to start a conversation with him, when all she wanted to do was close her eyes and drift into blessed sleep.

He looked over his shoulders at her, huddled like a waif beneath the rough blankets, her black hair spread out on the pillow like a thundercloud and his mouth deepened into a smile. A secret smile, meant not for her, but evoked by memories inside him from the past.

'Still awake? Your stamina impresses me. Or is it fear which keeps those eyes open? The tune? It's called "MacGregor's Lament". It's very, very old.' He continued to whistle for several minutes as he finished polishing, and Sian was struck by the sadness of the air. This was no victory song to be played by the pipers after a battle. This was a lament for lost ones, perhaps, or for the dead.

She dared not say more, lest she give herself away. 'MacGregor's Lament!' Why did he have to bear that name! 'It's very sad,' she said drowsily, and his eyes darkened until they were almost black in the candlelight.

'It was meant as a warning to all those who survived a battle. Glen Fruin was the place. A lament for the dead, a warning for the living, the hunted and those outside the law.' His voice was very quiet, almost gentle. ' "Make winter as autumn, the wolf-days as summer; Thy bed be bare rock and light be thy slumber." As appropriate for that time as for many times after. Culloden, for instance. The English made damned sure our slumber was light, our beds bare rocks. They took our food, our men, our women when it fancied them, and left us with nothing.'

'Why is it you Scots are always the only ones to think you lost loved ones in that uprising? I lost Richard,

my father, at Culloden . . .' Sian began, and then fell
awkwardly into silence as fire grew within his eyes. His
chiselled features hardened.

'So you have English blood in you! You would do
well not to remind me of that again, woman, or I might
be inclined to take myself off this instant and leave you
to the tender mercies of the landlord and his cronies.
Were I not here to protect you, there would be at least
three scum up here to slit your throat. When they had
finished with you, that is.'

With a choked cry, Sian turned her face to the pillow
and did not look towards him again. Without wanting
to, she slept. An uneasy sleep, plagued by nightmares
of the recent hours. The scream that rose in her throat
was stifled by the hand across her mouth. She struggled
out of the realms of sleep, thrusting down in renewed
fear at the arm round her waist. She was so weak!

'Do you want to rouse the whole place, woman?'
MacGregor whispered harshly in her ear. 'Stop struggling, or I'll knock you cold.'

His voice brought her to reality. She sagged in his
grasp, gasping for air, but he did not take his hand away
from her mouth for a full minute as he waited for her
to recover more fully. When he did, she sensed he was
ready to silence her again if she attempted to scream.

Her skin was unhealthily hot beneath the hand he
retained around her body, his fingers against the upward
rise of a firm breast. He frowned as he saw that her face
was filmed with perspiration. Large tears welled from
her eyes over flushed cheeks, yet she made no sound.
He had never seen a woman cry so before. Most gave
the performance of a lifetime, using their tears as a
weapon. He could feel great sobs racking her slim form,
and his arm tightened. Why he should feel protective
at such a time was beyond him. Sian rolled her head on
his shoulder, moaning softly as the movement brought
pain, and buried her face in the leather of his doublet.
It smelt of sweat and woodsmoke, and a multitude of
odours that eluded her, retained by the creased, aged
material.

'Dammit, woman, I hope you are not ill! I'll not waste any more time with you,' he growled, and at his words she slowly lifted her head and stared up into his frowning countenance. The desolation in the depths of her blue-grey eyes shocked him—and touched something in him he had not experienced for a good many years—pity! It came and went in the same instant. Sian became aware of his eyes wandering down over her naked body in the most insulting fashion, yet she could not move, or speak. She was transfixed by the hunger in his eyes. No man had ever looked at her in this way before! Terror, revulsion and fear all mingled inside her at once as, with a harsh expletive, he crushed her mouth beneath his. His hands moved over her shoulders, the slender line of her throat, her breasts and thighs—and still she could not move.

She hung suspended in his arms as he held her away from him, her head fallen back, her hair hanging down, her eyes wide, fearful, yet containing something else that he did not miss, and his features became derisive, his tone brutal, cutting her like the lash of a whip.

'As I said, Madame la Comtesse, you are no different from Madame de Brissac. Even the arms of a mercenary can prove attractive when no one else is around!' He dropped her back on the bed and strode across to his saddlebags.

Sian lay uncomprehending as he searched the contents for a long moment. She was shameless! How could she have allowed such a man to rouse passion in her and, worse still, to betray herself to him? What did he intend now? Her arms felt bruised where he had held her. Gingerly she touched her mouth and discovered the cut there had been reopened by his savage kisses. She shrank back as he came to the bed and held out a wooden cup to her, staring suspiciously at the contents.

'Drink it,' MacGregor ordered. 'It will ease the fever and help you to sleep.'

'You—you want me drugged,' she breathed. 'No!'

'You little fool, if I wanted to bed you, you couldn't stop me, and well you know it! From the reaction a moment ago, I'd say you'd rather enjoy it.'

When she still refused to take the cup from him, he seized a fistful of her hair and tugged back her head, forcing the liquid between her lips. It tasted of honey and herbs and was not at all what she had expected, but still she fought him. It was useless, however, and he succeeded in making her drink it all. Feeling wretched and humiliated, Sian slid beneath the blankets, accusing him with the silent gaze of her grey eyes. Suddenly she found herself shivering, and could not stop. Her teeth began to chatter and her whole body jerked and shuddered. The covers were pulled from her without warning. She felt a hard, masculine body slide alongside hers, and when the covers were replaced, she grew rigid with terror. He could not know her . . . yet!

'No! No!' she moaned as his arms enfolded her, pressing her tightly against him. His doublet had been discarded, so that her cheek lay against a bare chest.

'Ssh! Sleep. You'll be fine in the morning.' She felt his lips against her hair as he spoke. His hands were still upon her body and gradually she felt a strange warmth stealing through her. The shivering stopped and she relaxed against him, too drained to offer further resistance of any kind.

Somewhere in the trees outside the window an owl hooted, and its solitary call was answered by another. Laughter floated up from the depths below, but it instilled no fear in her. Entwined in the arms of Douglas MacGregor who, by his own admittance, thought her to be little more than a rich slut, Sian, Comtesse de Saint-Rémy forgot the horrors of the day and slept peacefully.

The man who held her lay awake in the darkness, as alert as he always was when in a strange place, and tried not to think of the softness pressing against him, the rise and fall of her breasts against his bare chest. She was everything he hated and despised, and there was English blood in her, too. That alone made his gentlemanly manners unforgivable. He should have taken her like the whore she was, and left her. She sighed in her

sleep, and he moved slightly to watch the first rays of
muted light play across her face. Eighteen or nineteen,
he mused. The cut beneath her hair had closed, but
looked ugly and painful. He had scorned her for her
helplessness, yet he reluctantly had to admit that she
had courage. The effort to overcome the enormous
brute bent on raping her had been no mean feat. She
must have fought like an enraged tigress.

Perhaps she was a little more innocent that he gave
her credit for. Perhaps not. Perhaps it would be worth
his while to wait and find out. Sian stirred, and pressed
closer against him in her untroubled sleep. Perhaps it
would!

# CHAPTER
TWO

A THUNDEROUS knocking roused Sian from a deep sleep. Through half-closed eyes—her lids felt as if great weights were pressing down on them—she saw a tall broad-shouldered man with a shock of blond hair approach the door and unlock it. She froze in the bed with horror and shock. Where was she?

He wore nothing but a pair of hide trousers! Who was he? Where was she? Why was she naked beneath these awful rough blankets? Her limbs, like her eyelids, felt like lead. She tried to sit up, but they refused to function, and she lay sleepily watching as the door was swung open to admit two men labouring with a large trunk. Her trunk!

The sight of it brought memories crowding back to her, and her hands clenched beneath the covers as she fought to retain her composure. Her trunk from the wrecked coach. The last time she had seen it, the contents had been scattered over the ground as the men who had waylaid her searched for valuables. They had found her jewel case hidden beneath one of the seats, and what little money she possessed for the trip was stolen from her purse. Dead servants! Timothy screaming for her to help him! Would she ever forget his pitiful cries?

A ruthless Scots mercenary had been her saviour from certain death. She closed her eyes, but when she opened them, it had not been a nightmare. She was still in the same bed, in the same room. The men had gone, but *he* was still there, watching her with an unnerving gaze. Douglas MacGregor, her rescuer! The man who had held her all night long in his arms, and she without a single stitch of clothing to separate her body from that of a man whose reputation left much to be desired!

'Are you hungry? I've ordered some food. I advise you to eat whatever is brought. You need strength if you are to travel this morning,' MacGregor said.

The hand laid against her cheek was cool and impersonal, as had been the hands which ministered to her the evening before. Did he really believe she would take pleasure in relating this incident to her friends, bringing down on both their heads malicious gossip and lewd comments? How the scandalmongers would enjoy this! He nodded in obvious satisfaction and stepped back.

'Please—before you leave me, send word to my brother Roland at the château at Saint-Rémy,' she implored. 'You cannot refuse me that small request, surely? Here—take these—send one to him. He will recognise it and come at once. Keep the other for yourself.'

He took the two rings she plucked from her fingers and held out to him. One was a blood-red ruby set in gold; the other a huge diamond Roland had given her for her eighteenth birthday.

'I do not want to be in your debt, monsieur,' she added meaningfully as he stared down at them in silence, his brows drawn together in a deep frown.

'They will go some way to compensating me for my trouble,' he replied, his tone heavy with sarcasm. They were thrust into a pocket of his trousers as he went down on one knee before the trunk and threw back the lid.

Sian stared in dismay at the jumble of clothes which had been bundled thoughtlessly inside, then her annoyance subsided as she realised she was lucky to have them back at all. She watched him sort through them. He selected several items and flung them on the bed.

'Get dressed. When you've eaten, we will leave,' he ordered, straightening. She could only stare at him in amazement. Was he offering to escort her?

'Leave? You are not abandoning me here?' She could not hide her relief, and he smiled thinly. 'Thank you.

You will not regret it. My brother will reward you, I promise.'

'Naturally. Is not money the prime importance of a man of my profession?' It was the first time he had even hinted he was what she thought him to be—a sword for hire. 'Besides, you have already taken me out of my way. I might as well be paid for my troubles,' he returned, and began to pull on his boots, his back towards her.

With an effort, Sian threw back the clothes and reached for the garments at the bottom of the bed. She was not accustomed to dressing herself. Awkwardly she pulled on her shift, wincing as pain seared stiff arms and shoulders. Somehow she forced down some of the bread and cheese that had arrived. There was more of the same unwholesome soup, which she refused. Douglas pushed a plate of oakcakes in her direction, and under his narrowed gaze she managed one. The only drink provided was more red wine. Douglas looked at it for a moment, then, to her relief, pushed it to one side. She had begun to believe he had a head as hard as the rock which took the place of a heart.

'How far are we from Saint-Rémy?' she ventured to ask as he strapped on the enormous broadsword. Suddenly she was afraid of him again. Afraid of what he was. The man who had been kind to her, despite his brusqueness, his rudeness, disappeared as she watched the slim-bladed dirk being thrust into his belt. This was Douglas MacGregor, the Scots exile with hatred in his heart and money on his mind. The mists were slowly clearing from her senses. Whatever he had drugged her with, it had been powerful and left her with a feeling of unreality. She wanted to thank him for the peace of mind he had given her, but no words came. Once again she felt ill at ease in his company.

'We shall be there by mid-day. It's lucky the coach is roadworthy, as you wouldn't last an hour on a horse,' he said, throwing her a searching glance. She knew it was the truth, but she still hated him for saying it. She could ride and hunt with the best horsemen in her part of the country, and she was proud of it. He made her feel an insignificant little nobody!

'I've hired a young lad to act as driver. It's better if I ride inside. I don't envisage any trouble, but if there is, I want to be ready for it.'

She nodded, accepting that what he said made sense. When they were ready to leave, he preceded her through the door. She was about to rebuke him for his lack of manners, when she became aware of the gathering below. At least half a dozen men were all gazing up towards the narrow landing where they stood.

'Stay close behind me,' MacGregor hissed. 'Yon rabble have no heart for naked steel. Watch my back.' Those words alone gave his life into her keeping!

In one swift movement he had lifted his sword free of its scabbard and was advancing down the wooden stairs. Not a hairsbreadth separated them as she followed. She did not like the way they were being eyed. A locked door had protected them last night, but this morning . . . She had not believed her life was still in danger. Now, seeing these hard, unshaven faces, the narrowed eyes, gleaming as they raked her from head to foot, she knew only his presence had saved her from further pain and humiliation—and death!

The men pressed close at the bottom of the stairs menacingly. No word was spoken, but she knew what was in the mind of each one. They were six or seven against one man and a woman. Easy picking. MacGregor's sword swung in a wide arc before him and they fell back, making a clear passage for them to pass through.

'Come on, my friends! Who will be the first to taste this fine steel, the finest in Scotland? You?' The tip caressed the shirt of a swarthy-faced individual, braver than the rest, who had moved forward again.

Danger sharpened Sian's wits. She cried a warning as a shadowy figure launched itself at them from an alcove. MacGregor wheeled about, sweeping her towards the open doorway. As she staggered out into the sunlight and collapsed, weak-kneed, on to the ground, he lifted his weapon and despatched the man to the hereafter with a single blow which cleaved his head open. She was hauled roughly to her feet and propelled towards the waiting coach, where a village lad in his early teens sat, white-faced, holding tightly to the horse's reins. MacGregor flung himself in beside her and for a moment his weight crushed her against the far side as they were driven away at high speed.

How long had it taken them to leave the inn? Five minutes—no more. Yet, in that short space of time, she had seen another man killed. A great sickness rose inside her. She thrust at him with trembling hands, nauseated by what she had seen, and his part in it. He looked into her ashen features and scowled, sensing the source of her displeasure and discomfort.

'I—I'm sorry. I know they would have killed us . . . I saw it in their eyes. But it was so horrible!' His movements had been swift, decisive and without mercy. His jaw tightened as she shivered and drew her cloak more closely about her, despite the warmth of the morning. 'It was brutal!'

'Life—and death—often are,' he remarked shortly. 'We have to contend with them the best we can. You are still alive, that's all that should matter to you.'

She drew away from him and huddled in the corner in a miserable silence. He pretended not to notice the withdrawal, but she knew he had by the tightening of his lips, the way he folded his arms over his chest and stared sightlessly out of the window. A man of violence! Violent in the way he lived—and loved. She closed her eyes and pretended to sleep, hoping to shut out the memory of his arms round her naked body. The fierce, demanding pressure of his mouth on hers, forcing apart her stiff lips, forcing a response from the depths of her. That was the most shameful part of all. She had answered him!

The journey to the château took less time than she had expected, for most of it was completed at breakneck speed. Whoever the young lad was in the coachman's seat, he was no novice where horses were concerned,

Sian realised, and decided to offer him a job in her brother's stables once they had safely arrived. That had to be better than returning to the inn where he must surely be chastised, or even killed, for his part in their successful escape.

She could have cried with relief when the coach swept at a dangerously fast pace through the tiny village below the château, scattering carts and animals in its path. Curious villagers watching it flash by and turned to wonder at the white face of the woman at one window, the bleak features of the blond-haired stranger at the other. Something was terribly wrong to bring Madame la Comtesse home in such a hurry—and who was that with her?

The château of Saint-Rémy had been in the possession of Sian's mother's family for countless generations. Norman knights had fought at its walls, battling between themselves for supremacy of this choice piece of land on the edge of the dense, desolate forest. Much of the design had been copied from the fabulous Palace of Versailles itself, but on a far more modest scale.

She loved this place. Always she felt welcome here, at peace. By comparison, Ard Choille was a prison. Not of her making, but of Phillip's. Oblivious of the hatred and misery existing around him, he had set himself up as Laird with the full approval and backing of the English government. The house and lands which came with it had been payment for his services during and after the rebellion of 1745. The MacGregors who survived had long memories. She saw it in their faces as she rode past—the contempt and loathing, the silent desire for revenge which might, one dark night, cause them to plunge a dirk into the back of the man they hated—or hers—or Timothy's. They cared not that he had been born at Ard Choille—he was the son of an English butcher, and there was no place in their cold hearts for him. She had tried so hard to reach them with gifts of food and clothes, even sheep to graze on the brown mountains which would clothe and feed them in the winter months. But still those faces were sullen and resentful.

The keen gaze of Douglas MacGregor missed nothing as the coach approached the house. She saw a smile touch his features—a smile of pure derision. She was as rich as he had suspected, and therefore she knew she would once more be the object of his scorn. A horseman came round from the back of the house as it neared the front steps. She glimpsed a surprised face beneath unruly black hair, and was unable to prevent the tears which sprang to her eyes. Roland! She was home! Safe!

He jumped to the ground as the coach came to a halt, wrenched open the door and caught her as she came tumbling out into his arms, almost making him lose his balance.

'Thank God! Oh, thank God,' was all she could murmur. Douglas was ignored—if he was even noticed —in those first hectic few moments as Roland carried his sister up the wide flight of steps where the servants stood and gaped at the sight of the pale, dishevelled girl in his arms, who clearly showed the marks of violence on her face and shoulders, where her cloak fell open.

They went through a hall panelled with mirrors and lighted by an enormous chandelier, and on, past more gawping footmen to the Peacock Drawing Room, where Roland laid Sian gently down on a *chaise-longue* covered in the most vivid shade of blue to match the curtains at the windows, the enormous carpets and the colourful tapestries on the walls, and turned to order wine to be brought immediately.

Roland Saint-Rémy had never been known to raise his voice above an authoritative tone, and, even now, only a nerve throbbing at the corner of one temple betrayed the agitation building inside him.

'*M'amie*, what has happened? I thought the devil's hounds were pursuing the coach!' Gentle fingers touched her bruised mouth, explored the cut on her forehead and the nerve throbbed more wildly.

'Roland . . .' Sian tried to speak, but huge sobs rose

in her throat. 'Hold me! Hold me! I never thought to see you again.'

Her brother gathered her into his arms and for a long while she remained there, silent and still. So still that he became alarmed and drew back, but she looked up at him, tears wiped away, eyes dry. 'Timothy has been abducted. The coach was attacked yesterday morning. They took him—and Effie. I was going to be killed . . .' She broke off, fighting to control a surge of panic. Over her brother's shoulder, she saw MacGregor, and withdrew from his arms, inclining her head slightly in his direction. Puzzled, Roland turned and he, too, saw him for the first time. He did not like what he saw. The man looked and smelt of death. 'I owe my life to this man. He—he found me afterwards . . .' She knew she was in no condition to give full details at that moment; besides, she was aware of the hovering figures in the background. Only her brother must know what she had endured and, even then, she wondered if it was wise to tell him everything? 'And this morning, when—when men attempted to detain us, he—he saved me again.'

'She means that I killed a man.' MacGregor's voice came mockingly towards her. Strangely enough she was not intimidated by the mockery there, the scorn that he had killed on her behalf. After all, he expected to be paid for it. She was home now, in her own territory, alien to him. Here she need be afraid of no one, accept insults from no one. Her word was law, as he would discover if he continued to act in this manner. 'I suspect, but I have no way of proving it, that several of the men she speaks of were members of the band who abducted your brother.'

'Step-brother,' Roland intervened softly, and Sian winced at his words. He had never accepted Timothy, never forgiven their mother for remarrying, never liked the home he had been forced to live in when she did. 'Go on, monsieur.'

'Not here,' she pleaded. 'There is too much to tell. Roland, you must get in touch with the authorities, and tell them what has happened. There must be a search.'

Her head fell back against the tapestry cushions. She was exhausted again, and in pain. Roland rose from her side.

'We shall talk later when you have rested. Monsieur here can give me all the details, though there's damned little we can do except make a search. If it's a ransom they are after, and I can see no other reason for them abducting him, then we can only wait until we receive word from them. It could be days—weeks. Don't worry.' He clasped her hands in his as she gasped, cursing himself for his thoughtlessness. Timothy was not his favourite, but she loved the boy, and he had no wish to add further to what she had been through. Once again he touched her cut lip, and his face darkened. 'When do we hear . . . I shall meet them myself.'

'No! No, not you. You do not even like to handle a sword, and you are a terrible shot,' Sian whispered pleadingly. 'I want nothing to happen to you too. It must be someone else. Someone who can deal with— with people like that.' She looked significantly towards the figure in the doorway as she spoke. Roland frowned, not agreeing with her choice. He did not like the look of him, no matter how helpful he had been. He was waiting to be paid, of course, and then he would leave without a backward glance. Men like that had no loyalties. 'Please.'

He looked down into Sian's ashen face and nodded, then bent to help her to her feet.

'Come, I shall take you upstairs. André will go for a doctor.'

'No. I need sleep, that's all. I have been well cared for,' she added, and he gave her a searching look. 'Treat him as a guest, Roland, for my sake. Ask no questions of me now. Later I will tell you everything, but not now. I owe him my life—twice. And we need him. Be careful of him.'

'The man's a mercenary, even I can see that,' her brother muttered as he guided her towards the staircase of green and pink marble, the banister inlaid with gold fretwork. 'Are you suggesting that we give him money to ransom Timothy? He'd be in Paris before we could blink, and we'd not see either again.'

'We need him,' Sian repeated determinedly. 'Do not let him leave until I can speak with him. His name is Douglas MacGregor.'

'I think the experience you have been through has addled your brain, little sister, but I shall do as you ask. I shall treat your mercenary as a guest. He shall eat at our table and drink our wine and sleep in a soft bed, and I'll have servants watching his room—and every move he makes. If he so much as looks at you again in the way he is looking at you now, I shall have him disposed of, and you will not stop me!' A MacGregor! Beneath their roof? Was she mad!

'Please, be seated, Monsieur MacGregor.'

The Scot turned away from the window to face the man who came into the room, closing the doors behind him. He glimpsed two dour-faced servants hovering outside. Protection, perhaps?

Roland motioned him to a chair and watched as he removed his broadsword before lowering his six-foot frame into a high-backed chair, laying the weapon beside him. Within easy reach, he mused. The man trusted no one. MacGregor! The name alone carried trouble with it—for them!

'Will you take a drink with me? Brandy? Wine?'

'Whisky?' MacGregor asked hopefully, and to his surprise Roland nodded.

'I think I have some.' He knew he had several bottles that Sian had previously brought out with her. He caught a flash of surprise on the face of his guest, as he filled two glasses and handed one to him. 'A bad habit I picked up while in your country, monsieur,' he said drily as he seated himself.

MacGregor held the crystal glass in front of him for a moment, a smile playing at the corners of his mouth as he gazed at the dark, amber liquid. Liquid gold! How long had it been since he had tasted good Scottish whisky? Too long!

'A taste of home. My compliments to you on your excellent choice! *Slainte*.' He toasted his host in the Gaelic before appreciatively swallowing the contents. 'Lacking the fire I have known in *usquebaugh*, but preferable to your cognacs and brandies any day.'

'Please feel free to help yourself. I drink very little until the evening,' Roland said, waving him to the open cabinet. Without hesitation, MacGregor rose and fetched the decanter and placed it on the glass-topped table beside him. 'Besides, regardless of what I told my sister, I fully intend to ride into Saint-Rémy this afternoon and have a search begun for my step-brother,' he added as he watched the empty glass being replenished.

'Even though you don't give a damn what happens to him?' MacGregor answered, a blond eyebrow arching in a gesture which implied contempt.

'Our family business is none of your affair, monsieur!' Sian had asked him to be civil to him, treat him as a guest. It was difficult. 'I am waiting to hear how you happened to find my sister, monsieur,' he said stiffly when the Scot made no attempt to speak, giving more attention to his glass than to the man opposite. If it was a deliberate attempt to make him feel uncomfortable, it was succeeding. Uncomfortable in his own house! 'I need details before I can go to the authorities.'

'There is little to tell. I found a wrecked coach and three men dead. Two in livery. The third had been killed by Madame la Comtesse when he attempted to rape her. No mean feat, I might add. The others were her servants. Her brother and maid had both been abducted. I found her about two miles away in deep woodland.'

'*Mon Dieu!* The hell that child must have endured,' Roland ejaculated. Then he frowned suspiciously. 'In deep woodland, you say? Not on the road? What prompted you to search for survivors?' It was in his mind that this man had contrived the whole thing in an attempt to extort money from him. To pretend to find Sian and help her. To return her to her home and collect a fat sum of money to share with his friends.

'I did not.' MacGregor gazed unflinchingly into the hostile face. He was no fool. He knew how Roland's mind was working. In his position, he would have deduced the same answer. 'I was taking a back path to my destination when I came upon her. She was unconscious and had been badly abused—but not raped. You may set your mind at rest over that. She was in no condition to travel. We spent the night at an inn—at my insistence, not hers. She was barely conscious by that time, and I knew she needed rest. She tells me that money and jewels were taken from the coach, yet surprisingly, the robbers did not strip her of her own personal jewellery. There is little more to tell. She is here, safe, and my obligation to her is discharged. If you will provide me with a horse, I shall be on my way. I can still make my destination by nightfall.'

Roland was silent, pondering his words. A simple, to the point account, with so much left unsaid. Deliberately? What was it he did not want known? Had he laid hands on Sian? He would kill him if he had. Where was he going? There were only two estates as large as Saint-Rémy in the area, that of the Duc de Bouillon, as remote as Saint-Rémy in its forest retreat, and that of Monsieur d'Artoille, a retired magistrate. He could see no reason for this man to visit either. The Duc would not hire mercenaries, although there were unconfirmed rumours that he was a close friend of the exiled Charles Stuart and had offered him sanctuary in his home, despite the Royal order banishing him from the shores of France. No, that would be too much of a coincidence, just because this man was a Scot.

MacGregor had made no mention of money. A subtle touch. The man was clever.

'Not without payment for your services, surely? What did my sister offer you to bring her safely back to me?' he demanded.

A strange gleam sprang into MacGregor's eyes, audacious in the silent suggestion mirrored there; otherwise he did not react to the barbed question.

'My sister has a soft heart. She trusts too easily,' Roland continued. 'I am the opposite. I tell you now, I neither like nor trust you, monsieur. We both knew why you brought her back—money.'

'Then pay me, and let me be on my way.' There was a sharp edge to the other man's tone which warned of rising anger. 'As it happens, the idea was hers. She persuaded me it would be worth my while. Am I to understand that you are not willing to honour that commitment?'

'My sister hired you. You will await her pleasure or leave without a *sou*,' Roland snapped. If he had said 'no' directly, he was sure he would have found that huge sword at his throat.

'I have no wish to linger here. A horse is all I require from you.' Somehow the Scot retained his temper in the face of Roland's high-handedness.

'It is my sister's wish that you remain as our guest until she has recovered sufficiently to speak with you again.' By his tone, Roland indicated he did not approve, and MacGregor did not blame him for that. Nor did Sian's request surprise him. The scent of danger had excited her as it did most of the women he came in contact with. They saw in him a challenge—a wild animal to be tamed for their pleasure. Tamed by dazzling smiles, tantalising promises, which they never meant to keep.

No woman had ever owned Douglas MacGregor, and never would. It was too late for the eagle's wings to be clipped. He would fly free and probably end his days on the sword of an enemy, dying as he had lived— alone, friendless, unloved. No one would mourn his passing. All those he loved were dead and buried in the mist-shrouded mountains of his beloved Highlands. He would never be with them again until death.

'I am sure your sister will have recovered by morning,' he said as he rose to his feet. 'She is a very resourceful young woman.'

He wanted to be away. Away from this fine house which was beginning to remind him of the luxury he had once lived in himself. Away from this protective brother who, if he stayed, might well become more difficult than he already was. And from her! Most of all away from her, with her softly curving body promising untold delights to a man reckless enough to reach out and take what she offered—but had not the courage to admit she wanted to give freely.

'I have had a room prepared for you.' Roland also rose, relieved to know that his guest wished to depart. When Sian was awake, there were questions he must ask her about this man's 'assistance'. He summoned a servant and ordered him to escort the Scot to the Green Suite. Also to have food taken to him, together with the remains of the whisky in the decanter. MacGregor smiled at the order. He inclined his head slightly towards his host, an acknowledgment of appreciation from his growling stomach—nothing more. 'I dine at six,' Roland added. 'Should you wish to join me.'

MacGregor glanced down at his attire and his smile grew, knowing that a refusal was anticipated and would be welcomed. He did not disappoint Roland.

'I think I shall sleep the remainder of the day away. A bath would be most welcome before I do, and a change of clothes afterwards. Could someone bring me the saddlebags they will find in the coach?'

'Of course.' Roland nodded confirmation to the waiting servant. 'André will be on hand for whatever you require.'

'One more thing—the boy.' The Scot picked up his sword, and noticed that the servant moved quickly two paces backwards. The sight of it affected most people like that. It had belonged to his father, who had taught him to use it as soon as he was able to lift it above his head at the age of fifteen. 'The young lad I hired to drive the coach. Without him, we could never have escaped from the inn. He can never go back there, of course; he would be killed for his part. I promised him money and work. The latter I shall take care of. He will come with me when I leave, but the other . . .'

'The boy shall be rewarded,' Roland replied. What

other demands did he have? 'About this inn . . .'

'As I've said, it is my belief some of the men about to waylay us as we left were part of the gang waiting for their friend to join them. They would have found what happened to him when I sent them out to bring back the coach and your sister's belongings. They thought to take my life for his. Thanks to your sister's warning, they did not succeed.' He had not forgotten how her cry had alerted him to danger. He had saved her life— she, his. They were even. Whatever happened between them from now on, there would be no talk of debts. 'They will be long gone by now, so there is little point in sending men to search the place. The boy will already be in Paris, well hidden in the jungle that also hides the thieves and murderers who kidnapped him.'

'Paris?' Roland echoed, taken aback. 'How so?'

'Strangers in this area would be noticed. Where do you hide a wisp of straw, but in a bale of straw? How many children do you suppose there are in Paris, monsieur? Where will you begin to look? Who will you bribe to bring you information and, when it comes, will you be able to trust the bringer—or act on what you learn?' MacGregor shrugged broad shoulders, his mouth a tight, grim line. 'The boy is as good as dead.'

'There will be a ransom note. There has to be!' Roland cried hoarsely. Suddenly he realised what Sian had meant. He lived a quiet, untroubled life at Saint-Rémy, caring for the estates and reading his books. When he wished for a change of scenery he spent a few days in the secluded hôtel in Paris. His extensive library at the château was the envy of the countryside for miles. Yet what good were his books to him now? The man who stood silently watching him, with mockery flickering in the depths of his eyes, could be of valuable assistance. If offered a large enough sum of money . . . 'I would like to speak to you further on this matter. If Timothy is killed, or even harmed, it would destroy my sister. She idolises the boy. He must be found.'

He was mad, Roland thought as he watched the tall

figure climb the stairs to his room. Quite, quite mad. A MacGregor aiding them! It was unbelievable—and dangerous!

# CHAPTER
# THREE

THE CHÂTEAU servants talked long into the night about the stranger who had arrived in their midst. They were puzzled by the ill-shod guest installed in a suite of his own on the first floor. He looked a rough soldier-of-fortune with his huge sword which was never far from his side—even as he soaked himself in a steaming hot tub—and scraps of conversation overheard between the master and the new arrival seemed to prove this correct. Yet here he was a privileged guest, and they had orders to be on hand to carry out his slightest wish.

They were not to know he had once lived in a fine house, had servants to wait on him, a stable of fine horses to choose from to ride the wild hills. He had eaten food from France and drunk French cognacs, although preferring the special brew distilled within his own walls—the nectar of the Gods the Scots called *usquebaugh*—a whisky distilled from malt which was always drunk undiluted. Fierce, throat-ripping liquor of which any decent, self-respecting Highland gentleman would consume at least two glasses before breakfast—and many more afterwards!

That night Douglas lay outstretched under a single silk sheet beneath a canopy of emerald green velvet. It was the first time he had slept in strange surroundings and not felt uncomfortable. His sword lay within easy reach as always, his dirk was beneath his pillow, but he knew he would have no need of either. Roland Saint-Rémy needed him. He despised him, but he needed him and he would ask him to stay. He would sleep in peace—a rare occurrence, but long before dawn he would be awake and dressed and restless. The pre-dawn time was always the worst, when his mind

was no longer fogged with sleep and memories came
creeping back to bring his body out in a cold sweat.
Hours reliving the bitterness of the retreat back into the
Highlands, the final great battle on Culloden Moor,
where the cream of his kinsmen, of Scotland, had fought
and died beneath English grapeshot and bayonets. The
long months of running, hiding, starving in the heather
with his wounded father and three loyal clansmen.

The death of his beautiful, gentle mother at the hands
of the English major who had first brutally raped her—
cut down without mercy as she tried to warn her husband
and son of the enemies' presence. The murder of his
father, frantic with grief, and the sacking of the village
by soldiers who had raped and looted their way through
the Highlands without quarter.

Throughout long nights he lay wounded, uncaring if
he died, in a cave on Ben Alder, waiting for a ship
to carry him away safely. Away from the death and
destruction, away from his beloved mountains and
streams, away from everything and everyone he had
ever loved.

Sian did not remember being undressed and put to bed
by her old wet-nurse, who made loud clucking noises
as she divested her of her clothing and burst into tears
as she saw the bruises and abrasions marking the soft
skin of her 'baby'. All she could recall was sliding
between silk sheets, her aching body soothed and
caressed by the gentle touch of a diaphanous chiffon
nightgown. She had allowed herself to be gently washed
and her hair brushed, but the latter had proved so
painful for her throbbing head that she had dismissed
the maid and declared she wished to be left alone to
sleep. She did not care what she looked like. She wanted
only to sleep.

And sleep she did, without a single nightmare, until
at last, managing to rouse herself sufficiently to look
across at the small gilt and ivory clock set inside a jade
elephant, the tusks and eyes studded with emeralds, she
found it to be two o'clock.

Had Roland gone to the authorities? Surely he could not sit idly and wait for a ransom demand? He could not hate the child that much! Her eyes grew misty as she thought of Timothy's impish smile, which always endeared him to her even when he was at his most mischievous—which was three-quarters of the day—the pale blue eyes and golden hair inherited from his mother. Suddenly the boy's image was no longer with her. Before her face was another who was also capable of invading her mind at will, despite the shortness of their acquaintance. Douglas MacGregor! Blond-haired also, but ruthless, arrogant, a wild animal who stalked the jungles outside the boundaries of her limited existence, seeking a way through the defences which surrounded her, seeking a way to destroy her world. He would destroy her if she allowed it. She knew it in her heart.

She drew herself up in bed, awkwardly because she discovered her whole body was as stiff as an oak beam, a hand gingerly touching the gash beneath her hairline. Now why on earth had she thought such an outrageous thing? He was nothing to her.

She must not allow herself to be browbeaten by his fierce manner again. She must ignore the mockery in those penetrating eyes and remember who and what she was. He was a hired hand, no more. But she was Sian, Comtesse de Saint-Rémy. A lady! She had not felt like a lady when she had lain in his arms and felt his hands on her. She had felt a woman for the first time in her life—and it frightened her. Excited her, too, and that in itself was frightening. She was not an experienced woman of the world like so many at Versailles.

Even Jeanne Poisson, Madame de Pompadour, had laughed not unkindly at her lack of knowledge, for they had been friends too long for her to do that, but it had hurt her nevertheless. Did friends discuss her behind her back? 'Poor Sian, she has never had a lover.' Did every man expect her to sleep with him the very first time they met? If so, she would never know a man. She had been brought up by strict Catholic parents who had

taught her that the sanctity of marriage mattered above
all things. Only her husband would ever touch her.

Yet, when Douglas had held her, subjected her to
the searching force of his kisses, the experienced touch
of his hands, marriage had been the last thing in her
mind. She had known an exquisite pleasure at his
caresses, immediately followed by a feeling of terrible
guilt that he could have roused her so easily. Accessible
women were a *sou* a dozen in Paris. They came in all
shapes and sizes, from all walks of life. She did not want
to join their ranks.

She rang for her maid, and then remembered that
Effie was not at the château. The realisation sent her
straight back into the depths of despair. When someone
came, she ordered a light breakfast and a hot bath to
be made ready, and had the closet doors thrown open
wide so that she could scan the contents. There was
only one way to combat the effect Douglas MacGregor
had on her.

After soaking for an hour in water scented with jas-
mine and lavender, she emerged refreshed and ready
for battle. She declined the awkward whalebone corset
laid out—her figure was so perfect that she rarely wore
one, even at Versailles. In Scotland she had given them
up altogether, much to the horror—or was it envy?—
of her friends. Over a shift of linen embroidered with
Brussels lace, the young maid slipped a gown of watered
silk. The colour was saffron yellow, and it set off Sian's
hair, with its sable sheen after such careful brushing, to
perfection. Round her neck she placed a single strand
of pearls. On her feet, dainty leather shoes, dyed to
match her gown, adorned with silver buckles.

Slowly she turned to and fro before the gilt-framed
mirror which dominated one wall of the bedroom. She
looked groomed, elegant, aloof: the image she had been
seeking.

As she passed her brother's room on her way downstairs, she saw that the door was open, and stepped
inside, hoping to find him alone. She was anxious to
discover exactly how much Douglas MacGregor had

told him. He came out of his dressing-room, fastening the buttons of a fresh shirt, and his face lit up in a relieved smile at the sight of her.

'My dear girl, no one told me you were awake, let alone up and about,' he declared, taking her in his arms and kissing her affectionately on both cheeks. 'When I looked in on you first thing this morning, you were sleeping like an angel. You looked so peaceful. After what you have been through, I can only marvel at your swift recovery. You have the constitution of a horse.'

'Are you hurrying off too, Roland? I would like to speak to you.'

'If you are worrying about Timothy—don't. The authorities have been informed, and the word will soon be out from here to Paris.'

'Paris,' Sian echoed, turning pale. 'Why so far? Surely he will be hidden in this vicinity?'

'Not according to your mercenary friend. He is sure Timothy is in the city. His reasoning is beyond me, too. I agree with you, but if anyone knows about the kind of people who took the boy, it will be someone like him. Anyway, there is nothing either of us can do— except wait.'

Sian bit her lip, and he was instantly contrite at his off-hand manner.

'Forgive me, little one. I don't care for the child as you do, but I don't want to see him harmed. I want him returned to you safe and well as soon as possible.'

'Then you agree I should ask Monsieur MacGregor to help us?' Sian asked hesitantly.

'He told me what happened,' Roland said. There was a questioning light in his eyes as he looked at her, but she chose to ignore it. 'He says you offered to pay him to return you here. Is that true?'

'Yes. He was most reluctant at first, but in the morning he agreed. Thank God he did, or I would never have left that inn alive! Oh, Roland, you should have seen the way those men looked at me!'

'Then I suggest we pay him and allow him to go on his way.'

'Not use him to find Timothy?' she cried. 'Why not? You said yourself that if anyone knows the kind of men who have taken him, it will be someone like him. Someone who can move in their dark world without suspicion.'

'Would you hand over the ransom money to him? Trust him to bargain on our behalf?' Roland frowned at her. 'You cannot trust a mercenary, Sian. He will take the money and run, and you will never see Timothy again. I don't know what he said or did during the short time you were together to make you feel you can trust him. He could be dangerous to you—to us. That name!'

'What do you mean? Nothing happened between us! I owe the man my life, Roland, and I am not about to be ungrateful. I don't like what he is any more than you do, but if he had not found me when he did . . . I might never have returned here alive. That is not something I find easy to forget.'

'And at this inn where you both stayed overnight?' her brother asked quietly, and noticed a wary look stealing into her eyes. Something had happened, he was sure of it!

'I—I remember very little. I was barely conscious when we arrived, and later on, I was feverish—or so he tells me. I really don't remember anything very clearly. You will have to ask him.' Sian had never been able to lie, and she failed miserably now. 'He bathed my cuts and put some kind of salve on them. I can recall that . . '

'And did not lay a disrespectful finger on you? I am not a fool, Sian! I may shut myself away here with my books, but that does not mean my mind is closed to what goes on in the outside world. I have seen the way men and women parade themselves at Versailles, and it sickens me. I am not saying MacGregor touched you, but I do know that something happened between you. Can you not tell me what it was?'

Slowly Sian shook her head, and at the misery mirrored in her expression he slipped his arm round her and held her close.

'He—he is like no other man I have ever met. He

frightens me, yet . . . He was kind to me, Roland, but he despises me and my money, my title, my English blood. He lost everything in the last uprising—home, family, friends—and can never return unless he wants to be thrown into prison or tried for treason against the English crown. His manner with me was one he would have used with a servant-girl, and I am sure his rudeness was deliberate, intended to hurt and humiliate me. But still he cared for me, fought and killed for me. I feel we have a chance of getting Timmy and Effie back alive if he is helping us. We have to risk the loss of our money. We can afford it.'

'Can we afford to risk their lives? Our own?'

'Are they not at risk at the moment? How do we know they are not dead already?' Her lips quavered as she spoke. It was something she had not had the courage to put into words before. 'Have we a choice? Can we afford *not* to use him?'

'Very well. I shall speak with him if your mind is made up—and I can see it is,' Roland said with a shrug of his shoulders. 'It is obvious that he does not connect us in any way with Scotland. We should be safe enough.'

'Why should he? We shall both speak to him,' Sian corrected. 'Tonight at dinner. I shall ask cook to prepare something special, and tell André to bring up a bottle of '45 claret from the cellars. We shall wine and dine our guest in style.'

'The sight of a bag of *louis* on the table might prove a stronger inducement to help us, but we shall tell him no more than is absolutely necessary.'

'Agreed.'

That evening Sian went downstairs early to take a last look at the dining-room before Douglas MacGregor and her brother appeared. As she inspected the table, checked the wines and refreshments for after dinner, she felt a pang of conscience. Here she was about to sit down to a mouth-watering array of food in elegant surroundings, when somewhere in some unknown place, probably frightened and uncomfortable, her little

brother and her maid Effie prayed and waited for someone to rescue them.

Why had there been no demands made yet on either
her or Roland? Two whole days! How many more would
pass before they heard? They would hear, she told
herself over and over again. They *must* hear. It was
unthinkable that she might never see her little brother
again.

Angrily she pulled herself together, pinching her
cheeks as she stared into a side mirror and saw how
white they had become. She had to believe everything
would be all right—had to believe she could persuade
Douglas MacGregor to act for them when the time
came. Until then, he could set out and make his own
enquiries among the very dubious friends of his
acquaintance—of which she was sure there were many.
Someone surely would know something . . . be persuaded to speak, or bribed . . . She would give him
whatever money he needed.

A movement from one of the other rooms caught her
eye as she was about to take a last look in the kitchen
at the preparations. His back towards her, Douglas
MacGregor stood looking out of the window on to the
darkened garden, then moved to one side as André
began to pull the heavy velvet curtains. As he turned
to face her, she hardly recognised him as the same man!
His close-fitting coat was of a deep burgundy brocade,
sewn with gold thread. The wide turned-back sleeves
showed a hint of ruffled lace which matched that at the
front of his white shirt. His waistcoat was again brocade,
pale grey this time and quite plain. His knee-breeches
matched the coat, with white stockings and black leather
shoes adorned with large silver buckles.

She stood quite still, astounded at the picture of
respectability he presented. He could be mistaken for
a gentleman at any time! Quickly she dismissed the
idea that he had changed solely for her benefit as she
advanced into the room, her fan fluttering rather nervously before her cheeks.

'I did not realise anyone was down yet. Would you

care for a drink before dinner, monsieur? André, bring
us a bottle of chilled Château Autille. It is a light
wine and will not spoil our appetites,' she said, waving
MacGregor to a seat beside her.

'I prefer whisky, if you don't mind,' came the annoy-
ing reply.

She did mind, but tonight she would never tell him
so.

'I am sure you know where it is. Please help yourself.'

'As you see, I have taken the opportunity at least to
appear somewhat respectable tonight,' he murmured as
he sat down with a glass at his side.

He allowed his gaze to rest on her for the first time
since she entered the room, and she found herself
undergoing the very same scrutiny that she had given
him. He made no attempt to hide the gleam of interest
which came into his eyes as they swept down from the
shining black tresses, wound on the crown of her head
and secured with jewelled combs, over the saffron
yellow silk which gave her skin an ivory sheen, with its
low curving neckline and tiny satin bows adorning
bodice and skirt, and to the rings which flashed and
sparkled on the slender hands locked tightly together
in her lap.

'I think you enjoy being unpleasant to people,
Monsieur MacGregor.' The words were uttered before
she gave them thought, and to her horror he threw back
his head and laughed aloud. 'What do you find so funny?
Do the misfortunes of others amuse you?'

'What do you know of misfortunes, woman?' His
voice was as soft as velvet, but the knife-like gleam in
his eyes cut her, wounding as it was intended to. 'What
sorry little mishaps befall you here, cosseted by your
brother, waited on day and night by servants? God,
look at you! Painted and perfumed like some Versailles
whore. Is this meant to impress me, Madame la Comtesse?' Sian sat transfixed. How could he be so cruel?
'Your civility astounds me. Why don't you ring for your
servants? Have me thrown out or whipped? Shall I tell
you why? Because you need me. That is the only reason

your brother has been so cordial to me when I know he loathes the sight of me—as you yourself do. All this is little more than cheese to attract the mouse into the waiting trap. I am too old to be caught at such games —and by amateurs! I have played with experts—and won.'

'I am sure you have.' Somehow Sian found her tongue. She put aside her glass and glared blue daggers at him. 'You are quite right in your assumption, monsieur. We do need you. At least, I thought we needed you. Now, I begin to think my brother was right and that, given the chance, and the money, you would take both and vanish, leaving my brother to die. You care for no one but yourself, and I was a fool to think I could trust you with his life. He is too precious for me to put him at risk in the hands of someone like you. If you wish, monsieur, you may leave. I, for one, shall be glad to see the back of you.'

'Will you?' There was no responding anger towards her. He emptied his glass and stood, setting it aside, before moving to stand in front of her. His eyes burned into her angry features, challenging her to continue with her assassination of his character. She swallowed hard, unable to do so, yet managed to hold his gaze. What was it he saw there? Regret, disappointment—condemnation? What right did she have to expect him to risk his life for a seven-year-old boy he did not know and would not like if he did? An Englishman's son! And she with English blood too. He was insane even to be contemplating remaining. He had a good horse now. If he left this minute, he could be at the Duc de Bouillon's estate by midnight, and within a few days he would have forgotten this woman ever existed. Or would he?

'Ah, good. I see my sister is taking care of you, Monsieur MacGregor.' Roland came into the room, looking handsome and debonair in a blue suit, a profusion of white lace at his throat and wrists. Sian marvelled how he contained his surprise at the change in his guest, for not a flicker showed in his expression, as he helped himself to wine. 'My dear, you look radiant!

Are you sure you feel well enough to dine with us? I still feel you should have stayed in bed so much longer.'

'I am not an invalid, Roland,' Sian protested softly, pleased by his concern. No one at Ard Choille cared if she was ill or not—except Timothy. Since the death of their mother, they had grown so close. A shadow crossed her face and she quickly averted her gaze, afraid he might see it and question the reason. She had just dismissed Douglas MacGregor from the house! Whatever had possessed her to allow him to upset her so? From the doorway, André announced that the meal was ready to be served, and she rose to her feet in relief. 'Shall we go in to dinner?'

Why did he not take himself off as he said he intended to do? she thought, as the three of them moved into the dining-room, to the splendid table awaiting them. She sought his face as she sat down. It was a closed book. Whatever he thought of the array before him, he would not allow her to know. After the meal, she asked, 'Shall we take our coffee into the drawing-room? Or would you prefer to remain in here and talk?'

There had been little flow of conversation while they ate.

'As the whole point of this very skilfully executed manoeuvre is to make me more amenable to discussing the abduction of your brother, why don't we begin?' Macgregor challenged both of them in turn with his piercing gaze. 'My sword is at your disposal—providing the price is right.'

'You may have dressed like a gentleman tonight, monsieur,' Sian said stiffly as she rose, 'but your manners betray the fact that you still belong in the gutter.' He gave her no chance to enjoy the moment of victory.

'We understand each other remarkably well, do we not?' he countered with a mocking smile, and her face flushed with hot colour. Without a word she swept into the other room and took a seat on the long, low couch beside the fireplace. André brought in a tray with coffee, and placed the decanter of whisky on it also, and then stood waiting. She had the impression he was longing to hear what would happen. When she indicated that he could leave, he went out, closing the doors after the two men, who came in, grim-faced, not speaking.

'Monsieur MacGregor says that you told him he could leave? Is that what you want, *mignonne*?' her brother asked, looking at her intently.

'I think it would be best. We—we can deal with whatever comes. He does not want to work for the likes of us, and I would not dream of imposing on him against his will.'

'Hardly an imposition. I shall be paid for my time,' MacGregor returned, lowering himself into a chair. He refused coffee and settled for whisky.

Roland handed Sian some coffee, poured a small brandy for himself and stood with his back to the huge chasm of a fireplace, which stretched almost ten feet in length behind him, his brows drawn together into a frown of indecision. For a full moment no one spoke or moved, and then he sighed and looked across at the Scot.

'My sister spoke in haste, monsieur. We have already discussed this matter of engaging your services to find Timothy, and she believes it to be possible, with your assistance. Why she places such faith in you is beyond me, and I admit truthfully that I do not want you to be involved. I neither like nor trust you. I have no reason to. Perhaps she has, and that is why I ask, in her name, that you use whatever skills—whatever methods—are necessary to help us to get him back. Alive, of course.' He prayed they would not regret such foolishness.

Oh, Roland, Sian thought, a lump rising in her throat. I could never have said it. No more could I explain why to you. Everything I say and do is wrong for him and he angers me beyond speech sometimes, yet I owe him more than my life. Her brother had asked in her name!

The Scot looked at the silent figure sitting upright on the couch. Trust did not exist between them. It was something far more earthy: need—desire! It went by many names, but amounted to the same thing in the

end. She did not want him to go. No more did he, yet
he wavered on the brink of acceptance. His sword was
for hire, and the money, at this precise time, would be
most welcome, for after visiting the Duc de Bouillon
and the guest he had ridden so far to see again—none
other than the exiled Charles Stuart himself—he had
no idea where he would go or what he would do.
Madame de Brissac had made it uncomfortable for him
at Versailles, and few people wanted to acknowledge
that they even knew him, let alone to hire his services.

Even La Pompadour had made known her displeasure at what had taken place at the Petit Trianon
that evening, and it had reached him in no uncertain
terms at his lodgings at the Coq d'Or! Without help, he
would never get back into the circle of people who
provided him with a not unprofitable existence. Sian
Saint-Rémy was the answer to his problem. With her
contacts, he would not starve this winter in some garret.
He told himself that was the only incentive which made
him sit and listen to what was being said, when he knew
the safest, wisest thing he could ever do in his life would
be to get up and leave the room, the château—and
her.

'You ask the impossible, monsieur,' he said, shrugging his shoulders, and caught the flash of horror in
Sian's eyes as she thought he was turning the offer
down. 'Where do I begin to look? Paris? It is unhealthy
for me there, and it is only instinct that tells me the boy
has been taken there. It may not be right. Are you
prepared to give me *carte blanche* to search until I find
him? Or will my every move be questioned? My motives
suspect? I do not work that way. I work alone—and
unhindered.'

'Surely there will be a ransom demand soon,' Sian
interrupted. 'There has to be. Why else did they take
him? And why Effie? Unless, I suppose, they need her
to look after him?'

'Why else indeed?' The light eyes grew almost black
as he pondered her question. 'I do not understand why
you also were not abducted and held. Can you think of

anyone who might have such a grudge against him alone that they would want to harm him?'

'No,' she cried, aghast at such an idea. Surely he was not suggesting that Timothy might be dead? She would never accept that! 'He is a sweet child. Kind and thoughtful, and everyone loves him here. And in Paris. Why, I took him to court one day with me, and even Madame de Pompadour loved him. Roland, there is no one, is there?' Except a Scot who bore a forbidden name. No, she had to trust him!

Only the brother who has some reason to hate him, he mused, watching Roland with a keen eye, but the other man gave no indication that he might have a troublesome conscience, and he dismissed the thought without dwelling on it further. Sian obviously doted on the boy, ruling her out also. It was a blind alley, and this worried him. So much about this abduction did not make sense. Was there a bigger fish to land than a mere ransom for the return of the child? If so, what? What was it he did not know about the Saint-Rémy family which could give him a clue to the mystery? He felt an uneasy feeling in the pit of his stomach that forewarned danger.

'Well, monsieur? Do you think the boy is dead?' Roland asked slowly. For Sian's sake he prayed not, yet he, too, had sensed something terribly wrong from the beginning. He almost spoke out, then checked himself. It was in his mind that MacGregor's appearance upon the scene had been too opportune, yet he knew his sister would not accept that. The man had been clever, if it was all his plan. Perhaps it had been his intention to find only Sian's body, and then deliver it to the château and be conveniently on hand when a ransom note arrived so that he could offer his help. If only that name was not between them? So much blood spilt already! How could he trust this man?

'An excellent bottle, this,' the Scot remarked as he sipped the whisky.

'I am glad you like it,' Roland replied. He could never tell the difference. 'Are you also an expert on whisky?'

'We used to distil *usquebaugh* in our cellars.' He had
learned to appreciate the potential of the undiluted
firewater which Highlanders regarded as true 'nectar of
the Gods'. 'It brings back memories of my last months
in Scotland in '46. Not a good year for me, or for
Scotland. It was the year the English soldiers pursued
us into the heather, burning, raping, plundering. God,
how they enjoyed their work.' Roland frowned at the
bitterness creeping into his voice, but MacGregor did
not notice. Shadows flitted across his face as memories
returned to haunt him. 'My father was wounded at
Culloden. It took us three months of fighting, of hiding,
to get home . . . and to what? The house was occupied
by an English major. A butcher. He had razed the
village to the ground, killed all the able-bodied men
there, no matter their age, and taken women to the
house for his men. He took my mother for himself.'

'I think my sister has heard enough!' Roland intervened, pouring himself another brandy. 'The past is
over and done with. Nothing can bring back what you
have lost.' He had grown exceedingly pale. Sian, too.

'Your father was also at Culloden, was he not?' The
softly-spoken question had a dangerous edge to it, and
Sian moved uneasily in her seat. She had seen this side
of the Scot before, and been afraid at the change in
him. When memories possessed him, they aroused the
jungle animal which lay dormant beneath the surface of
his character. 'Perhaps it was he who thrust his sword
into my father's back.'

'Take care,' Roland warned, turning pale. 'I will not
have you speak of him in that way. Have you not
thought it might have been your father who put a
pistol-ball through the heart of mine? I was very fond
of my father, monsieur. Speak ill of him again, and I
shall call you out this instant! I am no match for you,
of that we are both aware, but I will face you over sword
or pistol.'

'Roland!' Sian cried softly, and instantly MacGregor's
gaze was full on her, but she sensed he did not understand the silent message in her eyes.

'You and I have no quarrel. It could well have been as you say. So let us proceed to the matter in hand. To speak of the past further would only anger me more. You must forgive me my ill manners. I was raised with a sword in one hand and a glass of whisky in the other. Not the kind of upbringing that includes polite drawing-room conversation.'

He was laughing at them, Sian thought, silently hating him. He lifted his glass in her direction, and the eyes full of the devil's laughter held hers for a long moment, before he turned his attention once more to Roland.

Before her brother could speak again, the door opened and André stood on the threshold, a look of astonishment on his face. She gave a gasp as he was pushed roughly aside. The colour fled from her cheeks as a dishevelled, weeping woman flung herself across and room and collapsed on the floor by her feet, to bury her face in the folds of Sian's gown.

'Madam! Oh, madam! They let me go.'

Trembling in every limb, Sian bent and lifted the woman to her knees, her eyes wide with apprehension. They had let her go . . . But what of Timothy?

'Effie, where is my brother?' she demanded tremulously. 'What has happened to him?'

# CHAPTER
# FOUR

'HE IS SAFE, madam. They sent a man back with me to tell you their demands.' Effie looked up into the white face of her mistress, still clutching at the silken folds of her skirt. She was a woman in her thirties, pretty in a countrified way, with heavy dark curls falling about her plump face. She was tall for a woman, endowed with an ample bosom, but not fat. On more than one occasion Sian had been surprised at the strength she possessed.

'Why did they free you?' The question came from behind her, from MacGregor, who had not moved in his chair. His narrowed gaze took in her dishevelled appearance, torn blouse, and dusty skirt ripped at the hem. The graze on one cheek. Her eyes were red with weeping, but to his mind she in no way resembled the frightened woman *he* had found, whose body bore painful reminders of her ordeal. One or two faint bruises and a grazed cheek. She had fared well at the hands of men who had no scruples about rape and murder. The premonition of danger, that lurked deep inside him, raised its head once again to warn him to take care with his words.

'So that madam would hear of her brother's safety from my own lips and believe it, and pay whatever they ask to have him released. They will kill him if she does not.' She gave the Scot only a cursory glance, fresh tears spilling down over her cheeks. 'The child is so afraid. They are rough with him . . . He sleeps on dirty sacking, with rats . . . Oh, madam, you must do as they say!'

'Where is this man?' Roland demanded.

'He is waiting outside in the hall. He made me come in first to tell you that if anything happens to him,

Timothy will be killed. He must be allowed to leave here unharmed,' Effie sobbed.

Sian stroked her hair, her eyes seeking MacGregor's face as she did so. Timothy was alive! She would pay anything to get him back. Surely the Scot could not refuse to aid them now? He looked so strange as he stared at the woman huddled at her feet and weeping loudly. Poor Effie, did he have no compassion for her, either? Anyone could see how she had been mistreated. Any antagonism she felt towards her maid vanished as she stood up, lifting her to her feet.

'Come, someone will take you upstairs. You are to go straight to bed and rest.'

'We need her to tell us where she had been held, Sian,' Roland insisted, stepping forward to bar her path. 'When we have heard everything she knows, then she can rest.'

'The poor woman is exhausted, can't you see that? Tomorrow she can talk. This man they have sent will tell us everything we want to know. God knows what indignities she has suffered!' Sian replied, surprised at his stand.

'She is right. A hysterical woman is of little use.' MacGregor's gaze centred as he spoke on the woman supported in Sian's arms, and for a brief instant, there was a spark of defiance mirrored in the light eyes. And something more—was it hatred? 'Tomorrow, when she has rested, she will be able to answer the many questions I have to ask her. I shall bring in her companion.'

Sian handed Effie over to André, with instructions that she was to be put to bed immediately with a glass of warm milk and brandy. As MacGregor rose and advanced towards the door, she retreated nervously to the side of her brother and slipped her arm through his.

'Monsieur MacGregor seems to have taken charge of the situation,' Roland remarked in a dry tone, but she sensed he was not annoyed by the man's actions. He was as much in the dark about how to handle the newcomer as she was. To show fear was what he would want—and be expecting. To be defiant or difficult might

jeopardise Timothy's life. To refuse to pay whatever
ransom was asked would most certainly amount to his
death-warrant. A tremor ran through Sian's body, and
he managed to smile and pat her hand in a show of
reassurance.

The man who preceded MacGregor into the room
and stood silently, insolently looking at them, reminded
her of a weasel. Short in stature, balding slightly, with
eyes that stared out of a leather mask of a face like
black beads. The mouth was thin and cruel, and Sian
knew instantly they would know no mercy at his hands.
Closing the door behind him, MacGregor stood with
his back against it, arms folded loosely over his chest.
His expression betrayed no thought. The narrowed eyes
fixed on the newcomer were as merciless as those she
found herself looking into, and Sian shivered again.
Concernedly, Roland seated her on the couch and
pressed a cup of coffee into her hands. A look warned
her that now was not a time to betray her revulsion of
this man or his reason for presenting himself.

'You have news for us?' Straightening, Roland turned
and looked at the slight figure, wishing with all his heart
he could take that wizened throat between his fingers
and squeeze the life from it for all the pain and suffering
he and his friends had been instrumental in causing his
sister—and were, very likely at this moment, causing
to a frightened seven-year-old boy.

'Don't take that high-and-mighty attitude with me,
Monsieur le Comte.' The man's voice was little more
than a husky croak, as though someone had already
attempted what was in Roland's mind. 'I could do with
a glass of that.' He flung out a hand towards the whisky
decanter. 'I've come a long way on your behalf, and
I'm parched.'

'You will have no need of that or anything else if you
do not hurry and tell us what we want to know, my
friend!' At this, the man swung round with a hollow
laugh to face the blond-haired Scot.

'You wouldn't dare touch me! If you do, the boy dies.
If I don't return to my friends . . .'

'I have every intention of allowing you to leave here.' MacGregor smiled into his face, and the little man saw death mirrored in those steady eyes. This one was not like the others, he knew. He had not expected him to be *here*. But what did it matter? The family would never dare to harm him or allow him to be harmed. A momentary twinge of uneasiness touched him, intensifying as MacGregor continued. 'However, how you leave is up to you. I, for one, am willing to cut your throat as soon as we have the information we need. Do you really believe your friends will care if you are dead? Your share will be divided among them. Perhaps they don't like you, René, and that is why they sent you here. They want you out of the way.'

'You know him?' Sian gasped. She was unable to take her eyes from his face. Did he mean what he said? Or was he merely trying to frighten the man?

'Allow me to introduce to you René: thief, liar, arsonist and now abductor. He runs with a band of unpleasant fellows near the Pont-Neuf, headed by a man called Simeon.' He saw the look of horror which came into Sian's eyes, but hardened his heart against the suspicions he knew were stealing into her mind. She had to know what kinds of men she was dealing with, and accept the reality she might never see her little brother again. He was beginning to wonder if it could be done.

'I will not ask how you come to be acquainted with them,' Roland began, and the little man burst into high-pitched laughter.

'Him? He beds with Simeon's sister. She's been his mistress for the past year, on and off. Why, he's one of us, Le Blond is!'

Sian banged her cup down on the table so loudly that she thought it would break. Mistress! Yet what else should she have suspected? Of course he had a woman. There was a sharp cry, and she looked up to find René sprawling on the floor, knocked off balance by a fierce thrust of MacGregor's foot in the middle of his back. That name! The same one he had told her. The man *did* know him!

'Stay there!' he ordered, as René tried to rise. 'With your nose in the dirt is where you belong. Well?' He stared at the two hostile faces before him. 'Do we listen to what he has to say, or has he turned your minds already? We will not find the boy by standing here, dividing our ranks with suspicions.'

'Are you offering us your services, monsieur?' Somehow Sian found her voice.

'I am sure you can afford me.' The words were flung at her with quiet fury behind them. He was annoyed that his personal life had been exposed. It was not something he wanted open to comment. 'Without my help, you will not get the boy back alive, believe me.'

She did not want to, but she did. It placed her under further obligation to him, plunging her deeper into the quicksand of complex emotions she had sought desperately to avoid.

'I shall pay anything.' She ignored her brother's warning frown. 'Anything, do you hear?'

'Scum like René here are not to be trusted. If they knew that, they would extort a vast sum of money from you and still kill your brother. I have to get to them before they have a chance to do that.'

'Are *you* to be trusted?' she asked, lips quivering as she gave herself totally into his hands. His eyes gleamed at the question.

'You alone can answer that. Need I have brought you home?'

'A clever man, involved with this man and his friends, might have done exactly that,' Roland flashed, and he nodded, not disputing the fact.

'True. As I say, the question of trust remains with you and your sister. I shall not be out of place making enquiries in Paris. You would. Can you afford *not* to take a chance on me?'

'Either way, Timothy's life will be at risk,' Sian whispered. 'Oh, Roland, what are we to do? Tell me, I cannot decide such a thing.' Her brother was silent, as torn with doubts as she was. Suddenly she straightened her shoulders and looked the Scot squarely in the face.

'Find my brother, any way you can and I shall meet your price, Monsieur MacGregor.'

'We shall meet it,' Roland confirmed, unable to allow her to bear the full responsibility for the decision alone. Timothy was his brother too.

'Speak, René, before I grow more impatient than I already am,' MacGregor snapped.

'The boy is safe. I swear it, but you'll never find him unless you do exactly as I tell you. We want fifteen thousand *louis*. You are to return to Paris and stay there until we get in touch with you again. Have the money ready to be delivered as soon as we tell you where.'

Fifteen thousand! Sian silently mouthed the words, her eyes going in relief from her brother to MacGregor. She had been expecting—fearing—a huge amount. This was easily within the limits of her purse.

The tiny nerve throbbing at the side of Roland's forehead betrayed his relief, too. Only the Scot showed no sign of emotion. His foot descended savagely again on René's back, and ground between his shoulderblades with vindictive force as he demanded,

'Now tell us the rest of it! Fifteen thousand? How much the next time? Another fifteen? Thirty? One hundred thousand? That's more Simeon's mark. He'd spit on the paltry sum you've mentioned. What's your game, René? Speak, man, or I'll slit you from ear to ear this minute! We have no River Seine handy to dispose of your body, but the woods round here will keep our secret. Besides, who's going to look for a gutter-rat like you?'

Sian pressed a hand against her mouth, not daring to utter a sound. Each word he uttered condemned him further. It was well known that the Seine was the ultimate grave of many unfortunates waylaid, robbed and then murdered.

She had allowed herself to forget—or at least to dismiss from her mind—the fact this man was no better than the beggars and thieves who inhabited the city on the other side of the Pont-Neuf. She would be hiring a dangerous, unpredictable man who lived by his own set of rules and set no store by those of anyone else.

René squirmed and swore beneath the foot immobilising his back. His face was lined with sweat. Fear, not pain, Sian suspected, as he looked up at Roland.

'Who gives the orders here? You, Monsieur le Comte —or he? You will get nothing from me. I have told you all you need to know for the present.'

Roland looked across into MacGregor's grim features, hesitated for a moment, then asked firmly, 'Do you think he can tell us more?'

'With a little persuasion. If you have a cellar somewhere where I could question him further . . .' MacGregor suggested, and Sian came to her feet instantly.

'No, he must not be touched. You heard what Effie said. If he does not return to his friends, Timothy will suffer. We cannot risk it,' she cried.

'I do not think we have a choice.' The Scot did not look at her, but at her brother. 'René already knows I shall soon be in Paris looking for the boy. Do you want them to know it, too? We cannot allow him to return, and if he is to remain here, then at least he should be amicable and tell us more. I am sure he would tell me. Wouldn't you?'

The man beneath his foot cursed him in gutter language that made Sian blench. She had never heard anything like it before. MacGregor reached down and hauled the slight figure to his feet by the collar of his worn coat. René dangled in his grasp like a helpless leaf suspended in the wind.

'Wouldn't you?' he repeated softly, and shook him. Sian was sure she heard his teeth rattle.

'I regret to say I agree with Monsieur MacGregor, *mignonne*,' Roland said, looking into her distressed face. 'I am sorry, but we cannot afford to let him go. However, I think it advisable that I question him— alone. He may feel more inclined to speak to me without . . . without any pressure being put upon him.'

Whatever had possessed him, Sian thought, as he rang for André and ordered two servants to come and escort him and the cringing little figure of René down to the wine cellars? Situated deep below the house, with numerous passages leading off to small rooms where the vintage wine was stored for years to mellow, she knew no sound would ever be heard from the unfortunate man if 'persuasion' was necessary. Once he went down the narrow flight of stairs which led to them, he might never reappear! Surely that could not be what her brother intended. MacGregor, yes! He was capable of inflicting pain and torture, but not Roland. Why had he taken such a task upon himself? She sank back on the couch, as he followed André and the others from the room without a backward glance. The Scot swore vehemently under his breath, and she looked at him sharply.

'What is it?' He looked annoyed. Because René knew him, perhaps?

He rounded on her, eyes narrowed with anger. The thin white scar on his cheek taut, menacing!

'He'll get nothing from him. The likes of René were raised on violence. To break him needs a special talent you learn only in the gutter.'

'My brother is not a violent man, neither is he a fool. He hopes to make him speak without force—the civilised way. Is that such a bad thing?' She did not understand his attitude.

'He was afraid of what might have been said between us when we were alone,' he flung back, bitter lines deepening the twist of his mouth. 'Because I know the man . . . And he spoke of trust!'

'No, I did. Roland does not share my belief in you, and I cannot blame him for that,' Sian returned, instantly springing to the defence of her beloved twin. 'You live by the sword; you know no other way. Roland does. It is to his credit that he does not resort to inflicting pain if there is any other way.'

'Pain is the only thing René will understand. He knows what Simeon will do to him if he talks, and so he has to be shown a greater threat, which would inflict greater pain, to loosen his tongue for us. While your brother may well know how to persuade him to talk, he

will not do so. Whereas I would—and will, if he fails.
My neck is also at stake, if you recall, due to Madame
de Brissac. Once I set foot in Paris again, I shall have
Madame de Pompadour's hounds after me. My life is
of great importance to me.'

For almost an hour they sat in a strained silence, Sian
trying to keep her gaze averted from his bleak features.
What was happening down in the cellars? Roland was
so long. Several time she begun to rise from her seat,
determined to go and see for herself what was taking
place, but each time MacGregor threw her a withering
glance and she remained seated. She could offer no
help, no sensible advice, under the circumstances, so
she was better where she was. But how the minutes
dragged!

She asked André to bring a pot of herb tea to steady
her nerves. It lifted a little of the weariness from her,
but did nothing to instil fresh confidence in her. Confidence to believe that the other members of the band
would not care if René did not return. Would share out
his take between them, as MacGregor had said, and
forget he had ever existed. Honour among thieves!

Douglas MacGregor possessed a strange kind of
honour—if any at all, which she still doubted. He would
not break his given word, yet he thought nothing of
insulting her as if she were a common street whore. He
treated Roland like a child, and both of them as
inferiors. Honour? He did not possess manners, let
alone honour!

The door opened, and her brother came in. He went
straight to the table beside her and splashed a large
amount of whisky into a glass. Carelessly, Sian saw.
Why, his hand was shaking so violently that he could
scarcely hold the glass to his mouth. She knew instantly
that something was terribly wrong.

'What is it? What has happened?' she asked
anxiously. He looked so strange. Pale, yet with a fierce
light burning in his eyes which she had never seen
before. MacGregor, too, was watching him intently.

'I did not think it possible to inflict such pain upon

the human body without breaking a man,' he said, almost to himself. His eyes as he looked at him became empty, devoid of all emotion. 'You were right, monsieur. He is one of the gang run by this man you call Simeon. Timothy is somewhere on the other side of the Pont-Neuf.'

'You managed to loosen his tongue, then?' The Scot stood up. This surprised him. 'For a non-violent man, you seem to have risen to the occasion rather well. Even *I* would have had a hard time breaking a rat like René.'

'A little knowledge can sometimes go a long way,' Roland returned dully. 'Brute force is not always the answer, Monsieur MacGregor. I am ashamed to say I did make him talk. By methods I am not proud of, and which I hope, in time, I shall be able to forget. My book-learning came in handy, you might say. Science can produce some excruciating ways of inflicting pain, and I merely used one of them. Sian'—he came to her and caught her hands in his, and she could feel him trembling—'I had to do it—for Timothy. No, for you, so that you would retrieve the boy safely. I know how much he means to you.'

'As you do. Your peace of mind is important to me, too,' she whispered, laying a hand against his flushed cheek, which the whisky had coloured. 'He told you, then? Where Timothy is?' She must not allow him to dwell on what he had done.

'No, only that he is in Paris. We shall leave tomorrow for the city and await further instructions from them, but it gives Monsieur MacGregor a place to start.'

'You think they will get in touch again? Even if he does not return?'

'Yes. I don't think he knows exactly where the boy has been taken. He is merely a messenger, and of little importance to them.'

'What do you intend to do with René?' MacGregor asked.

'Leave him here, under guard. I trust my men to ensure he does not escape.'

'If he does, he will put everything at risk, you realise

that? He should be killed,' he insisted. Heaven preserve him from amateurs!

'No!' Roland answered sharply. 'No! I will not have his blood on my hands, nor will I allow you to kill him. I promised him his life if he told me what I wanted to know, and he did. There are, so he says, eight members of the band. All are completely without scruples. Simeon is their leader. They usually rendezvous at a tavern called the Coq d'Or. Do you know the place?'

'There are three. But yes, I think I know which one you mean. The back entrance runs down to the river. Very convenient for disposing of unwelcome customers,' he said, and gave a wry smile. He knew it very well! 'They will not be foolish enough to hide the boy there. If I was recognised at the inn with your sister, they will be waiting for me. I shall have to tread warily and watch my back.'

'But—but will you be able to find out anything if they know you are looking for Timothy?' Sian ventured to ask. How could they calmly discuss torture and possible death?

'The Coq d'Or is only one place. There are hundreds in that quarter where I can find willing informants, providing the bribe is right. Each one willing to cut someone's throat or steal their purse, or sell them to the highest bidder.' He smiled into the two rigid faces before him, tossed back the last of the whisky in his glass, and put it on the table. 'Do not fear for me, either of you. The devil never harms one of his own. We leave in the morning, you say? I suggest it be as early as possible. I could make better time riding ahead on horseback. My back still aches from the last experience in a coach! I shall prefer it.'

'We ride together, monsieur!' Roland was quite adamant. 'If there is any trouble over the detention of this man and they send someone else looking for him, your sword will be required. I want no word of his captivity carried back to Paris to warn the others. Not now . . . Not after what I have done.'

'As you wish.' For a moment Sian thought MacGregor

would refuse as she saw resentment rise in his eyes at the direct order. 'Shall we say seven o'clock?'

'Effie and our luggage can follow behind us in the coach,' she suggested. 'The ride to Paris is no great feat, and as Monsieur MacGregor has said, it would be much quicker. Like you, I am anxious to be there as soon as possible. I am quite recovered, Roland, truly,' she assured him as he stared at her undecidedly. 'And you know I am capable of the journey.'

He nodded agreement and she threw an almost challenging look at the Scot. He bowed slightly in the direction of them both, ignoring it.

'I shall take my leave of you, then, until the morning. Good night, Monsieur le Comte. Madame.'

As the door closed behind him, Sian turned and laid her head against her brother's shoulder.

'Put your arms round me, Roland,' she begged. 'Suddenly, I am very much afraid.'

She had undressed and was preparing to climb into bed when a soft tap on the door halted her. Roland slipped into the room, and came over to her. A hand against his lips, he led her to a chair and motioned her to sit.

'We must keep our voices low. They carry too well in this old place at night, and Monsieur MacGregor sleeps with his door open. I do not think he trusts us.'

'That does not surprise me. What is it?'

'I am going back to the cellar to talk to the man René again. Given another chance . . . I don't know. I have a feeling there is something he knows which could be of great help to us. It is only a feeling, you understand, but I can't rid myself of it. He was frightened of the mercenary, you realise that, don't you? That's why I questioned him myself.'

'He said you did not trust him. There is little between any of us at this time, is there? Surely you do not still think he is somehow part of this horrible business?' Sian breathed. 'If he were, he would not have admitted he knew the man—or suggested he question him himself.'

'What better way to get rid of him? A pretended

escape during the questioning. If he was dead, he could tell us nothing, nor implicate anyone. There is something here I do not see, Sian, and it worries me. The ransom is too small, so what else do they want from us?' Roland asked, his young face lined with concern. 'Do not worry. I won't hurt him anymore; I know that troubles you. And me. I did not think I was capable of such . . . Never mind. Perhaps money will loosen his tongue again. I am going to try, anyway. I just wanted you to know.'

'I shall come with you,' she began, but he shook his head.

'No, stay here. I shall come back to you as soon as I have finished with him. Pray I have more luck this time.'

'I shall, Roland.' She caught at his sleeve as he turned to go, her expression puzzled. 'What makes you believe this is not just an abduction—apart from the money? I sense you have been uneasy ever since I came home. As though you were keeping something from me. Is it because of his name. Because he is a MacGregor?'

He stared at her for a long moment, and then nodded, as if accepting she must be told what was troubling him. He had never kept anything from her before.

'A month before you arrived in Paris on this last visit, an attempt was made on my life.' Sian stifled a gasp against the back of her hand, sat white-faced, waiting for him to continue. 'I thought nothing of it at the time. A man attacked me as I was walking through the Tuileries, and hit me from behind. He had a knife, but before he could use it, someone came along. Whether he would have or not, had we been left alone, I shall never know. I thought he was merely after my full purse. I had been gambling at Danon's house and won quite a large sum. Everyone was rather drunk, and they went on to a . . . certain house. I decided not to. Perhaps the rogue thought I was an easy mark. Until Douglas MacGregor carried you through the front door the other day and I discovered what had happened to you, I never gave it a second thought. Now, I find myself wondering why you were to be killed. Only I would benefit from your death. But if the two of us were dead—I at the hands of a supposed footpad, you at the hands of men who waylaid your coach, then . . .'

'Timothy would inherit everything,' Sian said, unable to comprehend his train of thought. 'That doesn't make sense. He has been abducted.'

'That is what puzzles me, too. Someone is very knowledgeable about our family background, Sian. Perhaps this whole thing was an elaborate plot to dispose of us, so that Timothy inherits. As his father and therefore legal guardian, Phillip would be empowered to pay his ransom—he could afford anything asked of him.' Anything a man from the past with revenge on his mind would ask!

'It would not be difficult to find out about us,' she said slowly, considering the awful prospect. 'It is common knowledge that I come over here several times a year to visit you, that we have this château, a fashionable town house, lands and money. It could be anyone. You —you cannot be thinking Monsieur MacGregor . . . Oh, no!'

'Why are you so loath to believe him capable of such a scheme? We both know he is. He is completely without scruples. Yes, little sister, I do think this could have come from his clever brain. I have to prove it, however. Perhaps this man René . . .'

'Be careful,' Sian pleaded. 'You have made me more afraid than ever.'

'I did not mean to. I shall be back in a little while. Wait for me?'

'Yes, of course. Roland, be careful! I sense danger!,' she pleaded.

She tried to calm herself when he had left her, but it was impossible to concentrate after the things he had said, the ugly suspicions now wheeling in her brain. Cold-bloodedly to kill two innocent people, abduct a young child! Was the Scot capable of such brutality? She remembered the look in his eyes at the inn as he had waved the broadsword above his head, challenged the men menacing them to fight with him. He had

wanted them to engage him, she realised now. The light
in his eyes had been excitement, the thrill of danger
threatening him. She could not feel anything for such a
man, and she felt something for this one . . . She was
afraid to explain it even to herself, but it was there
inside her. The flame he had kindled that night at the
inn would never be extinguished.

'Who is it? Who's there?' Her head jerked up as she
heard a slight noise on the other side of the door.
Effie's face appeared. She was wrapped firmly in a thick
dressing-gown, long hair in two plaits falling over her
shoulders.

'I—I thought you were asleep, madam. I wanted to
tidy up in here for you. I shouldn't be in bed, I am quite
all right now.'

'Don't be silly, go back to bed at once,' Sian said,
rising to her feet. 'You look wretched. Someone else
can see to the room tomorrow after I have gone.'

'We are leaving, madam?' Effie drew the robe higher
about her neck, as if she was cold. Again Sian found
herself looking at the long, slender hands clutching the
material together. Such strong hands for a woman. Effie
had often laughed at the other servants at Ard Choille,
especially poor Robert MacNish, nearly in his seventies,
with not half as much strength in his body as she possessed in hers.

'Leaving?' Sian came back to reality with a jolt. She
could never like this woman. When she returned to
France again, she would not bring her, but find a young
village girl to train. 'Yes, early. About seven. We shall
be travelling on horseback, Monsieur MacGregor,
myself and my brother. You will follow later in the
coach with our luggage. Go to bed now, Effie. Sleep
well.'

'Pleasant dreams, madam,' the maid returned, as she
went out.

Those were not something she was likely to have,
Sian thought with a grimace. She could not settle. She
wanted to go down to join her brother, but was afraid
of what she would find.

She opened her closets and took out some clothes, laying them across the sofa in readiness for them to be packed in the morning. Still her mind was with Roland. After another twenty minutes had passed, she could stand the unbearable suspense no longer. If he had not made the man talk by now, he must give it up. She would not let him torture himself any more.

Her slippered feet made no sound as she crept down the staircase. As she passed MacGregor's room at the end of the corridor, she saw Roland had been right, the door was ajar. He was probably lying in bed, with his sword and dirk beside him, not sleeping a wink. She did not envy him his solitary existence. Yet it was not so solitary. He had a mistress. What kind of woman could hold him for a whole year? she wondered.

She turned in the direction of the door which led to the cellars, then froze in her tracks as the sound of someone whistling softly came to her from the direction of the drawing-room. She knew immediately who it was. That lonely, haunting lament would haunt her for the rest of her days, and those words, 'Make winter as autumn, the wolf days as summer; Thy bed be bare rock and light be thy slumber.'

MacGregor looked up at her from his chair as she came quietly into the room. A single candle burned in an ivory holder on the table beside him. His shadowed face showed no surprise at her appearance. Did anything take him unawares, she wondered, as she came closer, drawn to him like a moth to a flame. Sensing danger, disaster, yet unable to stay away.

She could smell whisky on his breath as he demanded ungraciously, 'Checking on the silver, Madame la Comtesse?'

'I was looking for my brother. You are making yourself at home, I see.'

'Your brother gave me the run of the house. I am only accepting the hospitality of his whisky bottle. You don't approve?'

'What you do is not of importance to me, monsieur. You will remember we leave early in the morning.' She was determined not to rise to his taunts.

'Whisky or not, I shall be up and about long before you,' came the mocking retort. 'Are you really a good horsewoman, or were you just trying to impress me?'

'You are unsufferable,' Sian said between clenched teeth. How she managed to suppress the urge to slap that grinning face was beyond her. 'You are drunk!'

'Insufferable and despicable and—yes, a little drunk, but still man enough for you, Madame la Comtesse, if you want to try me.' The invitation was tossed at her with the casual air of a man asking the time of day. Her hand flashed out and caught him a stinging blow across one cheek. His head snapped back, and as she saw the dangerous glint in his eyes, she stepped away. 'If you didn't come looking for me, why are you dressed like that?'

Sian looked down in dismay at the flimsy robe she was wearing. She had come looking for Roland, not this unsufferable, arrogant man, with devil's eyes and black heart. What she was wearing had not been important —until he looked at her and stripped her once again with his deliberately insolent gaze.

She took another step back, and the withering look she swept over him left him in no doubt about her feelings of contempt and disgust. It was the look of a lady, lifting aside her skirts to avoid the beggar at the roadside—revulsion, scorn—haughty indifference. Without a word she spun round on her heel and started back towards the door.

As she emerged into the hall, where only one candle torch had been left alight, suspended from the wall over the stairs, a shadowy figure slipped back into the doorway leading to the cellars. René dared not breathe as she came towards him. Damn the woman, she was coming to the very door where he stood! No matter. His fingers tightened around the hilt of the knife he held close against his body. She would be as easy as her brother. The fool below had died without a sound. Let Le Blond talk himself out of this mess!

Sian's footsteps faltered as the sound of soft whistling

came from the room she had just left. Even that mocked her tonight. She stopped and turned to look back into the darkened room, and at that moment, René stole up behind her and thrust a hand over her mouth, bearing her backwards. Before her terrified eyes she saw the candlelight glinting on the blade of a dagger. With all her might, she kicked back with her foot and was rewarded by a grunt of pain as her heel descended on a vulnerable place. She twisted free of his grasp, a single scream tearing from her throat before he grasped her by the robe. She heard it rip as he hauled her close, saw the knife descending towards her again. René's body against hers suddenly convulsed as if in agony. She felt the hold on her robe relax and fell away from him, flattening herself against the wall. Without support of some kind she would have collapsed, her legs were trembling so much.

With a choking, gurgling sound, he toppled to the ground at her feet and rolled over, staring up at her with glassy, sightless eyes. From his throat protruded the hilt of MacGregor's dirk. Blood stained the floor around him.

'You have killed him.' Her voice sounded a thousand miles away.

Withdrawing his weapon, MacGregor wiped it across the dead man's shirt with a callousness that made her shudder, before straightening to fix her with his steely gaze. There was a large tear in the silk robe, exposing the rise of a curving breast. Her eyes were wide with shock.

'Had I not acted swiftly, you would now be dead,' he replied harshly. What strange sixth sense had made him rise from his chair to follow her? From the doorway of the drawing-room he had had but a split second to throw his knife. Had either one of them moved, even fractionally . . . 'How the devil did he get free?'

'My brother . . .' With a gasp, Sian wheeled towards the door behind her, but in two long strides he was there before her, pushing her roughly aside. Dirk in hand, he cautiously descended the dimly lit, narrow

flight of stairs, Sian close on his heels, desperately trying
to see past him.

'Roland . . .' Her voice echoed through the half-
empty chambers ahead of them, and echoed into silence.
They found him face down in the passage, four deep
wounds between his shoulder blades. He was dead.

# CHAPTER
# FIVE

'STAY BACK,' MacGregor ordered and stealthily crept along the passage, disappearing from her sight in the darkness beyond. When he returned, he found Sian on her knees beside her brother's body. She had lifted him up on her lap and her robe was soaked with his blood, yet she did not seem to notice.

'Damn you, woman, don't you ever do as you are told?' he muttered, thrusting a hand inside Roland's shirt. There was no beat of life beneath his fingers; he had not expected any. 'Leave him. He's dead,' he added bitterly, and Sian looked up into his bleak features. Her lips moved, yet he heard no sound and he suddenly realised she was praying. He closed the dead man's eyes.

'Why?' she whispered. 'Why? He was a gentle man. He lived for two things only—his books and me. We were so close . . . He can't be dead! Send for a doctor! Perhaps there is life in him yet. Please, hurry . . . A doctor!' She bent her head and laid her cheek against his. It was still warm, but he was dead. She knew that in her arms she held but a body that must soon be taken from her for ever. Roland was gone! Murdered! She could not face life without him. First her father and mother, now her brother. Was everyone she loved to be taken from her? Who could be the perpetrator of such foul deeds? Who hated them all enough to kill without mercy?

Into the eyes which turned on MacGregor, kneeling at her side, came suspicion and fear and a burning desire for revenge against those responsible for depriving her of the only person in the world who had understood her. Only hours had separated them at birth—they

thought as twins—a pair with one mind. Had she come
down to the cellars the moment she sensed something
was wrong, she might have saved his life.

'Come, we can do nothing for him now,' he said,
laying a hand on her arm. 'Let André and the servants
take him upstairs.'

'You are wrong!' Sian cried, a savage fury gathering
in her eyes. She shook off his hand, recoiling from him
as if he was some venomous snake about to strike at her
with its deadly fangs. 'I can revenge him! Find those
responsible, and have them killed. He would have done
it for me.'

'You are overwrought—you don't know what you
are saying,' he said, his tone more gentle, more understanding, than he had ever used with her before, but it
fell on deaf ears.

'You!' Her lovely face was contorted with grief, but
no tears came. Why could she not cry when her brother
lay dead in her arms? 'You have brought death into this
house! He knew something was wrong when he came
down here to question that man again. Did you follow
him? Were you so afraid of what he might be told?'
Why, oh why, had she placed her trust in him?

'I have never dirked a man in the back in all my life.
If you were a man, I would kill you for those words!'

Sian could not deny the ring of truth in his voice, and
she crumpled into a sobbing heap over her brother. If
he was innocent, then who? Why?

She felt herself lifted and quickly borne away from
the darkened cellar and the other half of her which lay
on the cold stone floor, so cruelly deprived of life. She
railed at the man who held her, cried out threats of
vengeance as he carried her to her room and laid her
on the bed, where a weeping girl waited to attend her.

'You need something to make you sleep.' He stepped
back from her, silently shocked at the loathing blazing
out of her face, the accusation in her eyes. She thought
he . . .! A soldier of fortune he was, and had never
denied the fact. He had no reason to be ashamed of the
way he earned his money. The rules by which he lived

were scrupulously fair. At times he bent them to suit the occasion, but never—never!—had he killed in cold blood.

'No.' She lay unmoving, her hands clenched at her side as she fought to remain in control of her battered, shocked senses. 'I want none of your potions. I want nothing from you! Leave me to my grief.'

Leave! Yes, that was what he must do, before he found himself facing a murder charge. With René dead, he had no way of proving his innocence in this or in the abduction of the young boy. Perhaps this was what René had intended to happen after he had killed Sian. First her brother, then her and then, under cover of night, René would have slipped away, back to his lair and his brother wolves, leaving himself with two corpses on his hands . . .

André and another man came past, carrying Roland between them, and took him into his own room. Mac-Gregor watched them lay the body on the bed and cover it for the moment with a single sheet. Every movement told him of their love for their dead master. The glances thrown in his direction were not meant to be seen, but they were, and he did not like the feeling they stirred in him. One word from Sian and he, too, could wind up with a blade between his ribs.

'Monsieur, the other man?' André came to his side as he stood gazing down into the now brightly lit hall. 'What is to be done with him? I would ask the mistress, but . . .' He shrugged his shoulders meaningfully.

'Have him taken out somewhere and buried. At least three miles from here. He must never be found—or if he is, never connected with this château and your mistress,' he ordered. 'Do I make myself clear?'

'Perfectly, monsieur, but . . .'

'Would you prefer to lay him out beside your dead master?' he asked harshly, and the man's face tightened. 'Get it done before first light. I shall be downstairs if you need me. You'd best send for a priest, too.'

Those few words decided his course of action . . .

words spoken before he had given any serious thought
to leaving—to abandoning all commitment to Sian and
the brother she sought to ransom. It had been a passing
thought only. He knew he would stay if only to ram the
accusation she had flung at him down her throat. Would
that it might choke her! He had forgotten the last time
he had known such anger. He did not take insults like
that from men he considered friends—or as close to
being friends as he ever allowed anyone to come—let
alone some bitch with English blood in her! If anyone
knew about treachery, it was her kind. The English
were full of it.

'My lady, I have just heard!'
   Sian looked up into Effie's disbelieving face, and said
dully, 'What are you doing here?'
   'I came as soon as André told me about—about the
master. Can I bring you something? A warm drink?
Something to help you to sleep? You poor thing, you
have been through so much of late—to have to face this
horror, too . . .'
   Sian turned to face into the pillows, unable to bear
the gush of sympathy which she was sure was not real.
   'Leave me alone. I want nothing except to be left
alone.'
   'It is his fault.' The maid continued to fuss over her,
pulling the bedclothes over her shivering body, picking
up the bloodstained robe from the floor where Sian had
discarded it in revulsion. 'This house is cursed since he
came here. What do we know about him? Nothing!
Except that he's a MacGregor!'
   'Who do you mean? What are you saying?' Sian
glared at her with dull eyes. Why did she not go away
and leave her to her sorrow? She knew what was meant
by the words. Had she herself not accused him of
bringing death into her home? Obviously others were
as suspicious of him as she was, and not without just
cause. That accursed name! As fearful to her as Phillip's
was to the MacGregors of Rannoch.
   'My lady, how came such a man here? Where was he

going that he just happened to come across you stumbling about in the woods?'

'You know what happened, then? After you were taken?' Sian slowly sat up, staring into the woman's face. Perhaps she had heard something which might implicate him for certain. 'I have never dirked a man in the back in all my life.' His words had had the ring of truth in them, and she had believed him, but so much was against him.

'André talked with the boy he brought with him, the one who drove the coach. He was the inn-keeper's son. I did not know it, madam; we were both blindfolded for hours and hours, but it seems we were hidden at the same inn for a while. We could even have been there at the same time as yourself. Oh, don't fret yourself, you could not have known,' she cried, as Sian gave a distressed cry, a hand against her mouth. So near . . . 'He could have known though, couldn't he? When he came to the coach to make sure his men had done their work and found you missing, perhaps he thought it to his advantage to play the great rescuer. What better chance to give his scoundrels new orders than to take you to the very place they were hiding?'

'Then why was I not killed there?' she asked, with a shake of her head. 'No, it cannot be true. He protected me against those men.'

'Who knows what goes on in a mind such as his?' the woman replied with a shrug of her shoulders. 'I can only think, madam, that he saw greater rewards ahead by returning you safe and well to the château. Is it true that you have asked him to find little Timothy? You will see neither him, nor any money entrusted to him again!'

'That is what Roland thought—and now he is dead. I am alone, Effie. I have to make up my mind what is to be done. Dear God, how muddled my mind is. If only I could gather my thoughts—think what to do.'

'You must get away from here. Your life is in danger. I am sure of it. They have killed your brother. Why should they not kill you also?'

'Without the ransom money for Timothy? They would

not have gone to all this trouble for nothing.' If she too was dead, and Timothy inherited the fortune left to him, he would be a very rich young man indeed. Had her brother been right? Was that the ultimate goal of whoever was behind these terrible events? She was beginning to agree that her own life was in peril. Yet what could she do? Whom could she turn to for help? The village was very close by and full of willing men who would come to her aid, but she was now the only authority for almost a hundred miles.

Apart from her nearest neighbour . . . On a fast horse, she could make his estate in three hours. There before light, back again before breakfast, with men who would know how to deal with Douglas MacGregor, who could weigh the facts she gave them carefully and give her good advice. If she slipped away now, no one would miss her until it was too late to catch her.

'Go to my brother's room. Bring me a pair of his breeches, and boots and a jacket. Something dark-coloured,' she ordered, dragging herself from the bed. It was a mad idea, but the only one that offered any solution. She was in no condition to decide whether the Scot was guilty or not of any crime. Others would have to make that decision for her.

'You—you are not going out, madam? It is past midnight!'

'Don't stand there gaping at me,' Sian said sharply, pulling off her nightgown. 'Fetch the things I asked for. I shall ride to Monsieur d'Artoille. He was once a magistrate in these parts. He will know what to do. I shall be back before seven . . . to take care of things.' She had shut her mind to what would be happening in the harsh light of day. Her farewell to Roland. He would rest at peace, knowing she had acted wisely in his stead. She told herself it was what he would have wanted. She would never trust anyone again, she thought, tugging on a pair of slim-heeled leather boots. Luckily brother and sister had been of identical height. The breeches clung to lithe hips, the high-buttoned jacket slipped over a silk blouse accentuated the curve of breast and waist. A pretty-looking boy was reflected in her mirror.

As an afterthought, she took a small travelling pistol from the bottom of her closet. It was a cannon-barrelled, turn-off pistol with a silver mask butt plate that fitted snugly into her pocket with no tell-tale sign. Roland had given it to her on her last visit, but she had never carried it with her before. In fact she had laughed at the thought of menacing anyone with it, knowing she could never find the courage to pull the trigger and take the life of another human being.

That was before his own life had been cruelly ended. Now she would use it on anyone who tried to prevent her leaving the house on her quest.

'Go back to bed, Effie. If anyone asks, you do not know where I am. Is that clear?'

'Let me come with you?' the maid pleaded, but her tone betrayed that it was the last thing she wanted to do. 'No one rides through the woods at night without an armed escort.'

'I shall travel faster and safer alone,' Sian assured her. 'And I am armed. If necessary, I shall use this pistol. I have vowed to avenge my brother, and this I will do. Go to bed. I shall wait a few moments before I go downstairs. Remember, you have not seen me since early this morning.'

The maid nodded and slipped out through the door, cautiously looking to left and right, before she hurried off. She paused by the open door to Roland's room, where four candles placed at each corner of the bed shrouded the corpse in grey shadows.

'Rest in peace, Monsieur le Comte! Your sister will be joining you soon. You fool!' The sibilant hiss was full of hatred. 'Did you really think I would allow you to come between me and what I want? Soon, it will be over. Soon!'

On slippered feet she swept towards her own room, her face alight with excitement. With Timothy a prisoner in Paris and Roland dead, only Sian stood in the way. She would let her get as far as Paris, Effie mused,

pondering how she would kill the mistress she loathed.
It would doubtless prove as easy as killing her stupid,
trusting brother! No more would Phillip's eyes wander
in the direction of his step-daughter. And once Sian had
been dealt with, she would hold all his attention—and
keep it. She would be mistress of Ard Choille—and
all those who had looked down their noses at her,
threatened reprisals for her association with an Englishman, would pay dearly. She had a long list of scores to
settle in Rannoch.

Sian stole down the back staircase, which led past
the servants' quarters and the kitchen, to a side door
opening out into a small courtyard which adjoined the
stables.

A full moon lighted her way. As silent as the shadows
about her, she entered the stables, felt her way down
the numerous stalls until she came to the one that
held the horse she always used at the château. A fast
two-year-old stallion, whose coat was as black as jet.
Roland had often said how they matched each other:
both of dark colouring, both proud and independent.

'Perhaps a light would enable you to see what you
are doing, Madame la Comtesse,' a voice drawled
behind her. She heard the scrape of a tinderbox, and a
torch flared to life, illuminating the area where she
stood—and the grim gaze of the man who held it,
blocking her escape to the door. 'A strange time for
you to choose to go riding! Have you a particular destination in mind?'

'What I do or where I go is none of your business,
monsieur!' she stated. Then, quickly regaining her control, she snapped at the boy hovering behind him. 'You!
Bring out the black stallion and saddle him at once.'

The lad did not move. Instead, he looked at the man
questioningly.

'Go outside and close the door behind you. Allow no
one to enter while we are here,' came the countermand-
ing order.

'How dare you! Boy, come back. Do as I say!' Sian
watched the stable door open and close, leaving her

alone with him. 'Are you mad? Bring him back, I order you!' Icy fingers clutched at her heart.

'Are you in any position to give orders? I think not. I asked what you were doing out here at this time of the morning? Where are you going?'

Her mouth set into a stubborn line as she stepped backwards from him, her eyes seeking an avenue of retreat, but there was none. His tall frame blocked the only exit. What was he doing here? Spying on her? Ensuring she did not go for help? Roland had been right about him all along—and now she was alone with him . . . He meant to kill her!

'Keep away from me!' She tried to sound brave, but failed miserably. 'The servants know where I am. Effie was with me only a few minutes ago.'

'Of what concern is that to me?' he asked with a frown.

'If you lay one finger on me, they will know it was you!'

'Such trust in my loyalty touches my heart,' he said sarcastically. 'Of what am I being accused? Or do you not have the stomach to challenge me to my face? Shall I make a guess as to where you were going? The estates of the retired magistrate, Monsieur d'Artoille.' Sian gave a gasp, and took another step away from him, but her back abruptly came up against the edge of one of the stalls, and she could go no further.

'How could you know that?' she demanded, fighting down the panic that threatened to seize her. If she allowed him to see she was afraid, she was lost!

'I have not wasted the time I have been here. Your servants can be a talkative lot, after a little wine. Also, Monsieur d'Artoille happens to be a friend of the Duc de Bouillon, whom I know quite well. It was he I was on my way to visit when I found you.'

She stared at him disbelievingly, afraid to accept anything he said as the truth. If she had allowed Roland to send him on his way in the first place, perhaps her brother would not now be dead. It was not a pleasant thought.

'Very well. I was—am on my way to see him. Stand aside, monsieur.'

'And allow you to go off, half crazy with fear and grief, and lay on unwarranted accusation of murder against me? Have you no sense, at all, woman? Have you not even tried to think this thing out, or is your hatred of me so great that you care little whether an innocent man goes to Madame la Guillotine? René's friends would thank you for disposing of me. They might even let your brother return home alive after you had paid what they want, but I doubt it. You will have lost two brothers—and sent to his death the only man capable of helping you. Is that what you want?' he snapped.

'I want you to stand aside and allow me to pass,' Sian repeated through tight lips. How persuasive he made his appeal sound, but she had to go, at once!

Her fingers stole to the pocket of her coat, and fastened round the handle of the small pistol. With a defiant gesture she jerked it out and levelled it at him. A look of derision crossed his face at the sight of it.

'If you do not move out of my way immediately, I shall shoot. I mean it!'

'You have already killed once. I've told you the second time would be easier,' he replied humourlessly. He gave her the impression she did not frighten him in the least. Did he think she would not pull the trigger? She would! She must! If he detained her . . . She dared not consider the consequences. She had betrayed her mistrust to him now, and he would have no reason to keep her alive. 'I don't think you have the nerve to kill me, because deep in your heart you know your suspicions are wrong.'

'I know nothing of the kind!' she flung back. She tensed as he turned aside and thrust the torch he held into one of the wall-holders. What did he intend to do? Surely he was not mad enough to challenge her?

He moved so swiftly that she had no chance to fire. One minute he was turning back to face her again, the next he had flung himself across the space separating

them. The pistol was torn from her hand. She was
grasped roughly by the front of her jacket and flung
backward into the stall. As she caught at a post, trying
desperately to keep her balance, she caught sight of his
face, and she cried out. It was the face of a devil, with
blazing eyes that held murder. His fingers fastened again
in the front of her jacket. She heard buttons rip as she
struggled to be free of him. Her hair came free of its
ribbon and tumbled about her ashen cheeks.

She saw him lift his hand, and tried to twist away
from the blows which rocked her on her feet. Three
powerful slaps across her cheeks were delivered with
such force that she would have fallen had he not been
holding her fast. Tears blinded her vision. Anger
exploded through her mind. To strike her! She would
have him whipped until his back was raw. Did he think
this show of brute force would deter her from her intentions? Now, more than before, she vowed to ride to get
help.

'You animal! Let me go!' She squirmed and writhed
in his hold, but the hands that held her did not slacken.
She kicked out at him with her booted feet, but he easily
avoided the blows. 'Pig! You will pay for this.'

'Never point a pistol at anyone unless you are prepared to use it,' he derided her. 'Am I hurting you?
Good! A little fear may bring you to your senses. Be
glad it isn't René or one of his friends holding you,
otherwise you would discover what pain really is.'

'You are like him,' she breathed, eyes dilated as she
gazed into his furious face. 'There is no difference
between you.'

'No? Then you are expecting no mercy.' A boot
behind her legs sent her flying back on to thick straw.
As she began to struggle up again, he knelt over her,
pinning her to the ground with one knee. Torchlight
glinted on the blade he held before her horrified eyes.
'So, you think I am a murderer? If you believe that,
you leave me no choice. I cannot leave a witness behind
to give evidence against me.'

A terrified scream rose and died in Sian's throat. His

blade would silence her before it was ever uttered. How could she have been so blind to what he was? It had been easy—he had made it easy. What an innocent she had been! How he must have laughed at her, mocked her lack of knowledge.

'Are you not going to beg, woman?' The blade hovered dangerously near her cheek. The face behind it was taut, the scarred cheek quite pale, she saw, and found herself wondering why. Surely killing her would not touch his conscience?

'No, monsieur, I will not beg, from you or anyone else in this world. I have never begged in my life, and I will not begin with you, of all people.' She spat the words at him with the last of her weakening defiance. His grip made her feel sick with pain, but she gave no sign.

MacGregor cursed her in the most prolific Gaelic he could bring to mind at that moment, and she closed her eyes, believing she was about to die.

'You have too much courage, woman. Are you sure it's English and not good Scots blood you have in you? Open your eyes; I'm not about to slit your throat. You are in no danger from me—at least not in the way you think.'

When Sian did as she was bid, she found him sitting back on his heels. The awesome dirk was replaced in his belt. She lay quietly, uncomprehending—still afraid. And then, without warning, the tears came. Tears she had held back since those terrible moments when she had cradled Roland in her arms and known she was alone. Alone with her fear, her grief, her loss. Alone with the knowledge that this man could be not only a mercenary, but a murderer, intent on exterminating all close to her.

She thrust her arms across her face as the tears rolled silently down her cheeks. Try as she did, she could not stem the unleashing of her emotions. She had not cried so since her mother died, and even then, Roland had been on hand to aid her, comfort her, reassure her with his presence. Now he, too, was gone. She had no one!

'Lass, lass—don't greet so! Though if you do, it will ease your suffering, but I cannot bear to watch such tears . . .' He bent and gathered her into his arms, rocking her against his chest as if she was a mere babe. She had no strength to push him away, and although she hated herself for it, she gained comfort from his touch, the gentle voice as his lips touched her hair, her cheek. 'I've never known such a woman to anger me as you do, do you know that? You have a wild tongue in you. Take care when we are together. My temper is short.'

Together? What was he implying? Would the tears never stop! The more she tried to control them, the worse they became. She lay like a limp flower in his arms, exhausted. Her cheek lay against his shoulder. How firm it was. Strong, where she was weak. Why had he not killed her? She lifted her head and looked at him, and he read the unspoken question in her eyes.

'None of this is my doing,' he said quietly, without anger. That had gone from him at the sign of the first tear. She was so helpless, yet possessing such great courage. He would be damned for helping her, but he could not walk away and leave her to whatever awaited her in Paris. It was not in him. Whether he liked it or not, she was his responsibility now. She had no one else. 'I have never lied to you or your brother. I know nothing of your brother's death or the abduction of the boy. If you do not believe me, say so now, and I shall leave. You will never see me again. But if you send men after me, or accuse me of crimes of which you know I am innocent, I shall come back before they take me, and you will not escape my dirk again. Too many people have betrayed me in the past. No more! Do I make myself clear?'

'No.' Sian's voice quivered with indecision. Was he offering her help? 'Go. Go away and leave me in peace. I don't know what you want from me. I can't think.'

Douglas seized her by the shoulders, his fingers biting through the thick material of the jacket into her shoulders. 'You may not think you can go on now, but this will pass. I promise it will. You need to sleep. Soon you will be able to think clearly again. The grief will fade.'

'Did yours?' she asked challengingly, and wondered at her boldness.

His mouth tightened visibly, then, seeing the apprehension spreading across her face at his expression, he nodded, his countenance softening slightly. 'Yes, in time. There is still too much hatred in me for many people. Sometimes—sometimes I act too harshly with those who do not deserve it, but inside me there are so many memories. So much pain . . . Stop thinking of yourself, woman. Think of the boy. He will be wondering what is being done to ransom him. Praying that someone, somewhere, cares enough to rescue him.'

'He knows I love him, and will do anything to have him released,' Sian cried. 'I won't let him down.' Yet what could she do alone? Douglas was silent. Was he waiting for her to beg for his help, as she had refused to beg for her life a few minutes before? 'It's no use. I don't know where to begin. I can't go on. I feel dead inside . . . without hope.'

'You can go on,' Douglas snapped, drawing her up against him, so close that his face was almost touching hers. 'But, first, there is something we have to settle between us.'

He lowered his lips slowly to the stiff, unyielding mouth below his, and heard Sian's sharp intake of breath, but she did not move. He wondered if she had any strength left in her after what had taken place throughout the day. He had been brutal with her— deliberately so, in an attempt to bring her sharply back to her senses. He did not blame her for the suspicions clouding her judgment. She knew little about him, would never know everything, so how could she be in a position to judge him and his actions?

The touch of her lips should not have roused him as it did, and the shock which ran through him made him tense unexpectedly. She was like a cold statue in his embrace, tantalising, yet unresponsive. His hands slid beneath the jacket, against the smooth, firm breasts straining against the thin silk. He was aware of the momentary resistance that rose inside her as he used the expertise gained from countless affairs over the years—and women, too numerous to recall—to bring her out of her lethargy. But even as her lips parted and answered his, he pulled back from her, staring down into the pale face.

'At last we understand each other. I can take you whenever it pleases me, and you know it,' he taunted softly, and flinty sparks flashed into her eyes to wipe away their dullness.

'I hate you for that!' She did not deny it.

'I was merely showing you how capable you still are of experiencing emotion. And it was a warning. Never think of me in the same light as other men you know. That would be a fatal mistake. Now, do we work together to get your brother back, or do I ride out of here and leave you to your own devices?'

'I cannot answer you! I don't know you.' Sian looked at him pleadingly. 'I no longer know what is true or whom to trust.'

'Once you trusted me,' Douglas reminded her, and she nodded, her black hair dancing round her shoulders in a profusion of curls. He wanted to reach out and catch them between his fingers, but he knew that if he did, he would not stop there. He was safe, so long as he did not touch her!

'You say that this feeling will pass? How can it? I loved my brother, and now he is gone! Murdered! How can I rest until someone pays for that?'

'In good time. Simeon has your brother in Paris. He sent René here with his demands. It is he who must be brought to account for Roland's death. Once, many years ago . . . Douglas broke off, a look of intense pain flashing across his grim features. 'Once, I held my dead mother in my arms, as you held your brother. Not three hours later, my father, too, died in my arms. The only two people I cared for in all the world had been taken from me, and I desired revenge. I still desire it. One

day, God willing, I shall have the man responsible at
my sword-tip. But in the years in between, I have had
to learn to live. No, to exist, to survive in a world not
of my own making. I tell you this only so that you will
understand that, one day, you will be able to look back
on all this without grief, without tears. If I can help you
to exact your revenge, I shall. His death was unneces-
sary.' And not possible without the intervention of a
second person, he thought to himself. Sian had not
even considered the possibility of someone else being
involved, naturally assuming that he had released René
and had killed Roland when he appeared. 'I don't have
any answers for the way you feel now. No one that day
gave me an answer, either. But I do have questions
about the present. Questions I want answered and will
have answered. Between us, we shall find the boy and
release him, and there will be no more killing. If it is in
my power, then it shall be so.'

'Why?' Sian whispered. 'After everything I have said
—and thought—about you?' His family dead! Not at
Phillip's hands, she prayed.

He drew back from her, a smile masking his feelings.
It mocked her, washing away the momentary compassion she had begun to feel for him and his loss.

'Why? For money, woman. Why else?' He rose and
stared down at her for a moment, then spun on his heel
and went to retrieve the pistol he had wrested from her
grasp. Sian found it tossed into the straw beside her.
'Pick it up. Use it, if you still believe me to be a liar and
a murderer.'

'And have your dirk in me before my fingers touch
it?' she flung back.

'That is the chance you take when you accuse a man
of such crimes,' he retorted, then, with an oath, he
turned his back on her and stood waiting. 'How is that
for a target? You cannot miss from where you are.
Either use your weapon, woman, or put it away and let
us get back to the house. There is much to do before
we leave for Paris.'

He did not believe she would use it, Sian realised as

she pulled herself to her feet, the pistol in one hand. No more could she. Forgive me, Roland, she prayed, replacing it in her pocket. I do this for you and Timothy. And herself, if she was honest about it, but she did not want to consider just how involved were her own feelings in the decision. Head held high, she moved past him to the door and stood silent, waiting for him to open it for her. Douglas ushered her out, motioning the waiting boy to remain inside the stables for the remainder of the night. To ensure that no one else left —or that she did not make a second attempt? she wondered, as she preceded him back into the house.

Her footsteps faltered as she reached the spot where René's body had lain beside the cellar door. She felt Douglas's hand fasten over her arm, urging her on. She paused at the bottom of the staircase, looking into his hard face, and said quite calmly, 'If you ever give me cause to suspect you have lied, I shall have you killed.'

'Your brother threatened me with the same thing. My sword is for sale, woman—not my integrity. Remember that!'

'Whoever holds my brother and killed Roland in cold blood, or at least ordered his death, is a monster. I want Timothy returned to me alive, and I tell you now, I care not how you do it. Money is of no importance. Name your own price.'

'I take it I am being put in the same category. To deal with such men, you need someone as callous as they are, am I right?'

'You killed tonight without hesitation. To save me, you would have me believe. Or to save yourself from the accusation of abetting this heinous crime! I know not which. You saved my life—I grant you that, and I am grateful. How much is my life worth to you, monsieur?'

'At this moment, very little,' Douglas growled, and she knew she had gone too far.

'No matter. If you were in league with the devil himself, I would ask for your help. I have no one else to turn to, and I am desperate. We shall leave for Paris after—after my brother has been buried. Until then, I would be grateful if you would stay out of my sight.'

Douglas watched her climb the stairs to her room, saw her hesitate before her brother's door, and then open it and go inside. As she closed it behind her, he swore violently and turned in the direction of the Blue Salon.

Douglas stood by the window, staring down into the cobbled courtyard. He felt restless—and uneasy. But this time it was not nightmares, but concern, that had kept him awake. It was barely seven in the morning, the sky still flecked with the remnants of dark clouds which the night before had promised rain, yet had failed to fulfil that promise. Pale pink clouds edged with grey seemed to hover at tree-top level.

Under different circumstances, he knew he would have come to like this place. It was far removed from his world of violence and intrigue. He was at peace here within these ancient walls, or riding deep in the forest beyond the château.

A carriage was below in the drive. It had brought a priest, and three well-dressed individuals he surmised were the most prominent men in the village. What would Sian tell them? Ahead of them, a steady stream of villagers came and went from the chapel which adjoined the house, where their liege lord lay on a great catafalque, surrounded by his ancestors.

When he was sure everyone was below in the crypt, Douglas left his room. He made no sound as he moved quickly, purposefully, in the opposite direction, to the small staircase to the servants' quarters. Past the room André shared with the cook, his wife, to the one he knew Sian's maid used whenever she was at the château. He could not pin-point any one thing in particular that connected her with the abduction, yet he knew she must have been.

The act she had played out in the drawing-room upon her return had deceived everyone but him. How or why Effie should be involved was beyond him, and he did not waste valuable time pondering unanswerable questions. If she were part of the band, what would she gain from Roland's death? The death of her mistress? Perhaps Sian herself unwittingly had the answers. Once they were in Paris, he would talk openly and honestly with her and try to win her confidence. Without it, every move he made would be hampered by her suspicions.

The door was unlocked; not that it would have taxed his skill to pick the lock. He had learned many useful tricks like that from the little dumb pickpocket who had befriended him when he first arrived in Paris. He wondered what Sian would say if she knew he could enter her room at any time—should he so choose! The chamber was bare, for that of a woman. A patchwork quilt covered the bed, the only splash of colour in an otherwise dull room. He found that strange. Effie did not strike him as someone who would turn her back on the fripperies and feminine touches a woman usually used to adorn a personal place. His mother's rooms had been full of embroidered cushions in bright colours, with paintings on the pastel-coloured walls, a lace cloth on the table below the window. The room reflected her vibrant personality.

It took only five minutes to discover the assortment of jewellery and bottles of sultry French perfume hidden away at the back of a drawer. There was something else, too; something secreted in a piece of velvet cloth. A soft whistle escaped his lips as he unwrapped the contents. In the palm of his hand lay shining gold coins —over fifty of them. Effie had not saved those from her wages as a maid! Had she a rich lover? A fancy gentleman who appreciated her ample gifts enough to shower her with gifts and money? The jewellery—two necklaces and several rings—although not very expensive, were not items she herself could have afforded. And then he grew cold, stiffening in disbelief as his eyes locked on a diamond brooch, fashioned in gold in the shape of a letter 'E'. Trembling fingers detached it from the rest, curved round it so tightly that it cut deep into his calloused palm. He was oblivious to any pain. It was

not possible! Could there be two identical brooches?
No—this was the one he had had made for his mother
in Edinburgh two months before he left to join the
Prince. He knew it! 'E' for Eleanor. 'E' for Effie . . .

Eleanor MacGregor, who had died at the blade of a
man who had invaded her home, ravished her
drunkenly, and afterwards kept her locked in her room
for over two weeks, to be further abused at his pleasure.
Two weeks of hell until he and his father arrived to
discover the terrible atrocities which had taken place
and sought to free her. Her warning cry had saved them
from an ambush by English soldiers. It had resulted in
her death. The brooch had been pinned to the gown
she wore, soaked with the life-blood draining from her
as she lay dying in his arms. It *was* the same!

Effie's protector was rich indeed. Only one man could
have laid his hands on the brooch after her death.
Douglas had heard that he had been rewarded with land
and an estate for his butchery of innocent Highland
folk. Lord Phillip Blakeney! The name would be forever
etched in his memory in blood. Ten years had passed
since the day he had left Scotland, only half alive, below
the decks of a French fishing vessel, but his desire for
vengeance had not diminished. Nor would it.

And, now, a simple abduction was turning into a
something of a far greater magnitude—and it involved
his hated enemy. The man who had left him scarred
in both mind and body, who had turned him into a
wandering, solitary exile. Blakeney was involved with
Effie, the brooch was proof of that. Was he also somehow involved with Sian? The thought caused the blood
to course red hot through his veins. Did she belong
to him? And what was his connection with Paris and
Simeon? Why should he want Roland Saint-Rémy
dead? He dropped the brooch back into the drawer, and
turned blindly away as he fought to compose himself.
Replacing everything as he had found it, he stepped to
the door. One final backward glance ensured that the
room showed no sign of his search, before he left it.

Ten minutes later, he was standing at the back of the

crowded crypt, listening to the final words of the burial
service—his mind far removed from the scene before
him. He believed in neither God nor man. His faith had
been destroyed long ago, and nothing in his life had
emerged since to replace it. He placed his trust in
himself and his capability to survive—in the strength of
his sword-arm. Then a slim figure shrouded completely
in black rose from beside the catafalque, and immediately his attention was for Sian alone.

The black dress made her look thin, and accentuated
the pallor of her cheeks, he thought, as she bent to lay
a last farewell kiss against her brother's cold cheek. For
a moment she hung over the body, swaying, and his
fingers tightened over the hilt of the sword, blade down
on the stone floor in front of him. But she recovered
and turned away, and he saw that her eyes were dry.
Dull, empty grey pools where once he had glimpsed
fires of desire and passion. He suspected she had cried
the last of her tears in his arms last night in the stables.
He thought of her in Phillip Blakeney's arms. It incensed
him!

She looked up, encountered his gaze, and the eyes
were no longer emotionless, but blazing with anger as
she challenged his right to stand in this very special
place. Without a word, he turned on his heel and
returned upstairs. When she came into the drawing-
room, he was waiting for her. Beside him on a chair
were his worn saddlebags. The broadsword was once
more in its usual place along his back. Once more he
was the mercenary soldier, awaiting her commands.
Silent, withdrawn from the moments of danger, of fear
they had shared. A stranger! Once more she looked at
him, and was afraid of what she saw.

# CHAPTER
# SIX

SIAN LIFTED the long black lace veil covering her features and looked across the room to where Douglas stood. He was ready to leave. With or without her, she wondered? Did he have no respect for the dead, that he was in such a hurry? Then, as the first impulsive flare of anger died, she realised the wisdom of reaching Paris as quickly as possible. The absence of the man called René would not go unnoticed for many days. Two, perhaps three at the most, before his friends began to wonder what had happened to him. Then she would discover whether their greed for her money was greater than the loss of their companion.

'I shall be ready to leave in an hour. Effie and my luggage will follow tomorrow in the coach. André, too. I am closing up the house for a while. I do not know when I shall come here again.' Her lips trembled, but her voice was controlled and very calm. Too calm, Douglas thought, wondering how much more strain she could bear upon those slight shoulders.

'May I suggest you dress as you did last night,' Douglas advised her. 'You will be far less conspicuous. I am about to test your prowess as a horsewoman. We ride hard and fast. I want Simeon's spies to report that you returned to Paris in haste, as though you were acting upon their instructions. They may never connect you with René's disappearance.'

'You think the house is being watched?' she asked. Such a thought would never have entered her head. Yet she did not question what was undoubtedly an order.

'Most certainly.'

'And when they see you with me?'

'It will give Simeon food for thought.' Until Effie

arrived and filled in the details for the rogue, as he was sure she would. By that time he would be back at the Coq d'Or, where he lived in one of the upstairs rooms. It was not merely coincidence that this was the place René had named as the rendezvous for the band. Either he had used it himself, hoping to implicate Douglas along with him, or he had been ordered to do so. Only someone who knew him as Le Blond would associate him with that tavern, where he was never referred to as MacGregor. Or someone who had made it their business to inquire about him! He could say nothing of his suspicions about the maid to Sian without further deepening the suspicions she already harboured about *him*. She was walking a tightrope of suspense as it was, and he did not want her to lose all sense of balance.

He stood by the window until she returned, clad in the clothes she had worn the previous night. Her hair was tucked out of sight beneath a wide-brimmed straw hat.

'Will you take care of these for me?' She handed him a large envelope and a jewel case. 'Letters of credit to the bank Roland and I both use in Paris. He gave them to me when we discussed payment of the ransom. I can draw whatever I wish . . . Not that I need his permission any more. He left everything to me,' she added bitterly. 'Fifteen thousand *louis* can be raised without a problem. Should we need more, I can sell my jewels, or the town house if necessary. We talked of many ways . . .'

She turned away so that he would not see how close she was to breaking down. Her gaze slowly wandered about the room as if to take with her the memory of every single item in it, alongside the unforgettable memory of her brother being entombed for ever in the cold crypt below the chapel.

'I am ready, monsieur.'

Head held high, she walked stiffly to the front door where André waited to bid her farewell.

The sky outside was dull and overcast, and she looked up dubiously. It was like an omen warning her of danger ahead, but she did not allow her footsteps to falter, aware of Douglas close on her heels. She had to put aside her fears and trust him—at least until they reached Paris and she could enlist the aid of her very good friend, Madame de Pompadour. If Douglas betrayed her in any way, the Marquise had friends who would know how to deal with him. She had the ear of the King himself!

Sian had been torn with doubts whether to contact her step-father, Phillip, who was, after all, Timothy's father and should know what had taken place. But she reasoned the whole frightening incident might have resolved itself by the time word reached him in Scotland, and he would be sent into a panic for nothing. She would wait until something transpired in Paris. The thought of enlisting the powerful support of the King's mistress had greatly comforted her. She had thought herself alone, but realised she still had one person upon whom she could totally rely.

Two horses waited in the stable-yard, held by the boy from the inn. As Douglas helped her to mount, she looked down at the youngster who was staring appeal-inglu up into his face. He wanted to come too, she suspected.

'You will be safer here,' she told him. 'The château is your home for as long as you wish it.'

'Your brother gave him a job in the stables. He knows horses well. In a few days he will have transferred his allegiance to one of the horses, and I shall be forgotten,' Douglas said as he mounted.

He would never admit it, but he had grown quite fond of the boy, she thought, as she cast a quick look into his eyes. As they reached the huge iron gates which led out into the forest, he kneed his mount past her and galloped ahead. Without hesitation she urged her own on to keep pace with him.

The Paris house was situated in the fashionable Avenue Noblesse, close to the Louvre. Gaping servants rushed out to assist the dishevelled, reeling young woman who fell from her horse into the arms of a stranger. As soon

as her feet touched the ground, Sian pulled herself free
of him and sought other willing hands to help her inside
to the bliss of a soft chair, which, for all its comfort, did
not ease the soreness of her bruised hips. She was
unaccustomed to riding astride, her thighs pressed hard
against the leather saddle. Sian found herself aching in
places where she had never ached before.

He had driven her ruthlessly, without any consideration for her discomfort, she thought, as he came into
the room after her, shedding his sword and stretching
stiff arms. But she had not allowed him to browbeat
her.

'Prepare a room for Monsieur MacGregor, and bring
us something to eat,' she ordered. Out of the corner of
her eye, she saw him shake his head.

'I have a thirst which will not take long to quench,
but then I am leaving. I have someone I wish to see as
soon as possible. I trust if I run into any trouble from
La Pompadour's friends, I need only refer them to you?'

She nodded, not attempting to change his mind,
although she dearly wanted to discuss how they were to
proceed in the days ahead. Of course, he was anxious
to be with his mistress again.

'No, not her,' Douglas drawled, and she flushed at
the accuracy with which he had read her thoughts. 'But
someone who is a fountain of information, and will tell
me everything I want to know.' About your brother and
you, and perhaps even your connection with Phillip
Blakeney, he hoped silently.

'As you wish. Whisky for monsieur, Frederick,' she
ordered the hovering manservant at her elbow. He, and
three other servants—Suzanne, a maid, a housekeeper
and an odd-job boy—made up the small household. 'I
shall take a tray in my room. Have Suzanne prepare a
bath. I am going to soak myself for at least an hour, I
am so stiff.'

She waited until the servant had brought a freshly
opened bottle of whisky for Douglas and a large glass
of lemonade for herself before crossing to the writing
desk. Opening a drawer, she took out writing materials

and penned a letter to her banker. Douglas's eyebrows rose as she held it out to him.

'This will introduce you to Monsieur Le Strange. His address is on the envelope. He is empowered to give you whatever money you consider necessary. Use it in whatever way you see fit to gain information about my brother's whereabouts. If we fail in this, we can do no more than wait for those dreadful men to get in touch with us again.'

'Are you not afraid that I shall simply disappear? Why this sudden show of trust?' he asked, his voice heavy with sarcasm.

'I have no choice.' Sian shrugged.

'No, you haven't, have you?' He pocketed the letter with a grim smile, took the others she had given him, and dropped them on the table.

'I shall go and see Monsieur Le Strange myself this afternoon. Should I draw the money they have asked for and keep it here? Perhaps we might hear soon?' she added hopefully. Hope was all she had now.

'No. If, as I believe, they are watching the house, it could be stolen from you on the way back, and then they would be in a position to demand more. There are many ways to skin a cat, and I've a feeling in my bones they intend to take you for far more than they have asked.'

'Roland felt that, too.' But for a far different reason. *He* had been the reason!

'Why did he like the boy?' Douglas demanded, and she sat down in a chair again, a shadow passing across her face.

'He was angry when my mother married again. It was only a year after our father Richard had been killed— at Culloden. He was a cavalry officer with Kingston's Horse.' She stared up at him, prepared for a caustic comment, but his face was a mask. As if he were afraid to allow his true feeling to show, perhaps. Afraid? No, not he! 'Roland loved Richard very much. I suppose he never really forgave her for installing another man in his place. When Timothy was born, and she nearly died, he hated the boy . . .'

'Enough to have him abducted? Killed?' Douglas flung back, and she gasped aloud. Did he intend to take suspicion from himself by accusing her brother?

'No! Never! He lives here in France now and sees Timothy only once or twice a year. I think they have even become friends now . . .' She broke off, realising she was referring to him as if he were alive. How long would it be before she could accept that he was not? The room was full of him, she thought, allowing her eyes to wander slowly over the shelves of books, his collection of ivory statuettes on a mahogany table.

'It will pass,' Douglas murmured, and she flashed an angry glance at him as she climbed wearily to her feet, resenting his words.

'No, monsieur, it will not. I do not want it to. I want to remember how he was, how dearly I loved him, so that the desire for vengeance I have will not go away. Someone is going to pay for his death and for what is happening to my poor little brother. I swear it!'

'Revenge can sour the soul and degrade beyond redemption,' Douglas said, picking up his sword. 'I should know. I have harboured it inside me for the past ten years. After a while it begins to eat up every decent emotion a person has. It's a fatal disease. One I hope escapes you. If it does not, it will make you old before your time, ugly inside—and that would be a great pity for one so lovely.'

'Look to yourself, monsieur,' Sian retorted stiffly. 'We—' hurriedly she corrected herself '—I dine at six-thirty, should you wish to join me. Perhaps you will have news for me.'

'Perhaps,' came the non-committal answer. 'Perhaps.' He was making no promises until he had visited a certain old woman in the Avenue Ricard. So much depended on what she would tell him. Perhaps the life of Sian Saint-Rémy!

'Who is it? Who's there? Are you deaf, Louise? I told you I am seeing no one today,' a voice declared loudly from a back room as Douglas brushed aside the aged maid trying to detain him on the front step and headed towards the parlour.

'Not even me?' He stood under the wide velvet *portière* and stared at the woman seated in a rocking-chair before a blazing fire. Whether she was fifty, sixty or seventy was impossible to tell. The lined face was like leather, but rouged and painted in the fashion of the day as a younger woman might do. Several black patches, a star, a triangle and a large crescent moon, adorned—if it could be called that, for it made her appearance rather resemble that of a circus clown—the chalk-white cheeks where the rouge did not reach. Grey hair was piled high on her head in court fashion, powdered and ribboned. Her gown was a bright blue silk, lavishly trimmed with ribbons and lace, and blue leather shoes with diamond buckles peeped from beneath the hem of the numerous skirts.

A heavily ringed hand was extended towards him. The face stretched into a broad smile, threatening to crack the carefully done work there, but luckily it did not.

'Le Blond! Where the devil have you been these past months, you young rascal? Too good to come and see me these days? Or have you found yourself a woman . . . a decent woman, not one of these painted whores you've been messing around with at court?'

'Is there anything you don't hear about, Grand-mère?' he asked, with a loud chuckle as he took the hand, as cold as ice, in his and bent to bent to brush his lips over one cheek.

'I know you came close to killing Monsieur de Brissac over that stupid wife of his. Wish I'd been there . . . Never liked the man! You should have run him through. She'd have seen you all right.'

'I don't kill at the whim of a woman, Grand-mère—or of any man, come to that. You know me better than that, surely? Besides, she already had another fool lined up to take her husband's place. I was simply the instrument she used in an attempt to get rid of an unwanted irritation.'

'Like a dog having a good scratch!' Grand-mère smiled, revealing perfectly white teeth. 'I hope your time wasn't wasted with her, then.'

'Every precious second was put to good use,' Douglas assured her, pulling up a chair close to hers. 'Now, tell that maid of yours to stop listening on the other side of the curtain and bring us something to drink. The good stuff, mind, not the watered Burgundy you keep for your other clients.'

'Louise? You heard monsieur. Two glasses of my best cognac. You want something from me, no?'

'Information, Grand-mère. About many things.'

'And someone, I'll warrant. I hear you have been away from Paris? How was the hunting on the Duc de Bouillon's estates? I have also heard he entertains a very special guest—also an exile from your beloved Scotland. Royalty, no?'

'You old witch, have you been reading the Tarot again?' He grinned, not minding this intrusion into his personal life. He would never have allowed anyone else to do it, but she was different . . . and he owed her his life. More than that. She had taught him how to live again, how to survive in a jungle, and he would be eternally grateful to her.

It had been a year after he first came to Paris. His skill with a sword had been useful to many people during those lonely, miserable months when he felt his whole world had crumbled about his ears. Had it been his choice, he would never have left Scotland but remained to seek out the man who had murdered his parents, and take the life owed to him. But, on the Prince's own insistence, he had been put aboard a fishing boat and transported to France. Wounded and weak from loss of blood, he was in no condition to protest.

His loss had embittered him, and he had made enemies quickly among the very people he knew would offer him work, or provide money so that he could start a new life. But in those days he had had no interest in beginning a new existence. He sought only revenge. The sound of an English voice was enough to send him

into a black rage. He had lost count of how many duels
and fights he had entered into, until one night he had
been set upon by the relatives of a man recently
despatched by his sword and left for dead in an alley.

Grand-mère had found him, had taken him to her
house and cared for him. The discovery that he had to
survive yet another day had sent him into the blackest
rage he could ever remember—save for that night when
he watched his parents die. Yet his curses, his threats,
had had no effect on the frail woman who nursed him,
fed him with her own hands, changed his bloodstained
bandages and sat with him day after day until his fever
diminished and he began to recover.

Each day she told him a little of herself. How she had
been sold as an orphan of thirteen to a brothel on the
other side of the city, and kept there for a whole year
until a rich woman had bought her for her husband,
hoping she would supply him with a son, which the
scheming woman intended to pass off as her own once
the child was born. There had been no child, and she
had been packed off in anger to a cousin, who, finding
her more than willing to accommodate him in return
for security, set her up in a fashionable house close to
Versailles. She had never looked back.

Now, three marriages later, a very wealthy woman,
she had retreated from the society she despised and
lived quietly in a house in the Avenue Ricard, with only
a loyal maid, who had been with her for twenty years,
to care for her needs.

As amusement to pass the dull days, she had begun
telling fortunes—to the rich and titled only, and charg-
ing an enormous sum for doing so. She told them what
they wanted to know, mixing fiction with more than a
little fact gained from the Tarot cards that never left
her side. Douglas had scoffed at them once, and had
been rewarded with a startling insight into his past that
left him speechless.

She had never told him her real name, and he never
asked. No more had he revealed his. She had named
him Le Blond as she nursed him, comparing him to a

lover she had once had. A comparison which had earned her the unpleasant side of his tongue. She had only laughed, and still continued to use it. After a while he conceded that she would use no other, and found it an acceptable alternative to his own name in the Pont-Neuf district, where only a fool would reveal his true identity.

For a while they sat and drank the warming brandy, and talked of trivialities. It was her way, and he allowed her this one indulgence. When the bottle was half-empty, she looked at him with eyes like quicksilver and demanded,

'Whom are you interested in?'

'Roland Saint-Rémy,' he lied, and she looked at him sharply, disbelievingly.

'A bookworm, from all I hear. You could have asked anyone that. Now tell me the truth.'

'It was a slight deviation only,' Douglas replied. 'I do want to know about him—and his sister. I met her recently at Versailles, on the night Monsieur de Brissac and I had our—disagreement. I want to know more about her, and I don't fancy a troublesome brother— or husband—getting in my way.'

'Sian Saint-Rémy?' Grand-mère pondered his question, finished her drink and held out her glass, which was instantly replenished. Her head was harder than his, Douglas mused, hoping he could still enjoy such a healthy palate when he was her age. If he ever reached it! 'A quiet girl; aloof, I suppose you might call her. You have chosen a hard nut to crack, my friend. I've never heard of her being involved with any man, or even interested in anyone in particular. The last time I heard talk about her was well over a year ago—just after the death of her mother. A funny business, that. Suicide, I heard, but the cards said otherwise. Violent death shadows that one, as it does you. Two of a kind, you are—marked for death.'

'Someone tried to kill her a few days ago. Yesterday her brother was murdered,' Douglas said quietly. 'I want to hear everything you know about her, Grand-mère.'

'She interests you? She is pretty. No, beautiful, and

so unaware of the talents with which God has endowed her. Tread carefully, or you may frighten her away.'

'Her background, Grand-mère, not a lecture! Her brother lived in France—sometimes in Paris, but mostly at the château at Saint-Rémy. I also know her father was an English soldier killed at Culloden. Her mother married again. What do I not know?' Douglas demanded.

She watched him with narrowed gaze, sensing the tumult raging in him. 'Yes, she is of interest to you, poor thing! I feel anger in you—great anger. Something to do with her, no? She has not scorned you—you would not allow any woman to do that, neither would you come asking me to help you with information intended to advance a courtship. I believe her mother did marry again. Now, let me see. Her mother was Clare, the daughter of Armand and Céleste Saint-Rémy. I knew him quite well. The old devil tried to proposition me once, and him with an angel of a wife! Ah, well. That's men for you.'

'Grand-mère, do you try my patience on purpose?' Douglas groaned.

'It is true that Clare was married to an Englishman, the impoverished son of a lord. Her parents disowned her after the marriage, and when Sian was born, and Roland, they relented and gave her a large sum in settlement of the marriage dowry. For years afterwards they supported her and the children. After their death she inherited everything, of course, and became rich in her own right. She loved France. Hated Scotland.'

'Scotland.' Douglas was shocked at the harshness of his voice. His instincts had proved right once more. 'Go on.'

'She married again, the brother of her dead husband. Went to live somewhere in the Highlands. She rarely came back to Paris after that, but Sian and Roland did as soon as they were old enough. They loved the château, and made great improvements there. As you have said, the son moved back here last year. Sian comes and goes with her step-brother, but from what has reached me, her heart is torn between two worlds. The foolish girl is on some crusade. As if she could change the havoc wrought in your poor country. She wants to do good among the villagers, make them work for themselves so that they can earn enough to plough something back into their homes and lands. Something about spinning and dying sheep's wool!'

'They have no homes and no lands,' Douglas broke in sourly. 'Everything was taken from them. I should know. It was from me.'

'And still you seek to rectify that?'

'No, that I can never do. I return home under pain of death. But one day I will go, despite their laws meant to keep us away from the land of our birth—our heritage! Anyone who fought with Charles Stuart would choose exile to certain imprisonment—or death—or to living under an English yoke!'

'Then you are prepared to die?' Grand-mère said softly, and the eyes which turned on her blazed with fire.

'Yes. What name does she bear besides Saint-Rémy, Grand-mère?'

'Why do I feel that to tell you will lead you on a disastrous path? A path leading to your own destruction —and hers.'

'Blakeney,' Douglas whispered, almost to himself. 'That devil haunts me still!' She nodded, and he grew rigid, staring sightlessly into the flames before him. Her step-father! Touched by his guilt, accepting it by living under his roof. Did she seek to disperse some of that guilt by pretending to care for the wretched souls under his care?

'Lord Phillip Blakeney. He inherited both title and money on the death of his father. His younger brother Richard, Clare's husband, had nothing but a miserly allowance Phillip begrudgingly allowed him. I met Phillip once. A detestable man, full of his own importance. Highly thought of in London, I hear.'

'A butcher! One day, he and I shall cross swords again.'

'Yes, you will, Le Blond. It will cost you dear. Perhaps it will be worth it.' He looked at her, his mouth tightening as she spread the Tarot cards across the table in front of her. Her hands moved so quickly that he had not seen the first card down. Now she turned it over. He frowned at the sign of death staring up at him. It did not unduly surprise him. He had lived with death these past ten years—and two more before them.

'*La Mort* follows you both. *Le Diable*—for the violence in you, perhaps? The cards say you are destined for each other. Do not smile like that! See—*La Roue de Fortune* . . . and *Le Chariot* . . . for your vengeance, Le Blond? I believe you shall have it, but the cost to your love . . .'

'Love!' Douglas repeated in a hollow tone. He wanted nothing more to do with anyone tainted by Phillip Blakeney, but he would make good use of the opportunity about to come his way. Make good use of Timothy Blakeney when he laid hands on him. He himself could not go to Scotland, but if he held Blakeney's son. . . .

'I do not like the look in your eyes.' Grand-mère averted her gaze from the pitiless face, and continued to turn over the remainder of the cards. 'You cannot escape what is here, Le Blond. It is not to your liking, but Fate has a way of playing out the hand she deals whether you like it or not. The girl is in great danger. You both are. So close, yet . . .'

'You have told me all I wanted to know, Grand-mère. My thanks. A token of my appreciation.' He rose, laying a pouch of coins in her lap. She did not touch them. Her gaze reproved the gesture.

'I have never asked anything from you.'

'No, you gave when I had nothing and you had damned little yourself. Now I am in a position to repay you, and it pleases me to do so.'

'How proud you Highland men are! She has her pride, too. Take care. I know not in which direction the danger lies, only that it is all round you. I fear for you.'

He smiled, bent, and kissed the ringed fingers with a

gallant gesture that would have put many a courtier to shame.

'I shall watch my back, never fear.'

'She will watch it for you, Le Blond, as she has done once before. Do the same for her. She holds your life in her hands.'

'As I do hers,' he returned gravely, and she nodded again.

'How you will hurt each other . . . Come to me again.'

'Perhaps.'

'Perhaps. With you it is always "perhaps". Next time, bring her with you. Be good to her; she does not deserve your hatred.'

'Goodbye, Grand-mère. I shall see myself out.'

Sian slept until almost four in the afternoon. By the time she had washed and dressed, it would be too late to go visiting Monsieur Le Strange, she decided. It could wait until tomorrow. She had a letter to write that was far more important than a call on her banker.

An hour later she had despatched a letter to Jeanne Poisson, Marquise de Pompadour, asking to meet her soon in a private audience. She had known Jeanne for many years, and trusted her implicitly. She was thinking about a bath, when André informed her he had shown Monsieur Le Strange into the drawing-room. She learned that Douglas MacGregor had paid him a visit already, and withdrawn a large amount of money.

'That is quite in order,' she said with a stiff smile. He had wasted no time.

Douglas did not return to the house that night. She waited a full hour for him, then ate alone, feeling angry —and disappointed, and more than a little perturbed by his absence. He had taken her money. Had Roland and Effie been right in their criticism of him? Was that all he was after? She had to believe he would return soon and bring her good news. If he did not, she would find him again if she had to search to the ends of the earth, and she would have him brought to account for failing her. If she did not believe in him now, she

told herself, she had nothing, and no one capable of
concluding a successful agreement with the abductors
of her brother. And yet, as she went up to her room,
her mind once more reeling with conflicting thoughts,
she wondered if she would ever see Timothy again.

Madame de Pompadour reclined on a velvet-covered
couch; a table close by bore crystal glasses with lemonade, and beside these, a tall crystal bowl of fresh fruit.
She selected an apple from the carefully arranged struc-
ture and bit into it, eyeing with thoughtful gaze the
quiet girl seated opposite her. She had paid considerable
attention to her dress, even though this was only a
casual visit from an old friend. Many years ago she had
learned to pay great attention to her appearance. It had
brought her to the notice of the King, and made her the
first lady in the land. When she was too old to be of use
to any man, she would still have power over others.
    Her hair was powdered and adorned with tiny pink
bows—her favourite colour, to match her exquisite
gown of lace and taffeta. The décolletage was aud-
aciously low, but she enjoyed shocking people,
especially the fawning fops who came to gape at her at
court, hoping that her royal lover's eyes would stray
from the woman who had successfully kept him satisfied
for the past ten years. She was too clever for that. She
was thirty-four, but she looked no more than twenty-five
at the very most. She still had the figure of a young girl,
and her complexion was admired and envied by most
of the women at Versailles. She would not be toppled
from her position for a long time to come.
    From beneath the froth of lace and pink skirt peeped
narrow pointed shoes with dainty red heels and diamond
buckles. Long slender fingers each bore a ring. Sapph-
ires flashed at her throat and wrists and more from her
ears.
    Jeanne Poisson had not changed since the day they
met, Sian thought in admiration. Or was she a little
more lovely? Never in her wildest dreams would she
have thought the unknown woman to whom she had

once given a lift outside Versailles, when her coach broke down as it was following the royal hunt, would some day be mistress of the King of France. They never talked of her association with Louis. Sian, with her strict upbringing, had found the whole affair rather shocking, although it had not prevented their friendship from continuing and deepening. But Jeanne, understanding the girl's natural abhorrence of sleeping with a man outside marriage, was careful to invite her only to the soirées and balls where she herself picked the guests and could ensure that none of them were too outspoken or adventurous and might somehow arouse Sian's puritan instincts still further.

Poor Sian! What she needed was a man to make her begin thinking of herself instead of others. And what does she do? Find herself a surly, uncommunicative exiled Scot, like so many who hung about the court. If they struck up a friendship with anyone, it was for one reason only—money. Whatever had possessed her to hire the services of this man, of all people? Had she not seen what he was like the night Madame de Brissac brought him to her party? A violent one, that. Dangerous, like a jungle cat. Sian would never hold him—or control him.

'You say he has been to your banker and withdrawn money. A large amount?'

'Yes.' Sian nodded miserably. 'It has been four days now, Jeanne. I begin to think . . .'

'That you will never see him again? I am inclined to agree with you. Were you out of your mind to give him such authority? He can draw any amount he likes.'

'That is the intention. I want him to find Timothy, so that if I have to pay a ransom and they then demand more from me, he will know where they are holding him. I had faith in Monsieur MacGregor's ability to go in and rescue him. I have seen him fight.'

'Have you, now! And what was he fighting over—or for?' Jeanne asked with a slow smile.

'For me,' she replied, and decided it was best to tell her friend everything. Jeanne, who was so more experienced with men than she was, would be better able to assess if she had been a fool or not. She spared herself nothing, and saw her friend's eyebrows arch more than once during the telling of her story.

'Either the man is a clever rogue—and that would be my first guess—or he is not as black as he is painted.'

'Every word of it is true,' Sian protested.

'My dear girl, I know it to be so. You are so naïve when it comes to men—and that is not meant unkindly,' Jeanne returned, ringing a little golden bell at her side. She ordered tea to be brought when a liveried servant came silently into the room, ignoring Sian's protest that she should be leaving. 'Don't worry about him. If he has returned, it will do him good to await your convenience. Do not show him, on any account, that you are dependent on him.'

'But I am, and he knows it!'

'Even so, stay aloof from him. Remember he is naught but another hireling. Do not make a friend of him, Sian. You find him attractive, don't you?'

Miserably Sian nodded. Jeanne gave a sigh and stretched languidly.

'My poor lamb, I cannot give you the same advice I would give to others at court. I would tell them to sleep with the fellow and let familiarity breed contempt. Then send him on his way with a pocket full of coins. You would not do that, of course. So the only way to keep a safe distance between you—a most difficult undertaking when it is necessary for you to work in close harmony under strained circumstances—is always to remember who and what you are, and make him damned aware of it, too! At no time must you allow what you feel for him to affect your judgment. If, and now I give him the benefit of the doubt, he has some grain of decency in him, he will see how his connection with you could affect your life and your friends, and he will leave as soon as Timothy has been returned to you.'

'And if he is a rogue?' Sian asked softly, her lips trembling slightly as she forced the words past them.

'Then you will allow me the pleasure of dealing with

him! You have no one to protect you while you are
here, now that Roland is gone.'

'I have been thinking I should inform Phillip, but to
bring him all this way for nothing . . . It would be so
wonderful to take Timmy home and make light of the
whole thing. How—how would you deal with a man
like Monsieur MacGregor?' she asked. 'Your prestige
would not intimidate him, Jeanne. He has contempt
only for people in power—or those with money.'

'I promise you, if he is in any way connected with
what has happened to you, or Timothy, or the murder
of Roland, I shall obtain a *lettre de cachet* from the King
and have him confined in the Bastille for the rest of
his natural life.' She smiled slightly as Sian gasped in
amazement.

A *lettre de cachet* was enough to strike terror into the
bravest of hearts, for it was the ultimate in punishments.
The King never knew whom he was committing to a life
of hell, for the sealed letters he handed to ministers or
sent directly to prison governors, authorising them to
arrest and detain the person named therein, were, when
he handed them over, always blank. Names were filled
in afterwards, by whomever had requested the favour.
It was a way of disposing of unwanted relatives, of
bringing troublesome children to heel, of subduing
headstrong young heiresses who thought to control their
own fortunes in defiance of the wishes of their guardians.
A few months in a damp, dark cell tamed the wildest
nature!

'No matter what he is, you would not wish that on
him, eh?' Jeanne asked, watching her friend closely.

'I have sworn to bring Roland's murderers to justice.
If he is one of them, then you may do as you please
with him,' Sian said, rising to her feet. 'Thank you for
seeing me. I shall let you know immediately when
anything happens. Meanwhile, you will do as you
suggested and make some enquiries for me? I am clutching at straws, Jeanne. I shall take all the help I can get.'

'Will you not stay here tonight? For you, there will
always be a room. I have to be with the King this

evening, a little affair. He wants to impress some minister from Italy. Or was it Germany? I've quite forgotten.' She gave an amused laugh as she walked with Sian towards the door. 'You need to be taken out of yourself. Stay. At least have some tea?'

'No, but thank you for the kind offer.' When everyone came to Versailles hoping to be seen by the King or La Pompadour, to be given an apartment, as Sian always was when she came to visit, was the height of favour. Many found themselves sharing with six or seven other people, crowding into tiny attic rooms where there was hardly enough space to turn round.

'I am giving a little supper party next week. I want you to come to that,' Jeanne insisted. 'You cannot shut yourself away because of what has happened. Roland would not want that. I want to keep my eye on you, too.'

'I have no wish to be the centre of conversation by attending such an occasion when my brother has been in his grave less than seven days, and when I do not know if I shall ever see Timothy again. Dearest Jeanne, I know you mean well, but I could not face all those people.' Sian kissed her hostess on both cheeks, and clutched at the soft, white hands in hers for a moment longer. 'Pray for him. And for me.'

'Unaccustomed as I am to asking help from anyone else,' Jeanne returned without the slightest trace of immodesty, 'I shall pray for you both. Goodbye, my dear.'

La Pompadour, her brows drawn together in a deep frown, watched Sian move slowly down the corridor in the wake of a lackey. Clad completely in black, the long veil once more covering her pale, tired features, Sian reminded her of a figure out of a Greek tragedy. She had no time now to begin circulating her desire to know more about Douglas MacGregor and his unsavoury companions in the 'Beggars' Quarter', as that part of the city which stretched beyond the Pont-Neuf was often known—it would take her three hours to dress for this evening's festivities. But afterwards, if the King did not keep her too late, she would ask a few questions of the right people. There were many at court completely at her command, including soldiers, statesmen, men of the arts and literature. The next time she saw Sian, perhaps she would be able to bring a smile to those anxious features. If it was in her power to do so, she would!

'Madam,' Effie protested, staring in dismay at the full plate of food Sian put back on the tray. 'You have eaten practically nothing! You cannot go on in this way. I am going to fetch you some broth.'

'You will do no such thing. Take that away, and leave me. I wish to rest for a while,' Sian ordered, raising a hand to her aching head. She seemed to have had a headache ever since her return from Versailles.

How long had it been since her visit? Three days? No, five. And still no word from Douglas. Eight days. She despaired of ever seeing him again. He had taken her money and gone, leaving Timothy to his fate and her to the terrible realisation that she had trusted in vain. She had sentenced her own brother to death in doing so!

Another day, and then she would go back to Jeanne and ask her to arrange the *lettre de cachet*. He must not be allowed to escape unpunished. One more day . . . but that was what she had told herself yesterday . . . and the day before. Oh, God, she prayed. Give me the courage to do it. I must. He has betrayed me!

She lay back on the *chaise-longue*, drained and weary. She ate very little these days, and the mere sight of food made her feel ill. She spent hours alone in Roland's room, refusing to allow it to be dusted or touched in any way. She did that herself, when the doors were locked and she was alone with him and her memories. She tended for each item there with loving care as though she expected him to return at any moment. Only at night, in the darkness of her bed, alone and frightened, distraught beyond thought, did the horror return to her—and the loss became unbearable.

'Madam.' Effie was gently shaking her shoulder. Without realising it, Sian had fallen asleep beside Roland's bed. She had been going through some of the many books he possessed which always lay untidily about the room. He had made this one a replica of his study at the château, so that he could sit and read his beloved books in peace. No one was allowed to tidy the study, either. 'He's back! As bold as you please, without a word of apology for his absence.'

The maid eyed the sleepy, dishevelled figure on the rich baize carpet, forcing down the annoyance which threatened to show on her face. His return could ruin everything. Another few days, and Sian would have been willing to sell her soul—go anywhere—pay anything for the return of her brother. Been prepared to walk unsuspecting into the trap now being laid for her. Now Douglas MacGregor had returned to the house, and Effie was afraid what he might have to tell her mistress. She had no fears for her own safety. Only Simeon knew of her involvement with the band. But what if the hide-out had been discovered and the boy rescued? No. Surely she would have heard. Perhaps Le Blond had returned for more money . . . or her mistress's bed. That was more like it. Highland men always took what they wanted.

Sian blinked up at her, not understanding the words for a full minute. Then hope rose in her face. Back! He had not abandoned her.

'What time is it? It's dark outside.' Roland had never allowed a clock in the room. When he was there, time was unimportant.

'After seven. You have been up here for three hours, madam.'

'Lay out a fresh gown for me. I shall dine downstairs. Have another place set at the table for Monsieur Mac-Gregor.'

'He is staying, then?' The maid's voice was deliberately insolent, and Sian stiffened. With each passing day, she sensed a growing enmity she did not understand and could not control. It went deeper than the dislike they held for each other because of her dead mother. Much deeper. 'It's a cold night. Shall I have a warming-pan put in his bed, too?' Or will you be warming it for him? she added silently.

'If that is necessary, I shall order it later on. You may go.'

Sian came face to face with Douglas as she came out of Roland's room. As his bleak eyes inspected the black-robed figure, the paleness of her complexion, the shadows of tiredness ringing her listless eyes, she felt something sharp cut through her breast at the sight of him. The pain of her foolishness, perhaps. Longing to be with him again, to know his touch? To know him? He was dressed in dark colours, as when she had first met him, shirt and breeches covered by a heavy woollen cloak. She saw no sign of fatigue in his expression and no indication that he had spent sleepless nights of worry. She stepped back from him, and the accusation which rose in her eyes needed no words to accompany it.

His fingers clasped her slim wrist, pushing her unceremoniously back into the room. He closed the door and glowered at her.

'Are you trying to get your brother killed?' he demanded before she could reprimand him for his actions. 'By whose authority have there been questions asked about me across the river? Whose men were those making enquiries at all the taverns for your brother? Whoever sent them might well have signed his death-warrant!'

'I—I don't know!' Sian protested. Jeanne! It could be no other. She drew herself up haughtily, as the words of La Pompadour returned to remind her how dangerous this man was to her. 'Remember he is naught but another hireling.' If only it were possible to be so detached. But she must! 'Do not make a friend of him.' Even though he had twice saved her life, beware! 'Perhaps the Marquise de Pompadour,' she added, and Douglas interrupted her.

'Hell-fire! Is she involved? What did you tell her, you little fool?'

'You forget yourself, monsieur,' Sian snapped, but her indignation had no effect on the angry man. He looked as if he wanted to slap her for daring to interfere. 'You took yourself off, with money from my bankers, and it has now been eight days! What was I supposed to believe? Jeanne is a close friend and she has offered me her help. Which I have accepted,' she added, as her lips tightened into a grim line of disapproval. 'People of her acquaintance may prove useful . . .' And she will protect me against you—against myself!

'I have an acquaintance of my own. One in particular that was willing to sell his friends to me for a large sum of money and my safe guarantee to leave the city. Then *her* friends started poking their noses in, alerting all the wrong people. Last night this man was pushed into the Seine, with his throat cut. You and your meddling—and hers—have cost money and time.'

'I—I didn't realise!' Sian stammered uncomfortably. How dare he make her feel she was in the wrong? If only he had been more forthcoming. 'You could have sent word.'

'I thought it best to stay away from here until they communicated with you again. I expected it to happen before this. You have heard nothing?' He swore as she shook her head, ignoring her shocked look. 'I can see why, now, looking at you.'

'What—what is wrong with me?'

'You have not been sleeping, and that means you are tired and irritable. Time is on their side. They are cleverer than I expected, and that surprises me. It's almost as though they know you could lose your wits at any time. Then you would be willing to do anything, wouldn't you?'

'I shall not—lose my wits, as you put it,' Sian retorted, eyes flashing disdainfully. 'And, yes, I shall do anything to get my brother back. And I shall use anyone I see fit to do so.'

'Then you do not need me.'

'No, wait!' she cried. He had turned to the door; his hand was reaching for the handle. 'You are inhuman to

walk away and leave me, knowing the misery I am
suffering. Have you nothing to tell me?'

'What have I been doing while I was away, that
you consider so trifling and unimportant? Watching.
Listening. Finding people who will not sell me, as they
sell others. Now it will have to be done all over again,'
Douglas told her coldly. 'You may have to wait another
eight days, or perhaps longer. Pray they think you have
been stretched to the limit. If so, they may contact you
soon. If you wish the boy to be alive when he is found,
you will allow me to go my own way and do whatever
is necessary without any more of your damned unneces-
sary interference. And you will tell that to Madame de
Pompadour also. Do I make myself clear, woman?'

He was the master—giving her orders, subjecting her
to his will! She nodded, hating the weakness in her
which still clung to the frail thread of trust.

'There is a room here for you if you wish to stay.'
Eyes that were almost black in the shadowy candlelight
gleamed with mockery at her words. Only with a great
effort did she hold his gaze.

'You will have no need to lock your bedroom door
tonight. I shall not be here. Sleep untroubled—and
alone. I know the fear that haunts you. Not fear of me,
although you pretend it is. It is fear of yourself, that I
shall touch you again and rouse the woman in you.
Deny it if you can!' he challenged.

Sian's mouth quivered as she stared at his smouldering
features.

'I was merely offering you the hospitality of my house,
not my bed, Monsieur MacGregor. Do you honestly
believe I could find you attractive? A man of violence,
penniless; an adventurer?' she demanded haughtily.
Attack was her only defence. How easy it would have
been to confess the truth of his words, beg him to put
his arms round her and give her the love and comfort
she craved in her despair.

'Some women need the excitement of something—
or someone—different!' Douglas grinned.

'I need nothing of the sort.'

'You lie!'

She gasped at his accusation, fought for words strong enough to tell him exactly what she thought of his preposterous assumptions, true or not—but words failed her.

'I could take you in my arms now and you would welcome it, but I think I shall return to the place where other arms will be waiting for me, willing arms and a most satisfying body.'

'If you are trying to shock me, monsieur, you fail miserably.'

'Really? So the puritanical pose is as false as I've always thought,' Douglas mocked, and she shrank back in her chair as if afraid he was going to seize her and prove it there and then. 'My God, I never fail to be amazed at the deceptions women practise. Why they even bother, is a mystery. Do you know there is more honesty in the woman who lies with me than you will ever possess?'

Drawing her skirts behind her in a deliberate gesture of contempt which brought his lips into a grim line, Sian said cuttingly, 'Then go to her, monsieur! I have no further need of you. When you have word for me, send it by a messenger. I do not wish to see you again until it is time for me to deliver the ransom money to Timothy's abductors. Then you may accompany me. I shall, of course, pay you extra to compensate for any danger you consider you will be in.'

'You little fool! You think this is a game, don't you?' Douglas gave a hollow laugh. 'Your brother is dead! Two attempts have been made on your life, and the boy's hangs in the balance. It is no game!'

He wanted to take hold of her and shake some sense into her stupid head, but he did not touch her. He could not trust himself to.

'Ach, why am I standing here bothering myself with you! Go back upstairs to his room and your memories. You may have little else left. But before you go, my fine lady, I'll tell you this. I have never killed without reason. Nor have I ever taken an unwilling woman.

Force is the last resort of bullies and cowards, and the world is full of those. You have bought my sword, woman, and with that goes my loyalty for as long as you pay me. What more did you expect? A bleeding heart for your troubles? I left that behind me in Scotland, along with my dead. I have no conscience, so never try to appeal to one; nor do I possess a heart, or it would have been torn apart long before now by bitches like you. I don't give a damn for anyone but myself. I am willing to find your brother and bargain for his release because I shall be paid to do so—and for no other reason. You will have to come to me now. If they get in touch with you, send someone to the Coq d'Or. Remember to ask for Le Blond.'

'But—but that is the place . . .' Sian's voice faltered and broke as he nodded grimly.

'The place René told you of. For your information, I live there. Simeon has never frequented the place or used it for any of his dealings. René was trying to implicate me as best he could. Ask anyone on the Pont-Neuf where it is, and they will direct you. Good night, Madame la Comtesse.'

# CHAPTER
# SEVEN

IT WAS nearly light before Sian fell asleep, and it seemed she had barely closed her eyes before someone was shaking her urgently. She opened tired eyes to find Effie bending over the bed, waving a piece of paper under her nose.

'This was pushed under the front doors, madam. André found it when he unlocked them an hour ago. There's no name on it at all, simply a few words. What does it mean? Is it from them? Saints preserve us, the child is still alive!'

And was far too precious to have even one hair on his head harmed, the woman thought as Sian sat up, snatching the grubby paper from her. He was a means to an end.

'An hour ago? Why did you not bring it to me immediately? A whole hour has been wasted. Bring me a robe, quickly, and writing materials. No, wait!' Douglas was waiting to hear from her at the Coq d'Or, and she must send for him at once; yet she hesitated, remembering his withering words to her the night before that had plagued her thoughts throughout the long hours of darkness. It was more prudent to go to him, she decided, although rather undignified. The fewer people who knew what she was about, the better. The note was explicit, and left no room for deviation. *Rue Madeleine. Midnight. 13th.*

Tonight! No names, nothing but that one address, where she suspected she would be met. If she ventured there alone, the money she carried would never reach its destination. On her own, she was not safe on those dark, narrow streets.

'I am going out. Bring me a warm dress and boots,

and my ermine cloak. No, not that one, it will not do. Something plain. Hurry, Effie.'

'Yes, madam. You wish me to go with you?' It was the last thing she wanted to do!

'No, I must go alone.'

'Madam, you cannot! Let me hire some men.' Despite her seeming protection, Effie was enjoying Sian's moments of agony; the contemplation of what lay ahead for her.

'I have no need of protection. They say I am to come alone. I must.'

Even if she went to him, Simeon would ask a high price for his help, Effie mused. Sian was too proud to pay it . . . The maid sneered silently as she opened the closets and took out a velvet dress in jade green, petticoats, warm stockings, and leather boots, and last of all the plain cloak Sian had remembered just in time. She could hardly walk into a den of thieves in ermine! It would make no difference to what would happen to her in the end! When she had begun to execute the diabolical plans first evolved in Scotland during the early weeks of Sian's absence from Ard Choille, she had never imagined how well they would succeed, or how easy it had been to dispose of Roland.

Sian she had intended should die first in the coach robbery, and her brother later when he came to Paris to instigate the release of his step-brother. Instead, it had turned out the other way. Effie's lip curled as she gazed at Sian's reflection in the mirror. She was coming to the end of her tether. Simeon would have no trouble in dealing with her at his leisure. Perhaps she would appeal to some of the other men, afterwards. It was not too often that they had the chance to tumble a real lady.

When Sian's body was found, she would sow the first seeds of suspicion pointing to the mercenary whose strange association with her mistress had given cause for such alarm. He had been present at the château, and killed the only man who could have led help to the unfortunate Timothy. He had twice been at this very house, and had she herself not heard them quarrelling

the night before she was murdered—about money?
Phillip would love her all the more when she told him
how she had disposed of his hated enemy. He need
never look over his shoulder again!

Effie was humming quietly to herself as she closed
the front door after Sian's departing figure, never realising that her mistress's destination was not as she
thought, the bank and then the Rue Madeleine, but the
Coq d'Or tavern, which lay in the other direction.

As the carriage reached the edge of the bridge, Sian
called up to the driver to stop. He pulled over to one
side of the road and waited patiently for her to change
her mind again. Four times she had started out for this
place, and four times she had turned back. They had
come further this time, to the beginning of the Pont-
Neuf, and again her courage failed her.

It was like a different world across the Seine, she
thought, staring out of the window. People jostled and
bumped each other as they went to and fro. Ladies and
gentlemen, fans fluttering, skirts held high to avoid
the refuse underfoot, perfumed handkerchiefs held to
sensitive noses brushed shoulders with beggars and mer-
chants, street-pedlars and whores. Rich, monogrammed
carriages with high-stepping horses pushed past fully-
laden carts which looked as if they might fall apart at
any moment. She had to go on! Timothy's life depended
on it. What was her pride worth with so much at stake?
A minimal sum compared to the one he would have to
pay if she did not continue.

In a firm voice, she called up to the driver to proceed.

Did people really inhabit the squalid, filthy dwellings
she was passing? How could human beings live in conditions like these? Pestilence was surely rife, and the
poor souls could have no money to buy medicine or the
attention of a doctor. God have mercy on them, she
prayed, averting her eyes from a one-legged beggar
pleading for alms in the road.

Everywhere, to her surprise, even in the dingiest
places, there were flowers and flower-sellers, bringing

a touch of badly-needed colour to the drab surroundings. But their presence was offset by other features
that marred the narrow, winding streets, where the
houses leaned towards each other so perilously that they
almost touched. The smell of vegetation returned to set
her fan fluttering again. In the pit of her stomach was
an unpleasant churning sensation. Fear of this place or
of what lay ahead? Who awaited her at the Coq d'Or?
What if *he* was not there? She would have endured this
horrible journey for nothing. Where would she look for
him? The thought of going from tavern to tavern asking
if anyone had heard of or seen Le Blond sent her into
a near panic.

How much further? Her appointment was for midnight! Please, please let me find him soon!

'I think this could be it, madame.'

The carriage had halted outside a dingy tavern, where
through the open door she could see the dregs of
humanity seeking relief, or an escape, from the wretch-
edness of their existence. She alighted, her eyes full of
apprehension as curious faces peered out to see whose
carriage had arrived.

Pulling the hood of her cloak over her face, she said
to the driver, 'Go inside. Ask for a man called Le Blond.
Someone must know him.'

'And if I must give a name, madame?' the man asked
dubiously, and Sian paled. On no account must her
identity be revealed to those inside.

'If he is there, tell him it is the messenger he has been
expecting. If he is not, ask where he can be found.
Here.' She handed him several coins. 'These will loosen
a few tongues. Hurry! I feel as if I am being watched
by a thousand evil eyes.'

Sian leaned back against the coach, hugging her cloak
about her as several men came out a few minutes after
the driver had gone inside. They stared at her boldly
and she turned away, flushing uncomfortably. They
exchanged comments and walked away laughing. No
decent woman ventured here alone, she realised. They
thought she had come looking for an excitement which

could not be provided even by the immoral court at
Versailles or found in the corridors of the Louvre,
notorious for the clandestine meetings which took place
there, and she suspected there would be many willing
to oblige her if she paid enough. How could her friends
come to a place like this? She knew that some did.

A dwarf in a bright yellow shirt and matching trousers
tumbled out of the tavern, somersaulted in front of her,
and evoked roars of laughter with his grand bow. The
plumed hat he wore was swept from his head, the
weather-beaten face creased into a smile she found
almost pleasant, and as he bent double, she could have
sworn his nose touched the floor.

'My lady, do not stand there to be gaped at by those
ignorant fools. Come with me. I will take you to Le
Blond,' he added, as she hesitated. 'He has sent me to
fetch you. He said you would need proof. Will this do?'

Sian found herself staring at the diamond ring she
had given Douglas for saving her life on the road.
Without a word she nodded, gathered her cloak more
tightly to her and started after the little man, who had
disappeared into the crowd behind him again without
waiting to see if she followed.

A passage opened up through the onlookers, who
still gaped at her, some with hostility, others with open
thoughts written on their faces, which made her shudder
and quicken her steps. No one attempted to detain her,
however, or to touch her clothes as they had done
outside. The name of Le Blond was a powerful deter-
rent, she thought, and wondered how much influence
he wielded over the likes of this rabble around her?

Up a long flight of stairs to a room at the top, where
the door was slightly ajar. There were doors on either
side, these tightly closed. She heard the sounds of
laughter which told her far more than a hundred pictures
as she moved after the dwarf. He swung the door open,
motioned her inside, and the moment she was over the
threshold, closed it behind her. Sian came to a halt,
feeling trapped.

At the far end of the room, sprawled comfortably in

a battered leather chair, one booted leg flung over an arm, was Douglas. And he was not alone. On his lap reclined a dark-haired gypsy girl with eyes like coals of fire, glaring with unconcealed hatred at Sian. Her flounced skirt was hitched high over long, shapely legs. Her silk blouse, of black and red, slashed with silver, exposed firm rounded breasts and brown shoulders. Huge gold earrings hung from her ears, and bracelets by the dozen adorned her arms.

'I am honoured,' he said, and sounded the exact opposite. 'I did not expect a personal visit. Only last night . . .'

'That was last night,' Sian interrupted coldly, determined not to be intimidated by his manner—or that of the woman lolling on his lap in a most possessive manner. This was his mistress, of course. What chance had she against such a creature, she wondered? It was all there in the wild eyes and sensuous mouth—she could give him everything he wanted—make him want her. Passion—sensuality—knowledge—it radiated from her like a strong perfume, filling the room. Sian felt herself begin to sway unsteadily.

He frowned. 'Sit down, woman! Zara, fetch her a chair.'

'Let her get it herself. I am not her servant,' came the angry hiss.

The girl was unceremoniously pushed from his lap on to the floor. He rose and himself brought Sian a chair, positioning it close to where he sat.

'Get out, Zara! See we are not disturbed.'

'Yes, gracious master. Call me when you need me,' Zara said, her husky voice heavy with sarcasm, and Douglas slammed the door after her departing figure. He did not even raise an eyebrow. He was used to her tantrums and her possessiveness. It had never bothered him, nor would he allow it to do so now.

'You have heard?' he demanded, and Sian nodded. He wore only a loose shirt, open to the waist, revealing the strong muscular chest with its blond hair, and breeches, as well as his boots. Her eyes sought his broadsword, and found it hanging behind the door. 'It is still at your disposal, if you wish it,' he said, following her gaze.

'Yes, I do.' There, she was committed. 'This is the note I received this morning. I have been to my bankers, and the money will be ready for me this afternoon at five o'clock. I dared not bring it with me to this terrible place. Besides, I did not know if you would be here.'

'I said I would.'

'You have been waiting for me?' she asked, unable to hide her surprise.

'Of course. You wish me to accompany you to the bankers, collect the ransom and then take you to the meeting place, am I right?'

'Yes.'

'I could suggest I went alone. It will be dangerous for you, even if I came with you,' he said, watching her from beneath lowered lids. She looked so pale and drawn that he wondered if she was about to faint. Her nerves would not take much more of this cruel strain. Reaching out, he pushed the hood back from her face and looked at her for a long moment. 'But you do not trust me alone, so I will not suggest it,' he added mockingly.

Sian bit her lip. His fingers, light as they had been against her skin, seemed to burn it. How she longed for his touch again. No, she must think of nothing but Timothy! What was he waiting for? Why did he not put her out of her misery and say he would go with her? He was waiting for her to beg; she could see it in his eyes . . .

'I have come to you as you wanted. I have no one else to turn to, but then you know that.' She slid from her chair to her knees before him, her face twisted into a bitter smile. 'I am begging you to help me. Isn't this the way you wanted it? To repay me for all my harsh words, my suspicions?'

'Get up, dammit!' Douglas rasped, gripping her by the shoulders. But he did not pull her to her feet at once. Instead he bent his head, and his lips lightly brushed hers. He felt her shudder and strain away, but then she was still, allowing him his way, her lips soft and pliant beneath his, fired to an uncontrollable response as he slid one hand beneath her cloak against her breasts and gently caressed them. She had no strength to fight him, no will to resist the pleasure of his touch. She was tired and vulnerable.

'Perhaps we should talk of my price now, while you are in a receptive mood,' he whispered softly, moving his lips to the glossy curls about her neck.

'I shall pay your price, monsieur. I have already told you that,' Sian whispered. Why did he have to be so cruel? Could he not feel how wretched she was, how frightened of the chasm on whose brink she hovered? She was ready to cast herself into it—into the eternal fires of hell, she suspected—because of his touch.

'You don't know yet what I shall ask.' His hand slid over the satin smoothness of her shoulders, down to the curve of her breast above the neckline of the jade-green velvet and deeper until it encountered a nipple, hard with desire beneath his probing fingers. A mocking smile touched his mouth as she gasped and pulled back from him, cheeks flaming. 'You should,' he added.

She saw too late the trap into which she had unwittingly walked. But had she been so unaware of his intentions? Had he not made them clear from the beginning? His gaze on her was pitiless. She had played straight into his hands.

'Why do you hate me so much?' Sian asked, her voice little more than a whisper.

Douglas eyed her for a moment, the scarred cheek taut, even though he was smiling.

'On the contrary, I find you an attractive, desirable woman. I have wanted you from the first moment I set eyes on you. Why should I forgo a chance to have what I want?' he asked, with a casual shrug of his shoulders. 'I am a simple man. I take my pleasures when and where they are available to me. I cannot be blamed for that, can I?'

'I find that a contemptible attitude!' she said coldly.

'However, I shall pay whatever price you ask of me, monsieur. I love my brother enough to sacrifice anything, even my life.'

'A foolishly brave statement, which you hope I shall not accept as true. However, I do. I know you love him. I shall tell you what I want. As I shall be arranging matters, Simeon will have no need of the ransom money he has demanded. I shall have that for a start. It will help to pay those who go with us tonight. Without their help, we would surely fail in our venture.'

Venture? What was he talking about? Sian wondered, a frown puckering her chestnut brows.

'For—for a start?' she repeated. Her mouth felt as dry as dust.

'And you!' The ultimatum was delivered without mercy!

The blood drained from her face, leaving it a ghastly colour.

'Is there nothing you will not do to humiliate me?' she whispered. She had expected it, yet to hear him utter the words was like being doused with ice-cold water, and she began to shake.

'As I am only a Scottish exile who preys on unfortunate women, you must expect me to make the most of this opportunity! Douglas flung her own words back at her once again contemptuously. 'Besides, you must expect a high price if you ask a Highlander to do a favour for an Englishwoman! Do you agree to my terms?'

It was impossible! She could not—yet, to save her brother . . . Mutely she nodded.

'Is that a yes, woman? Speak! I want to hear what you say. I want a commitment from your own lips.' He was grim-faced as he studied her down-bent head. All or nothing. It was the way he lived.

'Yes.' Her voice was scarcely audible.

Turning away from her, he sprawled across the enormous bed, supporting himself on one elbow as he stared across to where she sat, her hands locked tightly in her lap.

Sian dared not look at him. He was enjoying his moment of triumph, and his next words confirmed it and filled her with even more horror as he drawled sardonically, 'In this quarter of the city, it is customary to inspect the merchandise before purchasing. Take off your clothes.'

'I will not!' She came out of the chair as if a thousand red-hot irons had suddenly branded her.

A dangerous smile played at the corners of his lean mouth as he surveyed her. 'Come here, little Sian,' he ordered softly.

She glared at him, but her composure, as well as her determination to fight him, was rapidly diminishing under the steady gaze which stripped her of all ability to think for herself, to act as she knew she should. It was as if he mesmerised her, compelled her with those cold eyes, seduced her without a touch! She would not obey him. He was not her master! She would not degrade herself to please him. Why did he have to make it happen like this? To undress in front of him, while his gaze devoured her bare flesh! Yet, as if pushed by an unseen hand, she moved like a sleep-walker to the edge of the bed.

'Perhaps you would like me to help you? Or one of my friends from downstairs?' came the threat, as she hesitated again. As if in a dream, her fingers reached for the fastenings of her gown.

Awkwardly, for she rarely dressed or undressed without the assistance of a maid, she discarded it and then the multitude of petticoats beneath. She could hardly breathe. She felt stifled. The room began to spin about her and her senses reeled. Only with a supreme effort did she regain control of them.

'The shift,' Douglas repeated stonily. She had not heard him the first time. 'Although I have seen you naked before, you left damned little impression on me. I might be wasting my time.'

With fingers of lead, Sian loosened the ribbons of her bodice. She felt unclean—and yet as those eyes continued to watch her, the gleam which came into them roused the first flicker of excitement within her. Ignited that first spark . . . She hesitated, hoping for a last-minute reprieve, but none came. Slowly she drew it away from proud, softly-tilting breasts and down over her shoulders until it was about her waist. Damn him, she would go no further!

'Now the hair.' How he restrained the wild impulse to grab her there and then, Douglas did not know. He regretted the anger and hatred in him which sought to destroy her courage and magnificent pride. If only she had not been connected with Blakeney. Damn the man. Even ten years after, he could still ruin lives! Douglas's lips compressed into a tight line. He had gone too far to back down now. Perhaps later—afterwards—he would be able somehow to explain the devil which drove him. He found that strange! He had never sought to explain his actions to anyone before. Why did he want to with this girl?

Free of the combs securing it, Sian's black hair tumbled in profusion about her shoulders, so long that it went some little way at least to hiding her shame and confusion.

Without warning, his hand snaked out and caught the skirt of her shift, tumbling her alongside him on the bed. She cried out as the weight of his body held her immobile. One hand fastened in her loose hair, so that she could not turn her mouth away from his. His lips swooped on hers and captured them without a battle, while his free hand moved down over her bare shoulders, caressing, stroking, seeking her breasts, finding and teasing the pink rosebud nipples.

'Court trollop, street whore or kitchen-maid who shares her master's bed, you are no different. You have a body, which you are prepared to use when the fancy takes you or you have little else to bargain with. How many men have you had before me?'

'None!' Sian's eyes smouldered as she stared into the cruel face above her. Her cheeks were in turn blenched by his continual insults, fired to fierce colour by the knowledgeable hand searching her body. No man had ever looked at her in this way, let alone touched her! 'I belong to no one!'

He gave a harsh laugh, but the ring of truth was undoubtedly in her voice and could not be denied. She sensed a momentary hesitation in him before he continued to kiss her, his lips wandering from mouth to cheek, neck and breast, to the glossy curls in wild profusion over the grey coverlet.

'No matter.' Still he could not break through that barrier of mistrust Phillip Blakeney's name had erected between them. 'All cats are grey in the dark. You are as much an alley-cat as all the others, and I shall prove it!'

Douglas gave an oath as a tear rolled down over one cheek and touched his. She did not know it, but he hated to see her cry. She cried so silently, the anguish inside her controlled. There was no hysterical outburst, no red-puffed cheeks to gain sympathy. Just huge, silent tears like glistening diamonds wending their way to his mouth. He raised his head, and the sight of them halted him in his moment of madness. He had not intended to go as far as this. To hurt her with words, yes! To show her that fine clothes and money gained no advantages from him.

'You are my woman,' he said quietly, and heard her sharp intake of breath. 'When I am gone from your life, you may take the devil himself to your bed, I'll not care. But now, until you are rid of me—and that may be a long while—you belong to me. My woman,' he repeated again slowly, and she could only stare up at him in astonishment. Was this his way of saying he cared for her? What did he mean when he said she would not be rid of him for a long while? Did he intend to stay with her after Timothy had been rescued? If only he would! She wanted to tell him she wished it, but the words would not come.

She raised trembling fingers to touch the lean jaw, trace the outline of the hard mouth. He turned his lips against them in a kiss that made her feel faint again, but this time from pleasure. He had changed . . . Why?

How? She could not define it, but there was tenderness in the eyes gazing down at her.

'I—shall—not—go back—on our bargain,' she said haltingly, and he gave a quick frown.

'No, you will not. But it is not of that I speak, and well you know it. I speak of what is between us. What we desire from each other.'

Desire! She had never known it before. How glad she was he had shown her the delights it could bring, the pleasures of his touch, his kiss. How dull he must think her, lying like a rag doll beneath him, yet she had no idea how to tell him, let alone show him, the depths of her own emotions. Or even if it was wise to reveal how utterly and completely she loved him. Love! Yes, she did love him. No matter what he was, how many women he had known before her, how many beds he had slipped in and out of under the noses of plausible husbands, she loved him. She was his woman! Such a feeling of pride swept through her to set her body tingling once more with the anticipation of becoming his woman in reality.

'You say nothing,' Douglas murmured, allowing his lips to wander across her shoulder. Her hands clutched at his arms, and then rose higher to caress the thick blond hair at his neck.

'Like a cornfield,' she murmured, and broke off as he laughed.

'I shall find one for us to lie in, one day.' If this was madness sent by the devil, he never wanted it to end! Never had he desired a woman so much, yet after only a few short minutes with her at his mercy, he had realised that she was as innocent as she had proclaimed. The joy that swept through him was so sudden, so overwhelming, that everything else vanished from his mind. Blakeney, the house in flames, his parents, Timothy . . . When the boy was safe, he reasoned at last, he would persuade her to return to the château, where they could be alone together, spend endless days exploring the wonder of what he was now discovering. Perhaps he might even tell her of this miracle that had happened to him.

He fought against the overwhelming urge to finish what he had begun in such a cold-blooded state of mind. She did not deserve such treatment from him. She had learned nothing from Phillip Blakeney, or she would not still have her innocence. He would not—could not —complete the seduction as he had intended . . . Not here, not in the same bed where he had lain with Zara. Where they had made love night after night, touching, arousing passion in each other without tenderness or affection. With Sian, it would be different. He would make it so. Yet to draw away from her now, to deny himself the pleasures offered by her lovely body . . .

Her hands were stroking his hair, his back, oblivious to his agony of mind, his withdrawal from her. With a groan, he sought her mouth once more with renewed intensity.

At that moment the door burst open. On the threshold, her eyes wide and blazing with hatred, stood Zara. She screamed abuse first at him and then at the woman who lay beneath him as she took in the passionate scene at a single glance. Sian gave a strangled cry at the sight of the curved dagger in Zara's hand. Douglas rolled away from her as the frenzied figure rushed forward, the blade raised high, gleaming wicked and deadly. His clenched fist caught Zara beneath the jaw, and she dropped to the floor like a stone.

Figures came crowding into the room. Peppito, more little men and women, customers from the tavern, all staring rudely, searchingly, at the unconscious figure of the gypsy girl—and then at the woman who lay on the canopied bed, shocked, silent, consumed with shame.

'Get her out of my sight!' Douglas snapped, and willing hands reached for Zara and carried her away. He swung round on Sian, but the words of comfort he was about to speak died unuttered as she drew herself back against the pillows, staring at him as though he had two heads and breathed fire.

'Don't touch me,' she begged. 'Not now! Please.'

He did not know if the anger which rose in him was for himself—or for her—or for the many eyes still centred on her naked loveliness. A savage arm outflung scattered them before him. The door slammed after his departing figure, leaving Sian alone, huddled miserably beneath the coverlet she had pulled round herself. Why she should have tried to cover herself from his gaze now was beyond her. If Zara had not appeared, she would have given herself to him freely. Her skin still tingled from his touch, her mouth ached from his soul-searching kisses. His woman! She would always be that. Would there be a next time, though? And could she accept him as she had done this instant, knowing that his desire stemmed from nothing more than animal lust? For her it was different, but he would never know it now. She knew she would not have the courage to tell him after this shameful encounter. Her eyes closed. She felt exhausted, drained of all strength, all will of her own. His woman! As his woman, she must await his pleasure. She lay back in the bed, running her hands over the places he had touched, remembering how wonderful it had been.

# CHAPTER
# EIGHT

SIAN AWOKE with a start, realising there was someone in the room with her. She lay still, eyes only fractionally open, hardly daring to breathe, until the small figure of Peppito came into view and bent before the hearth to throw more wood on the dying fire.

'You are awake? Good. I shall bring you something to eat,' he said without looking round, and she marvelled at his keen hearing. 'There, that will help to warm you. Now, what can I bring you? Chicken? Turkey? Goose? Lamb pie?'

'I thought this was the poor part of Paris,' she said, her fear vanishing as she sat up, pulling the bedclothes tightly round her shoulders. She had been gaped at enough for a whole lifetime, and there was not one inch of bare skin showing as he turned to look at her.

'My, my! Zara did put a fright into you, didn't she, pretty lady? Never mind, Le Blond will see to her. She'll not be so foolish again.'

'What will he do to her?' Sian asked hesitantly. Why should he do anything? Sian knew *she* meant nothing to him.

'She did try to kill you.' The dwarf looked at her with a wide smile. It was impossible not to like him. 'If she had found you alone . . .' He ran a finger across his throat.

'If I had been alone, she would not have been so jealous,' she returned, and his smile grew.

'She has reason, no? You are Le Blond's new woman.'

'I am nothing of the kind,' she gasped, colour rising in her cheeks.

'He has told me so himself. Put me personally in

charge of you until he returns. Come, now, tell me what you want to eat, and let me fetch it.'

'Nothing. I am not hungry.' Her stomach denied the words, while she thought that Zara would probably poison her! Peppito shook his head, and headed towards the door. 'Wait—something light, then. And to drink, something hot. I am so cold and . . . just cold.'

'Of course, pretty lady. I shall be back soon.'

She heard the key turn in the lock after him. She was a prisoner!

There was no timepiece in the room to tell her the time; only a small skylight above the bed gave her any indication by the darkness outside. How long had she slept? Was it time to leave yet? Where was Douglas? Why had he left her alone? She fought down the fear rising in her again, reached for her clothes lying across the coverlet and dragged them to her. Quickly she pulled them on and was fully dressed when the dwarf returned.

'Chicken pie, a thin slice only. Hot vegetable soup— and it's good, I made it myself—and a little something to settle your nerves.'

Sian stared at the tray and its contents in silence. The pie looked delicious, golden crusty pastry oozing with pieces of chicken in a cream sauce. The steaming soup smelt appetising, too. It was the cup which made her hesitate. It looked harmless, some watery-looking liquid which smelt of honey and cinnamon, but she did not touch it.

'Please, pretty lady? Le Blond will have my hide if you do not eat,' Peppito said, offering her the cup. Why that first, she thought in alarm? What did it contain? His gaze met hers squarely. 'It tastes as good as it smells, and there's a herb in it. Drink it, and that fluttering feeling in the pit of your stomach will soon go away. Simeon is a hard man, and you must show no fear when you meet him, or all will be ruined.'

'What will?' Sian asked. The cup was pressed into her unresisting grasp. Slowly she touched it to her lips. 'Tell me, or I shall ask Le Blond.'

'What will you ask me?' Douglas came into the room in time to hear her demand. 'Haven't you eaten yet? There are things to be done. Drink that brew, woman, and let's get on with it. And no arguments, or you'll not step foot outside this place tonight.'

The threat had an immediate effect. Without a word she swallowed the contents of the cup. It was strongly spiced: wine, cinnamon and honey, and another taste she could not name. Douglas's eyes narrowed as she reached for the chicken pie. He motioned his head and Peppito, smiling as he saw her take a hesitant mouthful, slipped unnoticed from the room.

Tossing his cloak across one chair, Douglas hooked another across to his side and sat down, watching her until she had consumed the last morsel.

Setting aside the platter, Sian raised her head and looked at him for the first time. She had not dared to do so until she had had time to compose her shattered emotions. The very sight of him again sent the blood coursing through her veins to remind her what had almost happened between them.

'Are we to continue where we left off?' she asked stiffly, and saw his mouth tighten.

'I'm in no mood for your sarcasm, woman. Get on with that soup, and listen to me.' She obeyed, deflated by his brusqueness. It should have been the other way round. Why was she feeling as if she were somehow in the wrong? He could manipulate her at will, and she was helpless to prevent it now. Helpless because she loved him and wanted him, and that made her no different from Zara, who had already shared his arms, his bed.

'While you slept, I went out,' he continued. 'I have the ransom money.'

'But—but how?' she asked in puzzlement.

'Did you not give instructions that I could draw whatever amounts I wished? And as you had already arranged for a certain sum to be ready for collection, I had no trouble. I simply said I had come in your place, that you did not want to transport such a large sum alone.'

'Monsieur Le Strange would never hand over any money without my authorisation,' Sian protested.

'But I had it,' Douglas returned with a hard smile.

'You—you forged my signature?' she gasped. 'That is unforgivable!'

'You were in no condition to go visiting, were you? Besides, it suited my purposes to do it this way. I left you—or a very good facsimile of you, wearing the clothes you now have on, in a carriage outside. I told Le Strange he was at liberty to confirm with you if he wished, but that you were not in a very receptive mood and would probably remove all your money from his bank if he did not do as he was told without argument. He was quite obliging, eventually. If I gave him the impression we are more than—how shall I say— employer and servant . . .'

'You did it deliberately,' Sian cried, aghast. What would the man think of her? She would never be able to face him again . . . and the gossip! 'You did it to entrap me!'

She broke off as his eyes gleamed with derision.

'Why should I need to do that? Do you not recall what was said in this very room a few short hours ago? Shall I remind you?'

'No!' She did not want to hear such words again. 'You are my woman. When I am gone . . . you may take the devil himself to your bed, I'll not care. But now, until you are rid of me—and that may be a long while—you belong to me.' His woman! She could not admit it to him, but she wanted to! How could she have sunk to this level? Did love always take so much and give so little in return?

Douglas rose and came across to where she sat on the edge of the bed, moving with the litheness of a cat. His boots scarcely made a sound on the wooden floor. That thudding she could hear, she realised, was her own wild heartbeats as she anticipated being gathered into his arms, held against his strong chest, subjected to his soul-searching kisses.

Light as a breath of wind, his fingers touched her

chcek, ran down the line of her chin to tilt it up towards him so that he could look into her eyes.

'Nevertheless, there will be another time when you shall hear them,' he said in a velvet tone, and she closed her eyes as his fingers continued down over her shoulder to her arm, sliding along with the same gentle pressure until they stopped at her wrist. It took a full moment for her to realise that they had closed round her pulse. 'Good, you are calmer now. Peppito's little brew works every time. You would have been no use tonight in your previous condition.'

He was right, she thought. She did feel better, but whether it was to have food in her stomach again or because of the potion she had drunk, she did not know —and cared even less. She felt well able to control her emotions again and face whatever lay ahead of her.

'It—it is almost time, isn't it?' she asked, surprised at how composed she sounded. Not one flutter of fear or uncertainty within her, no tremor in her voice. Douglas gave a nod of satisfaction before moving away. Suddenly she remembered what he had said, and a puzzled look came into her eyes. 'The woman who looked like me— why was that necessary?'

'Not for Le Strange—after all, I had your authoris- ation. No, she was for the beady little eyes of Simeon's watchdog. You have been followed everywhere. By one of his men—and one of mine,' he added. 'How else did I know of your visit to La Pompadour?'

'I suppose you considered it necessary, though I fail to see why. To have me watched, I mean.' His words sent a little shiver through her.

'I was not sure what you might do—or of his actions, either. He is a dangerous man, never forget that. He is completely without scruples, and delights in the tor- menting of other poor souls who fall foul of him. He is capable of anything, so heed my warning. When you are with him, act only as I shall instruct you, or you risk losing not only your own life, but that of your brother.'

'And you?' Sian asked. 'Where will you be? Are you not coming with me?'

Folding his arms across his chest, Douglas leaned back against the table, his eyes intent on her pale face. How he wished he could give her words of encouragement, of hope—but he dared not. With so much at stake, a single mistake could cost the life of everyone who sought to free the boy tonight.

'After I had been to your banker, I took you home. Or so it appeared to Simeon's man. I left you in the house and came back here. Your double will leave the house a few minutes before midnight, as if to keep the rendezvous, and she will be followed to ensure that she does.'

'But if Simeon thinks she is me—that she carries the money with her—you have placed her in terrible danger! You said yourself he might decide to waylay me, to take the ransom and then demand more. She might be hurt,' Sian protested, and was relieved when he shook his head.

'She will be well protected, don't worry. Tonight you must think only of yourself. We shall leave here as she is climbing into her carriage, with one of my men as driver and another as pillion. From here we will drive to the rendezvous, but I shall not be with you when you arrive. While you are keeping Simeon busy, my men and I intend to get into the house and reach the boy, so that we have him safe before any money changes hands.'

'And then you will return Timothy to me, relieve Simeon of the money, and everyone will be satisfied,' Sian said. How simple he made it sound!

'Something like that.' He gave a tight smile.

'Except Simeon. How on earth do you intend I should —occupy him?'

'By any means in your power. I am sure you will think of something! For at least ten minutes you must keep him talking. One hint of suspicion, and . . .' He shrugged. 'No doubt he has given orders to slit the boy's throat at the first sign of trouble. Be indignant. He will want to see the money first, so show it to him. Make him count it. Anything to buy me time. But don't think about me—don't let your concentration wander for one moment, because he's as sharp as a hawk.'

'You know him well, don't you?'

'We met for the first time about five years ago. I know him better than most, I suppose. It helps me to stay alive. I don't work for him—never have and never will,' he added, as she continued to stare at him questioningly. 'His ways are not mine, nor are his methods. They leave much to be desired, believe me. Are you afraid?'

'Yes.' What was the use of denying it? She was terrified. Not only for herself—for Timothy—but for him, although she could not tell him so . . . Not while those pale eyes dwelt on her so scrutinisingly.

'Then we must do something about it. You need a little light entertainment. Come, let's see if Peppito's friends can provide us with some,' he said, straightening. Without rising, she watched him move towards the door.

'Down there?' she asked, as he turned to question her reluctance, and a smile tugged at the lean mouth, mocking her reticence.

'Yes, Madame la Comtesse—down there. Among the dregs of humanity, the outcasts of society, émigrés from every country. You will find them all below. It is a different world: a world which accepts a face and asks no questions. Many young rich men and women come to this place for amusement, so you will not be out of place. You will be stared at, but you are beautiful, and men stare at you all the time. The women will want to scratch out your eyes and the men to make love to you. Not so unlike the little soirées you are used to at Versailles, no?' She sprung to her feet at the laughter in his tone. He was daring her to refuse—to proclaim herself better than the people below—better than those who were willing to risk their lives to help her in her quest tonight. Albeit they would be handsomely paid, but they were still willing to take that risk. 'I have men stationed in every street for a mile from here. If any of Simeon's men so much as shows a nose near them, I shall know about it. You will be quite safe with me until it is time to go.'

Safe with him? That she would never be. His hand
was extended towards her. Dream-like, she slid hers into
it, felt his fingers close tightly, somehow reassuringly,
round hers, as he drew her through the door. She froze
at the top of the stairs, gazing down at the sea of faces
below, finding the one she sought almost immediately,
who was glaring up at the two figures standing there,
with coal-black eyes blazing furiously. Zara! She slid
off the lap of the man she was with, pushed her way
through the throng of people and stood waiting. Hands
on her hips, head flung back, expression challenging,
she stood and waited and dared Sian to try and pass
her. She intended to show everyone that, despite what
had been witnessed upstairs, Le Blond was still her man
and that this interloper had no hold on him.

'Peppito, a table by the fire. We need to warm our
bones before we venture out into this cold night. Bring
wine. Everyone drinks with us tonight! To our success
—and afterwards we shall all get very drunk celebrating
our victory,' Douglas said cheerfully as they reached
the bottom stair. Zara continued to block the way,
ignoring the warning tug on her arm by another woman.
'You are welcome to join us, Zara. Perhaps the lady
would like her fortune told,' he said in a quieter tone.

'I need no cards to tell it.' Her gaze fell to the hand
locked in Douglas's grasp, and her lips twisted into a
sneer. 'We fight for him. Gypsy style.'

Sian's eyes flew to her companion's face, and saw his
eyes narrow sharply, angrily.

'What does she mean?' Did Zara intend they should
fight—over him? It was too preposterous!

'You and I have no quarrel.' He gave her no answer,
all his attention being centred on his mistress. Her
jealousy, like her so-called love, was hollow and meaningless—a show for those who watched. He had heard
the ripple of approval that ran through the crowd at the
thought of seeing two women fighting like cats over a
man. It was the way things were settled here, but it was
not his way, and certainly not that of the girl at his
side. How proud she looked! Even in the face of this

challenge, he thought, turning his head and looking into Sian's enquiring features. Like a queen—or a warlord about to do battle! Her pride would not be challenged by anyone, save him. His was the right, for she was his and no one else's!

'My quarrel is with her.' Zara spat, thrusting out long, taloned nails towards Sian's cheeks.

'Then it is also with me. She is my woman, Zara. Neither you nor anyone else here shall touch her. Besides—' he gave a slow smile '—the last man she killed was twice your size and doubtless twice as nasty. I doubt if you would last five minutes with this tigress!'

Sian gasped and stepped back, disbelieving what she had heard. Her fingers trembled between those of Douglas. Nor could she believe he had so openly declared that she was his property. Or proclaimed that she had killed. Unknowingly her eyes shone with a brilliance that would have put the finest jewel to shame. A hush settled over the room. The gypsies in one corner, with a huge black bear on a chain, ceased tantalising him with meat to turn and watch the encounter between one of their own and the blond-haired man from across the seas who walked among them unchallenged because he had proved his worth time and time again to their satisfaction.

Releasing Sian's hand, Douglas stepped forward, so close to his mistress that he could feel her breath on his cheek. His narrowed eyes regarded her, warned her, threatened her, as in silence he took her by the shoulders and turned her aside.

'Go and cool off somewhere,' he said, with a sudden unexpected chuckle, and slapped her smartly on the bottom.

She wheeled about, cursing him, and then, as she remembered her jaw that still ached from the blow he had dealt her earlier, the fist upraised to strike him fell to her side. He would knock her unconscious again without a second thought, and then she would have lost him. Cunning reason crept through the madness of her jealousy. To have him back, she must get rid of this woman. It was in her power to do so. She had not told Douglas of her brother's role in this affair, and she never would now. He had lied when he told her that, once they had rescued the boy, he would exact a large ransom from the sister so that they could live in comfort for the rest of their lives. He would pay dearly for that lie—and never know of her betrayal!

She smiled and stepped back, motioning him past with a sweep of her hand. Let him sit with his 'new woman'. Let him enjoy her company while he was able! She did not care if the boy was lost and, along with him, the ransom, so long as Sian died tonight leaving Douglas alone—free for her—longing for her as she was sure he would.

'When you are tired of her—and I think she has very little to offer you, my love—come and find me. I shall be pleased to show you the way a real woman makes love,' she laughed softly, and turning on her heel, melted into the crowd.

Sian felt Douglas take her hand again. He led her to the fire and sat her at a table. Someone gave her a glass, and she drank the wine, scarcely comprehending what she was doing, only aware that the terrible tension in the room was no more.

'To Madame La Tigresse,' a man laughed, as he bent to refill her glass, and Douglas's grin prompted her to ask furiously,

'Why did you tell her that? You made me sound like . . .'

'Like them?' he queried. 'There are many in this room who have killed. The reasons are not important. It is something you share—a bond—and in a place like this that is very important.'

'But *I* did so in self-defence,' she protested. 'You know that.'

'So did little Lisette. The redhead with Peppito. A certain comte tried to rape her when she worked in his mother's house. She resisted him, which of course was not the thing to do.' Sian looked away, wishing she had said nothing, but he had not finished with her. 'Look at the young boy juggling. In the brown shirt. He killed his step-father, who was attacking his mother in a drunken rage. It used to happen two or three times a week. One day he couldn't take it any longer, so he picked up an axe . . . Now, who else is there?'

'Please,' Sian whispered. 'No more.'

He fixed her with a steely gaze which softened at the sight of the distress in her expression. 'You judge too harshly; but then people of your background often do. There is a difference between you and Lisette and Paul. They did not have money and influence, a family who could hide their shame, their crime, and protect them from the law.'

'As I have,' she finished bitterly. 'You teach your lessons well, monsieur. You make me feel unclean for being born into the world I was.'

'That was not my intention,' Douglas returned quietly. 'Forgive me.'

She looked at him, startled by the apology, but he had turned away to watch the jugglers and acrobats crowding on to the floor, as if he had forgotten her existence. After a few minutes she turned her own attention to them, aware that she must now allow her mind to dwell on what would be happening later. Despite the doubts and fears which continued to lurk at the back of her mind, making it impossible to relax totally, she found she was beginning almost to enjoy herself in these strange, bewildering, fascinating surroundings.

No one gave her a second glance any more. She was Le Blond's woman, and he was accepted among them. So was she, now. When she was back in Scotland, this night would seem like a dream. She would never forget it, but neither would it ever be as real as it was now, with the sound of cheering and laughter coming from all sides.

Perhaps here it was possible to do just that, she thought, clapping vigorously at the gypsies and their bear, who gave the impression of being as gentle as a lamb, despite his red rolling eyes and the gleaming claws

on those massive hairy paws. Even Peppito had played
with him, leading him round like a tame dog, climbing
on his back and bouncing up and down to the delight
of everyone. A huge, cuddly toy—yet he was not. He
was a wild, dangerous animal, who without the chain
about his neck, the muzzle over his fierce mouth, would
resort to the instincts by which he had lived in the wild.
Animal instinct! The kind Douglas knew only too well,
and chose himself to live by. The kind Zara possessed.
One moment docile, the other ferocious, wild, untamed
and uncontrollable.

Peppito appeared at Douglas's elbow and bent to
whisper in his ear. Sian saw the bronzed features harden.
He dropped her hand and climbed to his feet, and
immediately the room was silent, awaiting his words.

'It is time. Those with me, come now. The rest of
you, go on enjoying yourselves. Sávan!' He addressed
a bearded jovial giant of a man who was sitting beside
him and had been consuming wine from the cask in
front of him at an unbelievable speed. 'Keep some wine
for me, or I'll send you out to rob the nearest wine
merchant when I get back!'

The man roared with laughter, almost upsetting his
chair, and his enormous frame rocked to and fro on the
spindly legs.

'I'll keep a glass for you, Le Blond, and for Madame
la Tigresse,' he flung back.

The smile on Douglas's face did not reach his eyes as
he turned to Sian. She felt as if she was suddenly
engulfed in a freezing wind. It was over. They had to
go. She would never see any of these people after
tonight. Why did she want to? What strange part of her
wanted to return here, to sit and listen to their noisy
chatter, the colourful language she had thought better
to ignore? Was it because their world was so far removed
from her own? Because here she was a face without an
identity? Roland had lost himself in his books—they
had been an escape for him. She was Le Blond's woman
here. A nobody—yet someone!

'It is time,' Douglas said again, wrapping her cloak

round her shoulders as she slowly rose to her feet, preparing herself for the unknown ordeal. The tenderness had gone from his eyes and his voice, from the fingers which closed over her arm as he escorted her to the door, lifted her into the waiting carriage. In the darkness as she sat beside him, silent and fearful, her huge tears rolled unchecked. She made no attempt to brush them away, knowing he could not see them. It was over. The spell was broken.

'You know what you are to do?' It seemed an eternity before he spoke to her again.

She nodded, then said tremulously, 'Yes, I understand. Why have we stopped?'

'This is where I leave you. Take this.' A heavy leather pouch was pushed on to her lap. She caught it to her, hugging it as if afraid it might suddenly vanish and they would have to start this hazardous undertaking all over again. Where was he going? Would he really be near, with Timothy? She had to believe him! He had what he wanted, he would keep his word. 'When the carriage stops again, you will be at the rendezvous. It's an old house in the Rue des Bergères. You will find no shepherdesses there, however. Oh, I don't know!' He gave a short laugh. 'In their way, I suppose they have a flock to tend. The houses are houses of pleasure,' he continued as Sian sat in silence. 'Simeon chose his meeting place well. Each one is connected to the other by a maze of passages, so useful if the law show their noses, or a rich customer wishes to come and go secretly. The boy could be in any one of them. I have to start at the beginning and work my way through. That is why I need the time. Five or six more men in there won't arouse any suspicion, even if he has men posted.'

'You—you know these places?' Sian blurted out, hating herself for asking, yet needing to know the answer.

'From time to time I have had cause to visit them.' His voice came out of the darkness, mocking her words. 'If I didn't know better, woman, I'd think you were jealous!'

'I leave that to Zara. She has cause. I care not what you do,' Sian snapped with a flash of the retaliatory spirit which had deserted her for so long.

Strong fingers caught her chin and held it fast, as, out of the darkness, his mouth came to find and command hers for a brief instant. Then the carriage door had opened, he had leapt out and slammed it behind him. There was silence again, no sign of anyone, no sound. She was alone!

Without an order—Douglas had ordered him directly, she suspected—her coachman whipped up the horses, and the jolting of the carriage jerked her back to reality, forced her to forget the hardness of his lips against hers for that short moment. Concentrate, she told herself, repeating it over and over until they stopped again and she forced herself to look out of the window.

They were in a narrow street, so narrow that the carriage wheels almost touched the walls of the houses. Somewhere out of the darkness of the night, a church clock chimed twelve long, melancholy strokes. She was on time, but then Douglas would not have allowed her to be otherwise. She had to reach the rendezvous well ahead of the woman impersonating her, who at this very moment was also on her way to this spot. She had to face the man Simeon, and for ten whole, tortuous minutes, keep him from her brother, keep him from suspecting she had not come in meekness and fear to hand over the ransom he had demanded. If she failed . . .!

'Madame,' the coachman whispered, his tone harsh and strained. 'Look!'

A door to the right of them had opened. A man stood there, holding a lantern, beckoning. Her legs felt like lead and refused to move. Oh, God, please give me strength! I have to go on now!

One steady step, another, another, until she was face to face with him. The light was held up to her face. A grunt of satisfaction, and the man stepped back. This was the place. They had expected her with the money, and she had not disappointed them. Did they think her callous enough to leave her brother to the mercy of cut-throats and thieves?

'Take me to Simeon. I will deal with no one else,' she demanded in the bravest voice she could muster.

No answer, just a grubby hand motioning her towards another door at the end of a long passage, lighted by wall torches, which gave her little indication of what lay about her. She heard a woman's laughter from somewhere above as she started along it, hesitated, and then continued, head held high. They had Timothy in a house of pleasure! What was the child being subjected to? Anger began to creep through the fear which chilled her bones and made her skin crawl as if there were a thousand tiny ants walking upon it.

Should she knock? She was expected. No, why should she announce herself? With a bold gesture, she clutched at the doorknob, turned it quickly and flung the door open. And then stood amazed on the threshold of the room, wondering if she had gone suddenly mad.

It was like an Aladdin's cave. Candles burned in cut-glass chandeliers from the ceiling, throwing a soft, muted glow over everything. An enormous Persian carpet covered most of the floor. The furniture would not have looked out of place in her own home, brocade-covered chairs, marble-topped tables with elegant gilt framework, some with carved feet in the design of a lion's head or that of a serpent. The couch before the fire, burning brightly, welcoming her from a hearth where brass and copper knicknacks gleamed and reflected the light above them, was covered in deep red velvet, as were the many cushions flung upon it.

She was to meet Simeon here? Had there been a mistake? This was where Simeon lived? the leader of a band of ruthless abductors, a murderer, thief, and heaven only knew what else? She leaned weakly against the jamb of the door, not knowing what to do next.

The door which opened at the far end of the room did so on well-oiled hinges and made no sound. She was aware of a man stepping towards her—an elegant man, whose grey hair was expertly dressed and powdered. There were rings on his fingers, diamond buttons fastening the rich brocade waistcoat, worn over a pale blue shirt and breeches. Feeling as if she was losing her mind indeed, Sian raised wide eyes to the face, and knew even greater confusion. It bore no hideous scars, and looked the face of a genial man, almost a fatherly face with the well-trimmed beard and grey eyes.

For a moment, however, something flickered in the depths of those eyes and she knew what he was, what could not be hidden from her. The look of death. She had seen it in Douglas's own eyes that night at the château as René lay on the floor beneath his foot. But for that one thing, she would have been deceived. She tried to speak, but no words came. Time . . . any way of stalling, bluffing, was better than no way at all. She raised a trembling hand to her head, sweeping back the hood from her face as she did so, allowing him to see it clearly for the first time. Now there was another gleam in those eyes. She knew that one, too. Anything, Douglas had instructed. Anything, but that!

'Come in, my dear Comtesse, you look cold.' The voice was quiet, yet commanding. The eyes devoured her.

'I do not see my brother.'

'He is safe. When we have completed our little transaction, I shall have him brought to you,' came the smooth answer, which she did not believe for a moment. She saw him for what he was, what Douglas had tried to warn her against. A man without pity. A vain man, she found, but still dangerous. Perhaps if she played up to that vanity? No, she was no match for him. She would be a child playing a woman's game with a man who knew what it was all about, and would not allow her to escape from him until she had finished what she had begun. She shivered.

'Come in, madame? Do not make me fetch you. Surely you have not come to be troublesome?' Simeon asked, regarding her with a smile. How she would have liked to slap it from his face!

'I have brought the money you asked for. Take it,
count it, and then let me see my brother. I do not
believe he is alive.'

'Come and sit down on the couch. We shall have a
glass of port together before we do anything. If you do
not, your brother's screams of pain may induce you
where my request does not.'

She gasped, moved past him to the couch, and fell on
it, with cheeks blenching.

'Oh dear, did I frighten you? A drink will soon
put the colour back into those cheeks. We shall drink
to the success of my venture and then to the safe
return of your brother. A fine lad. Gave my men
trouble, of course, but he's high-spirited. No more,
though.'

'What have you done to him?' Sian cried, her fists
clenching on her lap. 'He's only seven! You monster!
If I were a man, I would kill you.' She meant it, and he
saw that she did.

'A woman of spirit! I am so glad. So many of you rich
women have no backbone,' Simeon purred. He was like
a slimy toad, she thought, for all his finery. If he touched
her, she would scream. No, she could not. Not for ten
whole minutes. Her eyes fastened on an ormolu clock,
with two cherubs holding hands above the painted dial.
How long had she been here? Minutes only; it seemed
like hours. Five past twelve. Douglas needed more time
—as much as she could give him. Stay calm, she told
herself. Had another minute gone by? The clock had
surely stopped!

She felt like Daniel in the lion's den as she slowly
raised the glass of wine to her lips and sipped it.

'I see you have dispensed with the services of your
bodyguard,' Simeon said. 'Was he unsuitable?'

'Bodyguard? Oh, Monsieur MacGregor. I have
indeed.' She must say nothing which would lead him to
believe that Douglas was still involved with her. 'He
took too much upon himself. He made it necessary to
—to let him go after my brother was killed by your man
René.'

'Ah, yes. René.' A strange light flickered in the man's eyes. 'Le Blond killed him, I believe?'

She could not hide her surprise at the question. How did he know?

'He murdered my brother Roland and would have killed me, too, Why? Why do you want us both dead? Why was my brother kidnapped? I insist that you tell me!'

'Are you in a position to insist about anything, Comtesse?' Simeon asked with a throaty chuckle, and her blood ran cold at the sound.

He could see why the maid Effie despised her mistress so vehemently. The Comtesse had breeding and manners and courage, whereas her maid was a greedy, scheming bitch who thought to better herself in the eyes of her lover by disposing of both Sian and Roland Saint-Rémy in order to make him a very rich man. Controlling the fortune which would be inherited by his son would make Phillip Blakeney one of the most powerful men in the Highlands—and she would be at his side. Or so she thought. She even hoped that one day he might marry her. Stupid fool! Men like Blakeney did not marry their mistresses, or allow themselves to be blackmailed. There would come a day when he would dispose of her.

Simeon smiled as Sian drained her glass, and he reached for the decanter to refill it. Quickly she put it out of reach and grabbed up the money pouch.

'I demand that you count it now,' she said, thrusting it out to him.

'I can count it later—at my leisure. I am sure you would not try to cheat me. Take off your cloak and relax. I am not an ogre. You might find me better company than Le Blond.'

Sian hesitated, then unfastened her cloak and allowed it to fall on the couch behind her. She must not allow his attention to wander. What was the time? Twelve minutes past twelve! Douglas must be near at hand by now. Hope rose inside her, then died as Simeon's gaze raked her from head to toe. When he turned away, she was blushing profusely from the frankness of those bold eyes.

She sat like a statue as he began to count out the coins. The room was warm, uncomfortably so, and she was horrified to find herself beginning to grow drowsy. Simeon was watching her again. Was the wine drugged? Why had she not thought of that before?

'It is not doctored. You would be of no use to me if it was,' he chuckled, and she sprang to her feet in horror. 'You do not mistake my meaning! Sit down and be sensible. We have yet to negotiate the price of that name you require. But money—no, I don't need that. Look around. I am rich. I shall be richer still when I have been finally paid in full for tonight. You shall have your name, Madame la Comtesse, when you have paid my price.' And afterwards he would kill her!

'No!' Sian's eyes blazed with contempt. When she had taken off her cloak, the pistol became out of reach. She was not thinking clearly. The wine! Laughter outside made Simeon pause for a moment. Heavy footsteps overhead, however, brought a heavy frown to his face. He strode to the door, flung it open and bellowed for quiet. A drunken voice answered him, making obscene suggestions which made Sian tremble to hear them. She grabbed up her cloak, and fastened it. Thank God for the intervention! Whoever it was had given her the chance she needed.

Simeon's frown grew as he saw what she had done. 'Take it off and sit down. I have not finished with you yet.'

'You have the money. Give me my brother and let me go. I—I did not come alone.' She gave a shaky laugh as he advanced towards her, unable to move because the fire was to her back. 'My servants know where I am, and have orders to send help here if I am not back by two o'clock. And I have men in my coach outside. If you do not let us go this instant . . .'

She cried out as Simeon's thick hand fastened in the front of the cloak and jerked her against him. He was stronger than he looked, she realised, as her hair was grasped in his other hand, her head pulled so sharply back that it brought tears to her eyes.

'Do you think I didn't have you followed? My men have been watching you and your house ever since you came back to Paris. You should have retained the services of Le Blond, Comtesse. Now if he were here, I wouldn't be able to enjoy this evening as much as I intend to. I have made plans for us. More wine first— then I shall introduce you to the delights of one of my upstairs rooms. You will find it admirably furnished, like this one. Warm and comfortable. We shall not be disturbed. And in the morning, before you leave with your little brother, I shall tell you what you want to know.'

'No! No!' Sian tried to twist her head away from the mouth descending towards hers. His breath reeked of garlic and violets, his skin of some heady perfume which made her feel sick. With all her might she spat full into his face.

'You bitch!' As his hands flew to his cheek, she thrust him away with all her might, ran towards the door, blindly, without thought as to what she was doing— what her headlong flight would mean. She could not stay, allow herself to be pawed by this animal—allow her body to be used for his pleasure. She tripped on the hem of her gown and fell heavily against the wooden panels. Behind her, Simeon's voice froze her hand on the handle. 'Open that door, Comtesse, and I will have your brother's corpse delivered to you first thing in the morning.'

'Open it!' another voice declared. A voice which sent her spinning about with a gasp of disbelief. A voice which heralded her rescue from an inescapable predicament. Under such a threat, she knew she would have given in eventually.

In the open doorway at the far end of the room stood Douglas MacGregor. In his hands was his huge broadsword, and it was pointing directly at Simeon's heart. The steely eyes were without expression, the dark features holding a hint of a smile at her astonishment as he advanced slowly into the room.

# CHAPTER
# NINE

'DO AS I tell you, woman! Open the door,' Douglas repeated quietly, and her trembling fingers once again grasped the handle and pulled it open. 'Be still, my friend. One move, however slight, will be your last,' he added, as Simeon's gaze alighted on the swords hanging on the wall beside him. He was no coward, neither was he a fool. He remained still.

The cry that was torn from Sian's lips at the sight of her brother in the arms of Rudy the acrobat echoed along the dingy corridor. Timothy was wrapped in a blanket, his fair head cradled against the man's shoulder. His eyes were closed, and his face was as white as chalk. He was so still!

'He's alive!' Douglas watched her weeping as she kissed the child's waxen cheek. 'He's been kept drugged, and it will take several days to wear off fully.'

His tone betrayed none of the fury raging inside him. He had found Timothy in the third house they had passed through, guarded by four men. Not that he needed them. He lay covered only with a filthy blanket, despite the broken windowpanes which were allowing in a lusty gale of wind, and one look at the empty glass beside the makeshift bed told Douglas all he needed to know. The white dregs told him who had aided Simeon with her special potions. It was the same he had given to Sian at the inn. He had used it himself when an old wound in his back troubled him. Zara!

She had sworn to him she knew nothing of the abduction. He had not believed her, but she had never made any move to contact her brother, with whom she had quarrelled over him when she first became his mistress. He had forgotten her cunning: he had been too preoccu-

pied with other things—with Sian—and it could have
cost him his life. And hers, and those of the men with
him. Sian had done her part, and done it well. He had
failed to be as vigilant as he should have been. Thank
God Zara had been stopped by a guard when she tried
to leave the Coq d'Or as the rest of them were being
entertained. She had been coming to warn Simeon of
his involvement! She would answer to her own for her
treachery.

'Timothy! Oh, my darling, what have they done to
you?' Sian cried, laying a head against his cheek. 'He's
so cold. Like ice! We must get him home quickly and
to bed. He needs a doctor. You fiend! You inhuman
monster!' Eyes blazing, she stepped up to Simeon and
struck him in the face again and again with all the
strength she possessed. In doing so, she placed herself
between him and Douglas's sword, and he did not
hesitate to use the advantage she had unwittingly given
him.

She was flung violently backwards, and heard
Douglas curse her as she fell against him. He swept her
unceremoniously to one side as Simeon leapt for one of
the swords, plucked it from the wall, and wheeled to
meet him.

'Take her out of here, Rudy,' Douglas ordered. 'Now.
To the carriage, man, and wait for me.'

He sidestepped a well-aimed thrust and circled his
opponent, kicking aside pieces of furniture which
loomed up in his path, swinging the deadly, flashing blade
before him. Sian could not take her eyes from his face
as she struggled to her feet, gathering her cloak tightly
about her.

'Go!' he snapped, and she eased herself to the doorway where Rudy waited with her brother, her eyes still
riveted on him as if hypnotised by his fluid movements.

'Madame, come,' Rudy urged, but she shook her
head. 'Take flight, madame. We have dealt with those
men of Simeon's we found upstairs, but there may be
more. You are in danger and so is the boy. Leave Le
Blond. He knows what he is doing. Come!'

'Put Timothy in the carriage.' Half-way down the passage, Sian stopped and turned back. 'Wait for us. Go! Save my brother.'

She pushed him towards the door and cautiously made her way back to the brightly lit room, hovering out of sight of the men there to watch the encounter. Not that either would have been aware of her presence, she saw. The fight had become bloody and violent. Simeon had blood on his jacket, which was ripped open. Diamond buttons lay winking up at the chandeliers, beside smashed ornaments and shattered glass. Douglas gave an oath as Simeon's sword sliced his left arm, and she had to press her knuckles against her mouth to hold back a scream. He reeled away, his features contorting in pain, fighting to keep a firm grasp on his heavy weapon. Simeon laughed. It was the sound of a madman, Sian thought, gasping with horror at the eerie sound. He lunged at Douglas, his movements suddenly becoming wild and erratic, making it almost impossible for the Scot to reach him, even with the extra length of the broadsword.

Simeon's shirt was ripped, now, his face covered in sweat. No trace remained of the finely-dressed man who had greeted her on her arrival. He had been stripped of all pretence, exposed for what he was.

Sian averted her gaze, filled with disgust, and in that moment caught a movement from the back of the room. A shadow there? Beyond the half-open doorway where Douglas had appeared? Yes, a man, bleeding from a gashed head, dagger in hand! Behind Douglas! One of Simeon's men from upstairs, left for dead, but not dead. She stifled a warning cry; she could not distract Douglas now, but what could she do? Fetch help from outside? No, it would be too late. *She* must act! The silver mountings on the pistol she pulled from her pocket were ice cold in her palm. Ice cold like the awful terror in her heart. Nearer, nearer to Douglas's unsuspecting back crept the would-be assassin. She had never fired a pistol before. Even that time in the stable, when she had levelled it at him, she knew she could never have pulled the trigger and ended the life of another human being. Yet now, if she did not . . .

Clutching it in both hands, she took aim and fired. The report deafened her as it echoed up and down the passage. As the man gave a groan and toppled to the floor, the pistol fell from her fingers, and she did not retrieve it as she sagged, near fainting, in the doorway.

Douglas spun about. In one glance he took in the dead man behind him, the knife still held in one hand; Sian, white-faced in the doorway, the pistol at her feet. Her lips parted, her eyes screamed a warning. Simeon's sword again connected with his injured arm, and a red mist of pain rose before his eyes. The cry which rang from his lips in Gaelic had been shouted by his fore-fathers as they launched themselves into battle. She did not understand the strange-sounding word, yet at the same time realised she was seeing him as never before. This was Douglas MacGregor, born and bred in the Highlands of Scotland, not Le Blond who shared a room with Zara the gypsy girl. Proud, defiant, undefeated. Wounded and bleeding, exhausted, but undefeated.

Simeon must have realised it at the same moment as she did, for he staggered back, losing all momentum in his attack. Where before for a moment he had had an advantage, now he knew he was losing the fight, and open fear registered on his face.

'Mercy . . . For the love of God!'

Sian closed her eyes as the broadsword descended, turning away from the ghastly scene.

'Move, damn you!' Douglas was pushing her down the passage. Above them she could hear the sound of footsteps. She began to run as he said, breathing heavily, 'Reinforcements. They must have followed us through the tunnels. Run, woman!'

The moment she was in the carriage, the horses were whipped up. Douglas collapsed on the opposite seat, his sword at his feet as he clutched at his injured arm. A shot sounded behind them. She heard a groan and saw a dark shape fall past the window.

'Pierre,' Rudy said dully, Timothy still clutched in his

arms. 'That makes three we have lost. I hope she is worth it, Le Blond.'

Douglas threw him a look which silenced further comment.

'Find something to bind these wounds! I'm bleeding like a stuck pig,' he ordered Sian.

She forced herself over the shock of what she had seen, bent down and tore a wide strip of material from her petticoats, which she wound tightly round his arm. He sat in silence as she did so, but she was conscious of his eyes on her face. She wanted to reach out and smooth back the tousled blond hair which tumbled over the perspiring features, but dared not, so strange was the look in his eyes. Questioning and accusing both at the same time!

When she attempted to return to her own seat, he was holding fast to her wrist. She made no attempt to free herself, but remained where she was. He felt her begin to tremble as the full realisation of what she had done began to dawn on her.

'Did you stay, hoping to see me killed?'

She gasped aloud at the brutal question. Is that what he thought! 'No! Would—would I have killed for you if I wanted that?'

'Yes, you did kill for me, didn't you? That puzzles me.'

'Please,' Sian begged. She was no match for him now. The jolting of the coach was beginning to make her feel ill. She leaned back in her seat, overcome with an urge to weep on his shoulder, but his attitude deterred her. It was distant, withdrawn. 'You are wrong,' she said at length. 'It was not easier a second time.'

'For someone like you, it never will be,' Douglas answered, and she heard the pain in his voice.

'Are you so hardened to death, to killing, you feel nothing for your fellow men any more?' she whispered.

He shrugged his shoulders and did not answer. She closed her eyes, unable to bear his burning gaze on her, unable to bear the sight of her brother, unconscious in the arms of Rudy, unable to bear the anguish in her heart. Where was the tenderness he had shown her at the Coq d'Or? Did he now know how she needed his strength? And then she realised suddenly that he had none to give her—none to spare after the violence of his fight with Simeon. He, too, was drained.

As the carriage came an abrupt halt, her eyes flew open in alarm. Where were they? She could see the river. Why were they not crossing the bridge?

'Take the men back to the tavern. I'll come later,' Douglas ordered, and Rudy opened the door, still holding Timothy, even though Sian stretched out her arms for him. 'Leave the boy.'

'But I thought . . .' The man looked startled.

'Give her the boy,' Douglas commanded.

'You're the master. What do I tell the others—about payment?'

'You will be paid when I return. Zara is to be kept at the tavern. She is not to leave. I want her there when I return. Understood?'

'Whatever you say.'

Sian drew Timothy's cold body close against her, hoping to instil some life into him, but he did not move for the remainder of the journey to the house. Douglas sat in silence. She did, too, pondering his words and those of the man who had left them. Where had he expected Timothy to be taken? Her questioning looks in the direction of her companion were either not noticed or ignored. The latter, she decided as he helped her to alight, wincing as his wounded arm came in contact with the carriage door. He had been aware of her every movement!

He was going back to Zara! He wanted her to be waiting for him when he returned.

'Come inside and have that arm attended to properly,' she said as he turned to climb back into the carriage. 'You will not keep her waiting very long.'

She regretted the jealous words the instant they were spoken, as a familiar mocking smile spread across his features, wiping away the pain and tiredness there.

'Thank you, Madame la Comtesse. I accept your

generous offer. I don't think I have the strength to stand much longer, let alone to tumble a lively wench.'

Cheeks flaming, Sian hurried into the house. Servants came clustering around her, questioning, touching Timothy's blanketed figure, some crying with relief for her safe return and the miracle that had brought him back alive. No miracle, Sian thought, fighting back the urge to weep with them, but the force and determination and the tremendous courage of the man who stood swaying in the hall beside her. He was disoriented, she thought, looking into the strained features, no longer smiling. He had left his sword in the carriage!

'André, go outside and tell Frederick he will not be required again tonight, and bring in Monsieur Mac-Gregor's weapon. You will find it on the floor. I suggest you clean it before returning it to him, for it has been well used this night. Had it not been, neither I nor my brother would be here now. Suzanne, take monsieur into the sitting-room, give him whisky, and stay with him until I return.' She started towards the stairs with her burden, stopped and looked back at Douglas, seeing his eyes full of amazement at her swift recovery. 'You are sure he will suffer no ill effects from the drug?'

'You did not,' he returned, and she caught her breath, enlightened as to his meaning. 'Let a doctor examine the boy in the morning. He may suffer a chill from the abominable conditions I found him in, but nothing more serious,' he assured her, and saw the servants exchange relieved glances.

'Yes—in the morning. But your arm . . .'

'I have no need of a doctor's services while I have yours.' He tossed a wicked grin at her, but it lacked his usual insolence, and he turned away to the sitting-room.

Calling for Effie and the others to come and help her put Timothy to bed, she went upstairs. She would minister to him. He would not leave her to go back to Zara—not until she had paid her debt to him in full!

It was an hour before she left her brother's room. He looked so fragile, as he lay silent and still in his huge bed, that she could not bring herself to leave him.

Suzanne would sit with him all night and be relieved by herself in the light of morning. He would not be alone for a moment, and she had left instructions to be woken if he so much as opened his eyes.

Sleep, she thought, as she undressed and put on a fur-trimmed robe and leather slippers. She would not be sleeping this night. Effie brushed her hair in silence, which was unusual, lately, for her. Sian was too preoccupied with her own thoughts to take much notice. She was not to know the great shock her maid had suffered to see her mistress returning to the house, not only safe and well, but with Timothy safe, too. And accompanied by the mercenary! Effie had misjudged Sian. She knew it now. Sian was his mistress! She had bought his help with her body . . . It was not what she would have expected of her innocent, virginal mistress, whom she hated as no other woman she had known before, but she was sure it had happened. Or was Le Blond infatuated with her? Either way, from the looks he gave her, Effie was sure he intended the relationship to continue. This spelled doom for her plans. Sian could be manipulated, tricked, deceived by someone she normally trusted . . . Not so by the man who had chosen to remain at her side. He was no fool! He trusted no one.

Sian should have been dead, and Simeon would have returned Timothy to her the following day. Effie would have gone back to Scotland, to her lover, with news of the unfortunate happenings in France—and the joyful news that he was now a very rich and influential man. She could not do this! All because Sian had shown greater initiative that she ever thought possible and because a man had shown interest in her. Not an ordinary man. There was nothing ordinary about Douglas MacGregor. He was the product of the Scottish Highlands, wild and unpredictable, and even though she, too, had been born in his homeland, she did not think as he did. He had the cunning of a fox, like his father, who had been named 'the *Sionnach*'—Gaelic for 'the animal'. They had outfought and out-thought the English soldiers as they hid in the heather and brought men

to them with their staunch loyalty to the stupid Charles
Stuart's cause. She had no time for the idealistic young
man who had landed on the shores of Scotland and
raised an army to invade England. He was and always
would be a loser, and Effie Campbell had no time for
losers. She had cast aside one husband who had not
come up to her expectations—luckily he had been killed
at Prestonpans—to relieve her of the worry of disposing
of him later!

Phillip Blakeney had found her in Inverness, when
he brought his soldiers to the town, along with Captain
Caroline Scott, as notorious for his infamous treatment
of the poor souls he encountered in the mountains as
was his commander, the Duke of Cumberland. He had
had men of the Campbell militia with him, her brother
among them. Angus, who was now steward at Ard
Choille. So came Effie and her brother to Rannoch,
to share the wealth and power of the man who had
devastated the area in the uprising and made its people
little more than slaves to his will. Slaves, that Sian in
her ignorance, her kindness, had tried to reach. Given
time, she might have achieved her aim, but she had no
time. Effie and her lover had decided otherwise after
the death of Sian's mother. She was a danger to them,
as was Roland. Both had to be disposed of. And so, in
those first few months as Clare Saint-Rémy lay restlessly
in her grave on foreign soil, the plans were made. Once
investigated, there was no going back.

Sian descended the stairs to the sitting-room. She
found Suzanne standing beside Douglas's chair, white
and trembling, and immediately she was alarmed. He
lay back in his chair, eyes closed, his wound untouched.

'Why has he not been cared for?' she demanded.
'You stupid girl, he is bleeding!'

'Don't take out your anger on her, woman. I'll have
no one tend me but you,' came the dry answer. He did
not even open his eyes to look at her as he spoke.
'You may go, Suzanne. Please sit with Timothy. Tell
the other servants to go to bed.'

She knelt at the side of the silent man, her brows

puckered in a fierce frown as she ripped the sleeve of his shirt away to reveal the ugly cuts Simeon had inflicted. The pieces of the petticoat she had bound round them were soaked with fresh blood.

'You fool!' She was furious with him. 'You are losing blood still.'

'I have much to spare! Do your worst, woman. I am sure you will enjoy causing me pain,' Douglas said in a low tone. His voice was slurred with agony, and all the anger disappeared from her in an instant. She should have been able to enjoy this moment when he was so easy to hurt—as he had hurt her in the past with his words, his touch. Yet it was not in her to return all those other times. She owed him so much—and she loved him. There were times when they would hurt each other, she knew, regardless of the love she held for him, but tonight was not one of them.

'Be quiet. Have a drink, and let me tend you,' she snapped, and he opened his eyes and looked at her with a tight smile.

'Tonight we have shared much, haven't we? It was not easy to keep Simeon at bay, I know . . .' Was he acknowledging the hell she had been through?

'You saw . . . You were listening!' she accused. How could he have watched and waited, while she . . .

'It is over.' A firm hand fastened over hers as she replaced the bloodsoaked linen with fresh strips of bandage. 'Your brother is safe.'

'And I am in your debt. I have not forgotten it,' she returned dully.

'What a compliment you pay me. You think me capable of collecting it with this arm?' He was laughing at her, as he always did when she was stricken with indecision!

'You are more of a man than I have ever known before,' she said, sitting back on her heels and looking him squarely in the face. The shock that registered there took her aback. Had he not expected capitulation? Embarrassment made her tone sharp. 'Come now, why are you so loath to accept something you were so willing to take from me before? Have you no audience? Is that it?'

'Pour me a drink, woman, and one for yourself. We'll see who is not willing,' Douglas said heavily, and she rose, hating herself for having provoked him and returning the sharp edge to his tone.

Had she been more careful . . . Yet to do so would have given away completely her own feelings, and that would have placed her forever in his power. Why did she deny it? She was in his power. She was his, and she longed for that moment when their union would couple her with him in the final binding act! Yet, to say so in words!

There was a decanter of whisky on the table, and glasses. Boldly she poured some and brought it to him. He stared at her coldly, and she turned and poured another for herself. She never drank strong spirits. Her head still swam from the amount of wine she had consumed while with Simeon. Did he know this? Was it his way of bringing her to heel?

'*Slainte!*' He tilted his glass towards her mockingly, waiting until her own glass touched her lips, before emptying his. The liquid went down her throat like nectar, then suddenly ignited a burning fire which threatened to choke her. Douglas chuckled as she gasped, her cheeks glowing at the warmth aroused in her. 'Another will deepen your appreciation of it,' he said meaningfully, and she replenished his glass and then her own as his eyes fixed on her.

She could not drink it—her head felt as if it was about to burst!

'Drink,' he ordered quietly, but she did not. The hand he extended to her was ignored for a full minute, then she allowed her own to be taken, allowed herself to be drawn down beside him. His fingers tilted the glass towards her mouth, forced the contents down her throat, took the glass from her lax fingers as her head fell back against a cushion.

'No more, please,' she begged.

He smiled down into her apprehensive features, and

she saw his eyes were kind. As they had been at the Coq d'Or. 'Tonight you will sleep without nightmares!'

He had a head like a rock, she thought, wishing her own would stop swimming. She had intended to be in full control. To remain aloof, somewhat icy in her attitude, at the same time paying him her debt. But, now, he was making it impossible for her to think, let alone to act, rationally!

'Do you not think me woman enough to keep my bargain with you without this?' she asked tremulously, and Douglas's light eyes became riveted on her flushed cheeks, and his burning gaze made her feel weak. Weak —afraid—yet excited. He had looked at her this way many times before, and she had chosen to ignore him. With hunger, longing, sometimes almost desperation he had stared at her . . . She could ignore those looks no longer!

'You are—all woman—and tonight, if I touch you, I shall not walk away. Which is why you are going to bed now—alone!'

As she was lifted into his arms, she glimpsed his face for an instant before the reeling room sent waves of nausea flooding over her and she tightly closed her eyes, turning her face against his shirt. The naked desire there should have terrified her, but it did not. In a way she felt a strange satisfaction to know that he desired her as strongly as she did him.

She did not open her eyes again until she felt herself deposited on the softness of her bed. She was in her own room, not—as she had expected—his! He drew back, rubbing his injured arm. And then, without a word, he left her.

How long had she been asleep? It was light outside the window, yet she had no idea of time. Her vision was fuzzy, her thoughts disoriented. What had happened to her? And then, slowly, it all began to return as it had done once before. Another nightmare . . . Simeon, Timothy, the terrible fight between Douglas and her enemy—his enemy. How gentle he had been when he had carried her to her room. She would have allowed him to come to her bed, and he knew it, yet he had not taken her. Why? At every turn, his actions confused her. He seemed to hurt her—to destroy her totally—and it was in his power to do so. Yet, when the opportunity arose—and what better chance had he had than the night before?—he had walked away and left her to sleep alone.

How her head ached! Even the dull light coming through the half-closed curtains hurt her eyes. The door opened, and Effie came in with a tray. Sian pulled herself upright, wincing at the pain in her head. She would never touch whisky again. He had done it deliberately! But not to render her more accessible to him. Rather the opposite, she suspected. How she wished she could understand him.

'What is that? It looks horrible.' She stared at the glass being held out to her.

'*He* sent it,' Effie replied. 'Two eggs and brandy.'

A great feeling of sickness rose in Sian's stomach, and she quickly looked away. 'Ugh! I won't drink it. Bring me some coffee. Is he trying to kill me?'

'He said it would get rid of the headache. Do you have a headache, madam? I have some powders far more suitable.'

Something in the woman's tone stopped Sian from admitting the condition she found herself in this morning. Why did she think these days that Effie was always trying to be superior to herself? She stared at the glass, and then tentatively took it from the tray. Brandy and eggs. My God, she would be ill for a week!

Strangely enough, it slid down her throat without effort. She waited a full minute, expecting the worst to happen, and then a smile touched her lips as she looked up at her maid.

'I think monsieur has had many such mornings! Convey my thanks to him.'

'His instructions were given to André last night, madam. This morning monsieur has a fever. Little Timothy is still sleeping soundly,' she added, and colour

flamed into Sian's cheeks at the realisation that her first
thought had been for Douglas, not for her brother. How
dare Effie remind her so cruelly!

'If it was not for Monsieur MacGregor, he would
not be sleeping soundly,' she said, throwing back the
bedclothes. 'Fetch me a robe, and then send for a
doctor. I want him here within the hour. Don't stand
there gaping at me, Effie. I am well aware you disap-
prove of my relationship with this Scotsman—which I
find strange, as he is one of your kind—but that is not
important. Without you, Timothy would not be alive.
No more would I. My debt to him is too big ever to
repay, but I shall try. You will tell everyone his every
wish is to be granted. It would have been my brother's
wish, too, had he lived. Go! A doctor within the hour!'

She had never spoken so sharply, with so much authority, as she did now. Why? What had Douglas done to
her? She felt more in control of everything, and yet not
. . . not when it came to him! A fever?

Quickly she dressed and hurried to his room. André
was with him. He lay tossing and turning in the bed,
his dark features wet with sweat. She felt a terrible
helplessness as she came to his side and looked at him.
He was the strong one, but never before had he looked
so vulnerable.

'Fetch me cold water and clean cloths, lots of them,'
she ordered, sinking on to the edge of the bed. This was
her man. Nothing could ever change that!

'Can I help, madame?' Something in the manservant's
tone brought a sudden touch of warmth to Sian's
expression. He did not condemn, like Effie with her
remarks and knowing looks.

'Yes, André. Bring the doctor here the moment he
arrives. And if Timothy stirs, call me at once.'

'I have been watching him myself, madame. He sleeps
the sleep of the dead. I shall be glad when the doctor
has seen him. It is not right he should be so still.'

'Monsieur MacGregor has seen the drug before. I
have experienced it also. Don't worry. He will recover.'

How sure she sounded, yet she had only Douglas's

word for it. How did he know so much about this strange drug that kept her brother unconscious? If she listened to her maid's sly words, she would believe him to be responsible for all the awful things that had happened to her since the day her coach was attacked. She redressed his wounds and covered him with blankets. He muttered in his fever, names and places which were strange to her.

The doctor came and went. First, on her insistence, he examined Timothy. His diagnosis was somewhat complicated. He had seen such a thing before, he told her, and had been amazed and confused by the symptoms. The victim could recover after being in a semi-coma from the drug, even after a whole month, he told her. Or he could die. It depended on the dosage. Sian felt frantic. She had no way of knowing how much Timothy had been given during his captivity, only that it looked as if he had been kept totally incapacitated. It was in the hands of God, she was told.

As for Douglas MacGregor? The doctor shrugged, as if he had been called to examine a man with nothing wrong with him. Strong, and well able to recover without help, was his verdict. His, or that of Douglas himself? Sian wondered, afraid he would not take kindly to her seeking assistance for him.

Her suspicion was confirmed that afternoon when he appeared in the sitting-room as she was writing a letter to Jeanne. His arm was in a sling, which made him look awkward and uncomfortable, and after a few minutes in her company, he discarded it.

'The boy?' It was the first question he asked, and she warmed towards him instantly. He was not as hard-hearted as he pretended.

'It is the drug. The doctor doesn't really know. Tell me?' she begged, and he stared at her for a long while before answering.

'There will be no after-effects, as I told you.'

'But he lies so still,' she protested. 'Douglas, for the love of God, is he going to die? Tell me!'

She was not even aware she had used his first name

until she saw the gleam in those steely eyes, the rousing of interest she longed for, yet feared.

'No. The treatment was continuous since they first took him, I suspect. If he was a lively lad . . .'

'He was. He would have played havoc with them . . .'

'Then his spirit had to be curbed. The drug would do so, and keep him immobile and silent until it was time for him to return to the world of the living. He will be all right,' he assured her, and she gave a deep sigh. 'You believe me, then?'

'Yes. You—you have knowledge of this drug. You gave it to me!'

'And you wonder who administered it to your brother?'

'Yes.' There was no denying it, and he did not attempt to evade the issue.

'Only three people I know have the knowledge, and the access to the special herbs which made this potion. One—Grand-mère—would not harm me or anyone connected with me. The other is an abortionist, and the same applies to him. He has no reason. The third . . .' He frowned, angry at some thought within him, Sian thought. 'She had no reason then, but now . . . I have just killed her brother.'

'Zara?' she gasped. 'But she is your woman.'

'No, you are my woman. I have never called anyone else that—not even her.' Bright gleaming fire challenged her suspicions, and they melted before the desire there. Nothing could alter what was between them, however disastrous it was for her. 'You don't believe me? Why should you? No matter. It is the truth. How did you come by such a name—Sian? In the Gaelic, it is the word for "storm". Did you know that?'

'Yes, my mother told me. We—my parents, I mean —were on their way back to Scotland from France when my mother's pains began. There was a midwife on board, an old Scotswoman. It was she who named me. There was a storm at the time . . . She took one look at the colour of my eyes, and said they were the grey

of angry storm-clouds and heralded much disturbance
in my life.'

'It suits you.'

'Am I possessed of such a stormy nature?' He did not
miss the nervousness of her laugh. How he wished they
could be at ease together, yet the fault was his. He had
made it impossible.

Later that afternoon she insisted he went to rest. Sian
returned to Timothy's room to sit at his bedside, and
during the evening, before dinner, his eyes flickered
open and he knew her. Within minutes he was asleep
again without uttering a word, but most of her fears had
gone. She knew he was fighting back. Douglas had not
lied. The drug would wear off with time, and her brother
would recover.

# CHAPTER
## TEN

SIAN WAS overjoyed the following afternoon, when not only did Timothy wake up and know her, but she was able to persuade the boy to take a little freshly-made broth. She read to him until he fell asleep, and then, more reassured in her mind, went to her own room to try to snatch a few hours herself. She was exhausted, drained by the events of the past weeks.

It seemed her head had scarcely touched the pillow before a loud hammering on the bedroom door brought her upright in bed, reaching for her wrap.

'Madam! Answer me, for the love of heaven.'

Effie! She sounded hysterical.

'It's Timothy. He's acting like a wild thing. Crying, throwing himself about the bed. Oh, can you not hear me? He will harm himself if you do not come.'

Sian struggled into her robe, her cheeks paling at the words. She should not have left him. Tired though she was, she should have sat with him through the night.

As she flung open the door, Douglas appeared from the direction of his own room. He, too, had been resting, she saw, for he wore no shirt and his feet were bare. Without a word he followed her to Timothy's room. The boy's frightened cries reached them both even before they entered and found him cringing at the far end of the bed, while Suzanne wept a few feet away. There was a bloody scratch on one cheek, and her nightcap had been torn off.

'He has gone mad,' she whispered, backing towards the door. 'He will not let me touch him. When I tried to reason with him, he did this.' She touched her cheek, white with shock.

'André, take her downstairs and give her something

strong to drink.' Sian turned to find everyone clustering in the doorway, all anxious to help. 'Then she is to go direct to bed. Bring back a glass of warm milk.'

'Lace it with brandy,' Douglas added, and she nodded confirmation.

'The rest of you go to bed also. I shall stay with him. Including you, Effie. So many people are confusing him.'

'Or frightening him,' Effie replied, staring at Douglas. Look at him standing there in only a pair of breeches, as if he were master in the house!

'Where I come from, servants are not so free with unwanted opinions,' he snapped, and she spun on her heel and pushed through the other servants, who silently turned and followed her.

'Gently.' Douglas's hand was warningly on her arm. 'The lad is frightened. Delayed shock, if I'm not mistaken. I've seen it happen to men after they've been in battle for the first time. Days, weeks, even months later, they suddenly take in what has happened to them, and those not strong enough to cope with the reality are sometimes driven to the point of madness. I'm not saying this is so with him,' he said quickly, as Sian gave a gasp of fear. 'Only that now the drug has almost left his body, his mind is clearing. He will remember those days when he was alone and frightened, remember the way he was treated . . . The hunger, the fear of being shut up in a rat-infested room. Talk to him quietly, let him come to you. Quietly, woman, or he will withdraw from you.' Perhaps for ever, he thought, but did not say this to her. He could not. Never had he known anyone to have been drugged for so long with this particular potion and come out of it as quickly as Timothy had done. Too quickly, perhaps. Was his little mind only now beginning to accept those dreamy days among strangers? What had he seen during his captivity to give him nightmares such as now troubled him?

'Timmy! Timmy, my darling, it's Sian. I've come to sit with you for a while. I couldn't sleep. Would you like that?' No answer. No sign of recognition on the

rigid features, or in the staring eyes looking past her at
Douglas. Why did he stare so? 'You know how wretched
I become when I can't sleep. I long to talk to someone.
Do you remember when you were a tiny boy and you
used to steal into my room and curl up in bed with me?
Would you like to do that now, Timmy? In my bed,
with me. Will you keep me company?'

Good girl, Douglas thought in admiration for her
calm approach—to tempt the boy not for his sake, but
for hers. He watched her stretch out a hand to him. It
was ignored. But then the lips moved slowly, barely.

'Yes.'

Sian moved carefully forward and drew him into
her arms, not daring to hurry her movements lest she
frighten him again. His body was rigid against hers as
if he had suddenly beheld some terrible sight too awful
to bear. And then, as she stood up, her eyes widened,
as a possible explanation offered itself. It was nothing
that had happened to him afterwards, although those
days must have been terrifying for him. That day on the
road when their carriage was stopped and their servants
butchered. He had seen that! The head of a friend,
severed from his body and rolling in the dirt. The head
of Lucien, the coachman, who had taught him to ride
at Saint-Rémy! Sudden, uncomprehending, bloody loss!
How could a seven-year-old accept such a sickening
sight? It remained to haunt her dreams still, along with
so many others.

Holding him close, she went to her own room.
Douglas followed a moment later, having intercepted
the maid bringing the warm milk.

'Try him with this. But first taste it yourself, or he
will think it is something else again.'

She threw him a grateful smile. He thought of everything. How she wished Timothy would not continue to
look at him so strangely. The small mouth puckered as
she raised the glass before him. With a whimper of fear,
he pulled back from her.

'It's milk, Timmy. With a little something special that
mummy used to put in for us both, do you remember?

To keep out Mr Jack Frost when he howled up and down the valley, and we hid beneath the bedclothes so that he would not see us. Look, I'm going to have a little.'

'Who is he?' Timothy did not even glance at her.

'This is Monsieur MacGregor. Douglas . . . He found you for me. He took you away from that nasty room and brought you back here.'

'MacGregor? Do you know my father? He knows lots of MacGregors.'

'Does he? Ay, it's possible we have met—a long time ago.' He was aware of Sian stiffening, of the alarm flashing into her eyes.

'Your father doesn't know everyone, darling!' Sian laughed shakily, forcing her gaze away from his hard face. 'Drink this milk. Look, I have only taken half. You don't have to drink it all if you can't manage it . . . A little will do.'

Over the rim of the glass, the boy's eyes searched Douglas's face.

'I'm a Scot, too,' he said, and there was a note of pride in his young voice that made Douglas look at Sian enquiringly. She was busily tucking the bedclothes round her brother and appeared not to notice. Why did she have to prove to him she knew more than she should?

'Are you, indeed?' He managed a tight smile. 'With an Englishman for a father, how does that come about?'

'I told you, my mother remarried,' Sian said dully.

'Of course,' Douglas murmured, and anger tightened her lips.

'She fell in love again. That is not a crime. I did not blame her—no more will you.'

'Who am I, an exile without a future, to judge anyone for seeking happiness where they can? I have been guilty of it myself.'

She looked at him sharply. Was she to be as unlucky as her poor mother with love? Within the space of a few short months, Clare had discovered not only that her new husband was unfaithful to her, but that his sole reason for marrying her was to lay his hands on the vast

properties and wealth she had inherited on the death of
her parents.

Only then, when she discovered whan an ogre she
had married, did she tell him of the stipulations in her
parents' will. That he could never lay hands on a penny
of her inheritance without her written consent. They
had at last realised that her first marriage had been a
love match, her loss . . . total. So, upon their deaths,
she had been given everything, with additional huge
legacies to both Sian and Roland. They wanted her to
choose again, to seek a father for her children and
live a life of comfort, knowing she would have the
companion of her choice. All his needs would be catered
for by her money, and he would be powerless to steal
it from her as so many husbands did when wedding
heiresses.

She chose again. Not out of loneliness, but out of
love. Seeing in Phillip a strength, a maturity, his younger
brother had lacked. She loved him in a different way,
but blindly, as she had done his brother. She married
him in ignorance, and regretted it until the day she died.
Her last act was to ensure he inherited nothing from
her. Everything was to be shared between her two older
children. Only upon their deaths would Timothy inherit.
She had hoped they would live long, fulfilled lives, such
as hers had never been, so that when their little brother
became rich and powerful, he would have grown older
and wiser and be beyond the reach of his scheming
father.

Yet only she now stood between Timothy and a
fortune, Sian realised. She had tried not to think of
Douglas's words to her. His suspicions that someone
was plotting to kill her, too. Phillip was greedy, but to
have her murdered? If anything, he wanted her in his
bed—not dead!

'When I grow up I'm going to be a soldier,' Timothy
said. He yawned, but resisted Sian's attempt to tuck the
clothes round his shoulders. He was a fighter, Douglas
thought, admiring his pluck. What a pity he had such
blood in him! It would show one day. It was sure to,

under Blakeney's guidance. A reflection of himself.
God help the poor souls under him! 'Father says I'm
too puny to be a good one. He won't even let me have
a sword. He wants to send me away to school—to learn
to fight. Did you go away?'

'No, bonny lad. I fought with my father and friends.
Many a good game we've had together in the heather.
Do you not have friends of your own?'

'No one will talk to me.' The mouth pouted, and
Douglas had a sudden glimpse of ten years hence. A
mirror image. 'Father says it doesn't matter. That they
are only peasants. But I would like someone to play
with. Rolly used to before he went away, but only
because Sian asked him. He never liked me either, did
he, Sian?'

His words cut her like a knife. She was deeply
ashamed that those so close should have caused him
pain. She would never do so.

'Rolly—has . . .' She balked at telling him of
Roland's death yet, to add to his nightmares. 'He never
liked Scotland, you know that. He—he is at home only
here.' At home for ever now. Never to leave the shores
of France again. She blinked back a rush of tears. This
was no time for sentiment! 'Do I not play with you? Do
we not spend hours together riding? We do not need
others. It is for them to seek your company, and they
will when they see what a fine young man you are
becoming. When they hear of your exploits over here,
they will come flocking to your side, asking to be told
of your great adventure.'

'Father would not allow it,' Timothy said, blinking at
her tiredly. He was fighting against the overwhelming
desire to sleep. They could both feel his struggle. A
losing one, Sian hoped, looking into Douglas's closed
features. Whenever his thoughts turned to Scotland,
how stern he looked. How unapproachable! 'Do you
have a sword?' Douglas nodded. 'Can I see it? Will you
show me how to use it? You have saved my life, and so
you are my champion. My paladin.'

'I—I used to tell him stories about King Arthur, and

Charlemagne,' Sian explained, with a faint shrug of her shoulders. 'Would you mind . . . if it will calm him?'

'A good Scots lad should be reared on tales of Robert the Bruce! Now there's a tale of determination for you. Or tales of Montrose, of Glencoe, of Bonnie Prince Charlie.'

'Don't you think he has had enough of bloodshed and murder?' Sian said, and the smile he directed at her mocked her show of anger in a way that told her if he chose to tell his stories, she would not stop him. He was changing before her very eyes. Harder, colder, somehow frighteningly different. Dear God, she thought, in a moment of panic. Could he have known Phillip? He was a MacGregor, and so many had suffered at that man's hands as he and his men roved through the Highlands in 1746. No, of course not. He did not even connect the name Blakeney with her and Timothy. Why should he? She had never mentioned it. Never would . . . To see the same hatred in his eyes as in those of the villagers at Rannoch would be more than she could bear.

'Am I not the boy's champion? Let him keep his illusions a while longer, woman. He will grow up soon enough as it is. If I fetch my sword, you are to go to sleep and get well.' He fixed Timothy with a look which, for all its sternness, was not the grim-eyed threat of a parent, and to Sian's amazement, a faint smile touched her brother's lips. Without a word he slipped beneath the covers and lay with the look of an angel upon his face. She had seen that look before. Usually it heralded a great mischief!

'He is getting better,' she murmured, too happy to prevent him having his way. 'Fetch your sword. Let him see the champion he has.'

Douglas fetched his broadsword, and Timothy's eyes fixed on it disbelievingly. Never had he seen such a monster!

'Father has nothing like that,' he breathed. 'If you were with me, no one would be my enemy. They would not dare,' Timothy murmured, his eyes closing for a moment. 'Will you come home with me? Be my champion?'

'Fear is not the way. Earn their respect.'

How could he, when he was the son of Phillip Blakeney, the butcher of Rannoch, Douglas thought with anguish.

'Make him come, Sian,' Timothy whispered. He could not longer stay awake. His fingers reached for hers. She caught and held them fast, across the gleaming blade of Douglas's broadsword. It was like an omen! It separated them. 'He would like Ard Choille. Perhaps I would like it then . . .'

'What did he say?' Douglas demanded. His hearing was playing tricks on him. Fate could not be so cruel!

'Ard Choille. Our home,' Sian said, releasing her brother's hand as he drifted into an untroubled sleep. Looking into Douglas's face, she knew something was terribly wrong. There was accusation in his eyes, but of what? What was there between them, that she had always sensed was between them, that now opened a deep abyss between her and the happiness she had known in his arms? 'My step-father was given land and a house for his . . . for his loyalty to the Crown,' she finished lamely. For his butchery and the lining of his own pocket to which the English Government had turned a blind eye, for there had been no witnesses to come forward against him. 'But I think you already know that, don't you, Douglas?'

'My God!' Douglas exclaimed. He drew back, pulling his sword from beneath Timothy's outstretched hand. Instinctively Sian rose, as if afraid he was going to render the boy some harm. His mouth curved into an unpleasant smile. 'I'll not touch him, though if I did, no one could blame me. Ard Choille does not belong to Phillip Blakeney, woman! It belongs to me. Douglas MacGregor! It always will. He killed my parents to have it. Raped my mother and then nigh sliced her in half with his sword when she attempted to warn my father and me that he had soldiers lying in wait for us. He

killed my father. Dirked him from behind while he
fought another man. And did this to me.' He touched
his cheek, the livid scar searing one brown shoulder.
'My memory is long . . . My nightmares many, too.
One day . . .'

'You knew who Timothy was,' Sian said in a small,
disbelieving voice. 'Who I was. I prayed you did not
. . . You have lied to me!'

'Comtesse de Saint-Rémy. *His* step-daughter! I knew.
Why did you not tell me? Were you so afraid of what
you would learn? Or did you seek to protect him? He
has a way with women, or so he thinks. Has he with
you?'

She drew back her hand and struck him without
thinking, only conscious of the deliberate insult, the
insinuation that she had shared Phillip's bed.

'No more than I expected, to salve your wounded
pride!' he sneered.

'Do you think pride is all I have lost?' she cried.

Timothy stirred, and she drew back from the bed,
not wanting him to wake and hear what passed between
them. He had suffered enough. Now, more than ever
he needed her, she realised. He had no one else. She
had no one, either. The sight of Douglas's murderous
expression was proof of that. He had known her identity. The suspicion that he had deliberately set out to
entrap her stole into her mind.

'What I've had was given freely, woman, little though
it was. I took nothing. Remember that.' Why was he
being so harsh with her, when he wanted to be gentle?
To take her in his arms and soothe her fears? But he
could not. The past rose up before his eyes in flames of
red mist and hatred, gave his tongue the venom of a
snake. A deadly bite that would strike her down for
daring to live in *his* house! Beneath the roof that was
denied to him, the rightful master. 'You stayed silent
because you were afraid I might have suffered at his
hands and sought revenge. You are right, woman. And
I've had it—in part, at least. It will be complete when
he lies dead at my feet. Tell him Douglas MacGregor

returns you to him with his compliments. I have no
further use for you.'

Brutally he flung the words at her and watched her
flinch. Hate me for God's sake, woman, his heart cried.
Hate me, curse me! Set me free!

'It is a pity I have neither the time nor the interest in
what you have so far offered me, to remain and teach
you how a woman should act with a man. You are an
ignorant child!'

'You knew,' she said again softly, and into her mind
came Rudy's reaction when Douglas had ordered him
to return to the tavern, handing Timothy into her charge
as they sat in the darkened carriage. He had been
startled by the order. Had it not been Douglas's intention to return him? What had changed his mind? 'Give
her the boy,' he had instructed. And Rudy's startled
answer. 'But I thought . . .' What had he thought? Dull
fire sprang to her eyes as she looked at Douglas, and
he caught his breath at the sudden loathing there. This
was what he wanted . . . 'You knew, and you planned
to take Timothy from Simeon and keep him for yourself.
I would have given you anything to get him back. Or
were you planning on holding him for Phillip to grovel
at your feet?'

'At last you begin to understand.' He admitted
nothing. Denied nothing. Desperately she fought to
keep control of her reeling senses. This was a nightmare
of a different kind. One that, when she woke in the
morning, would still be with her. Would always be with
her. To be used by such a man!

'Why did you return him to me? Did I offer something
better? Myself? You know it would have been more
. . .' She broke off as shame swept over her. It would
have been more—much more. Anything he asked of
her, she would have given.

'I thought it would be amusing to have the untouch-
able Comtesse de Saint-Rémy, who is so fond of looking
down her rich little nose at mercenaries like me. I
promised myself that at Versailles. You made it easy
for me, although a little dull!'

'Get out!' Sian shivered in disgust, her lips quivering. She flung a hand towards the door. 'Out of here. Out of this room. Out of my life. If you stay, you will find yourself answering questions you may not like, monsieur. Your involvement with René, for one. Your association with Simeon, another. La Pompadour would like your head on a spike for the embarrassment you have caused her, and if you give me cause now, I shall see she has it.'

'Hell hath no fury,' Douglas mocked, his mouth deepening into a twisted smile that mocked her brave stand. She would never cause him harm, and suspected he knew it. Yet to allow him to stand there and tell her how inadequate she had been in his bed . . . 'You are not even woman enough to accept what has happened and put it down to inexperience. The next time . . .'

His taunt broke the thin thread of Sian's restraint. Like a mad thing, she flung herself at him, nails reaching for his cheeks. He swore as she drew blood, snatching his head back so that her wild attempt to reach him a second time failed. He gave her no more chances. She cried out as he coupled her wrists behind her back in one hand and thrust the other in her loose hair, brutally tugging back her head. His eyes flamed as he stared down into her tortured features, gazed at them for one moment longer, drinking in the loveliness which he had deliberately destroyed in his hatred of one man. His insane desire for revenge, which had kept him alive for the past ten years . . . kept his sword-arm strong and ever ready for the day they would come face to face again.

'The next time, I will choose a man!' she breathed, hating him with every fibre of her body. Loving him with every fibre. Each fought for supremacy.

'You will never find another like me, that I promise you. You will lie awake in your bed thinking how it might have been with me.' He bent his head until his cheek was close to hers, with its three lines of red blood drying now on the sunburnt skin. She had left her mark on him as he had on her, but in time, his would fade.

Hers never would. She fought against his hold, but she was like a child in his grasp. 'I could take you now and you would welcome it—even knowing what I am . . . what I have done.'

Sian's mouth opened to scream as his hand left her hair. His fingers fastened in the front of her pelisse and ripped it open from neck to waist, baring her breasts. It was never uttered as he took her mouth in a cruel, savage kiss that shocked her very depths. She fought against it, against him, against the fingers roving over her bare flesh, stroking her breasts as he held her helpless. Against the fire that rose inside her, the urge to melt against him and return kiss for kiss until he took her. Timothy was forgotten in the wildness which seized her and turned her legs to water. Her lips parted as she sank against him in surrender . . .

With a short laugh, Douglas thrust her away, turned back to the bed and retrieved his sword.

'This steel is more honest than you,' he taunted. His eyes swept over her, and the look in them made her realise how she had degraded herself in the name of love. To have no mind of her own! Nothing mattering to her but that she belong to him! God help her! She would be doomed to the eternal fires of hell for tonight . . . and for the words she was about to speak.

Slowly she drew herself upright, gathering together her gaping robe.

'If you are in Paris after tomorrow, monsieur, I shall have you killed.'

'You will try!' He crooked a smile at her as he opened the door. 'You will try as others have tried before you. They did not succeed; no more will you. If you do send anyone after me'—he paused and looked back at her —'I shall kill them, and then I shall come for you, Madame la Comtesse, and it will not be to share your bed. Think well on that before you risk not only the lives of others, but your own.'

The closed door separated them. Sian stared at it for a long while, without being aware of time passing. Her wrists and arms felt bruised from his touch. Her breasts tingled with the momentary pleasure she had experienced, even as a prisoner of his hatred, his scorn. Slowly she became aware of the room about her, the fire burning in the hearth, the sleeping boy in her bed. She had been prepared to give up Douglas once again, but not like this! Used, humiliated, discarded—as Phillip Blakeney had once done with Clare! There lay the crux of it. An eye for an eye. Not Phillip, but *she*, had paid for his heinous crime. She sank on to the bed, shocked, unable to gather her stunned thoughts. When André knocked timidly on her door to tell her the Scotsman had left the house without a word, he found her sitting beside her brother, holding one frail hand in hers. It was a full minute before she even recognised the man, and then she astounded him by beginning to weep . . .

She was done with the tears now. Done with weakness. Done with love. She had money and position, which in turn gave her power. She would use both as she saw fit to make a new life for herself, devoid of sentiment and stupidity. So Sian decided in the cold light of dawn. She had not been to bed, but remained at Timothy's side throughout the night. How could she sleep? How could she ever rest easily again, knowing what she had done?

When she rang for some food to be brought, she had cried her last tear. Her face was dry, her eyes devoid of emotion, her manner distant when Effie arrived and set it down before her.

'We leave for the coast at the end of the week,' she said flatly. The hot chocolate warmed her cold bones, but did little to restore her flagging spirits, yet outwardly there was no sign of distress. No signs of the terrible pain which still lingered inside her, alongside hunger and disillusionment. 'Have everything packed and ready by then. Send for Dr Devereaux when you leave me. I want him to look at Timothy and make sure he is well enough to travel.'

'Are you, madam?' Effie asked, looking into the white face. What had happened she did not know. Like the other servants, she had learned of Douglas's abrupt departure from the house without an explanation. Had he deserted her? It served her right, the high and mighty little minx! Did she think her looks could hold a man? 'You do not look at all well.'

'Your concern is touching,' Sian retorted sarcastically, 'but a little out of character, don't you think, Effie? We have no love for each other, and we shall part company as soon as we reach Ard Choille. If Phillip wishes to keep you on—in another capacity—that is his choice. I shall be glad if you will keep a civil tongue in your head and speak to me as little as possible. Do I make myself clear?'

'Perfectly, madam.' The maid did not turn a hair at the frosty tone, for it told her all she wanted to know. The mercenary had left her, and now she was running back to Scotland to seek sanctuary from the gossip and rumours that would soon be flying about Paris. What a pity she would miss them, Effie thought maliciously. After all, most of them were due to her. She would have liked to have heard what results her mischief had produced!

Sian was about to go along to Timothy's room, when André announced that a visitor was waiting below in the salon. Hope rose and died within her in the space of a heartbeat. *He* would not have waited to be announced.

'I am expecting no one, and I have no wish to see anyone. Ask him to leave a message. Say I am indisposed . . . anything . . .'

'*She* was very insistent, madame. Says she knows you . . . that you have a mutual acquaintance.'

Sian caught her breath. Only one woman would dare to visit her and proclaim such a relationship.

'A gypsy girl?' she asked slowly, and the man nodded. 'Tell her to wait, I will be down in a while.'

The reflection which stared at her from the mirror was of a woman who had lost interest in all around her. Dull eyes, pale cheeks, hair not even brushed this morning. Ten vigorous minutes changed all that. No matter how bad she felt, Zara would never know it! The woman was standing by the windows when she entered,

covered from head to toe in a scarlet cloak heavily
trimmed with fur. Her long hair was piled high on her
head and secured with jewelled combs. Apart from the
heavy gold earrings and the abundance of glittering
rings on the long, taloned fingers which betrayed an
extreme bad taste for gawdy objects, she could have
passed for a lady, Sian thought, as she closed the door
behind her.

'Madame la Comtesse. Thank you, I shall not sit
down, I shall say what has brought me here, and then
I shall leave,' she said with sarcasm as Sian said nothing,
not even offering the courtesies of the day to her unexpected guest. Would she have expected any?

'Please be brief, then. As far as I know, we have
nothing to discuss.'

'He has come back to me, you know. Last night . . .
after he left you.' She gave a soft, triumphant laugh.
'Didn't I tell you that you couldn't hold him?'

'You are quite right in assuming that Monsier Mac-
Gregor is no longer in my employ,' Sian said stiffly,
showing none of the pain which ripped through her at
the information. 'Where he is now, with whom—or
what he does, is of no importance to me. If that is all
you have come to tell me, you have wasted your time
—and mine. Goodbye, mademoiselle.'

She picked up her skirts to leave, then froze as Zara
declared,

'Not so high and mighty now are you, now that you
know the truth? Did you really think a man like Le
Blond could be interested in a milk-white nothing like
you? Why, he wouldn't have even looked at you if it
hadn't been in his plan.' She ran a hand lovingly over
her cloak, touching the fur to one cheek. 'He gave me
this when he came back—and much more—to make up
for being so neglectful of me. He had to, of course, or
you would never have believed he was helping you.'

'He seems to have taken you into his confidence. I
find it strange that someone of your limited intelligence
could comprehend the workings of his devious mind.'
It was an insult intended to provoke the woman before

her, and it succeeded. Zara's face grew red with anger.

'I knew everything from the start. Did I not give him the potion that kept your brother drugged until his release?' A wild look came into her eyes as Sian blenched and stepped back. 'He did not tell you that? Did he tell you he planned everything? Simeon was acting on his orders. But the fool had no ambition, he was content to have just the ransom money. Le Blond wants more . . . has had more already, has he not? Do not look so shocked, Madame la Comtesse, he has told me everything. Last night, as I lay in his arms, how we laughed about you . . . and him.'

'I grant he may have returned to you, that he prefers to wallow in the gutter with his own, and that he—he may have told you . . . It is of no importance any longer,' Sian said in a contemptuous tone. She had to maintain her composure at all costs. 'I still fail to understand why you have come to see me. You have told me nothing I did not know, or at least suspect. I shall inform the authorities of what I know before I leave Paris. He—you both—will answer to them for your crimes. Do not think you will escape punishment I have the full authority of Madame la Marquise de Pompadour backing me in my determination to bring to justice the men responsible for my brother's death and Timothy's abduction.'

Zara's laughter echoed and re-echoed around the tiny room.

'Justice! You little fool, you will never live to see him lose his head. He has not finished with you yet. Don't you think it strange he left so suddenly? He was bored with the charade, but that doesn't mean he has finished with you. He intends to wait for you on the road to Calais and take the boy from you. He will keep him until his enemy—this Blakeney—comes with much money. Although he does not want money only . . . He wants this man dead.'

'I won't let it happen,' Sian cried. 'I'll send word to Phillip!'

'You will not send word to anyone—or receive help

from anyone. You will simply not arrive at the coast. When you are found, it may be a little difficult to recognise you . . . Le Blond's men have been known to be animals with a beautiful woman.'

'What are you saying?'

'So now you are interested, no?' Zara came close to her. There was an aroma of strong perfume about her which made Sian feel nauseous. She felt stifled in this woman's company, and very much afraid by what she had heard. 'He has told them they can have you. You have nothing to offer him, you see. With you dead, the boy inherits everything . . . all that money for the taking . . . from his old enemy. It is justice, no?'

'Why do you warn me of this?' She had to get Timothy to safety, but how? If the Calais road was watched . . . 'You care nothing for what happens to me!'

'That is true. I should want to see you dead for trying to take him from me . . .' The swarthy features broke into a complacent smile. 'But I can afford to be generous.' Then the mouth was tight, unsmiling; the eyes cold. 'If he could use you to bait this Blakeney, I believe he would. I do not want you under my nose . . . under his. I share him with no one!'

'And so, out of the kindness of your heart, you have come to warn me.' Sian said in a sharp tone that betrayed the anguish inside her.

'As you please.' Zara shrugged her shoulders and brushed past the still figure to the door. 'Tonight we go to the theatre, Le Blond and I. We go in style, in a fine carriage, and I shall sit among all the fine ladies, dressed as they are with jewels better than they will ever see. He would do anything to please me now. He appreciates what he gave up, if only for a short while. If you stay in Paris, I wouldn't give a *sou* for your life. Go while you can . . . or you will find him waiting for you on the road. Are you anxious to repeat the disaster? I shall find my own way out.'

Effie was waiting as Zara came out of the salon. Sian had sunk on to a chair, her face in her hands, and so did not see the maid slip past and close the door, then

take the gypsy's arm and hurry her out to the front
porch where no one could see them.

'Did she believe you?'

'Why not? She will believe anything of him now!'
Zara raised a winged eyebrow in contempt of the figure
she had left behind. 'I want her dead!'

'We both do,' Effie murmured. 'You have my
brother's message? You will give him the powder and
tell him to leave at once?'

'As you told it to me. And my money?'

'He will give you sufficient upon delivery. I have
agreed a price with him. Go now, before we are seen
together. We shall not meet again.'

'There is no reason. You will have what you want,
and so shall I.'

Sian looked up as Effie entered the salon, and instant
displeasure registered on her ashen face. Coldly she
said, 'We are leaving Paris tonight.'

'Tonight!' Somehow Effie managed to contain the
triumph that rose inside her. 'But the packing is not
finished . . . and the doctor is coming to see Timothy
at six.'

'We shall leave around seven, when he has gone. It
will be dark then. No one must see us go. We must not
be followed! Our lives are in danger,' Sian exclaimed.
'There is an inn outside Paris where Roland and I often
stayed. We shall rest there tonight and go on to Calais
tomorrow.'

'Saints preserve us!' The maid crossed herself, a most
convincing look of fear on her face.

'Whom are we fleeing from, madam? Who is there
who would want to harm you? Not—not he! After all
you have done for him?'

'If I am to believe the gypsy, Zara, yet, he! Tell the
rest of the servants they are to help with the packing.
It may be a long time before I am here again, so we will
take all the clothes. If they wish, they can close up the
house and go to the château. See to it.' She recalled
how she had stood in the château and said the same
words to Douglas. 'Come back to me in an hour—no,

half that. I have a letter that must be delivered to
Madame de Pompadour immediately. Have a man
ready to ride. I shall tell her everything I know. Everything. She will know how to deal with the—the persons
responsible for all this. I vowed that Roland's death
would not go unavenged. Monsieur MacGregor will
discover he is not the only one to keep his word!'

She sat down and wrote to Jeanne in a feverish haste,
baring her soul to the only person she felt she could
now trust. She left nothing unsaid—even the hours she
had spent with him. Jeanne was a woman of the world,
and would understand. She told herself she was not
doing this out of hatred, or a wish to punish the man
who had abused her love, but that her vow to Roland
was the sole reason. He would not have allowed sentiment to cloud his judgment, had the positions been
reversed. No more must she.

She gave the letter into Effie's hands and went to her
room to supervise the hurried preparations going on
there. The maid appeared a few minutes later to say
that the letter had been despatched by a rider in all
haste to Versailles.

'Finish the packing, Effie. All the things from the
closet must go into that trunk beside the bed. I am going
to sit with Timothy for a while.'

'Yes, madam.' The woman's fingers touched the
paper still in her pocket. She had never intended it
should reach its destination—at least not yet. By the
time Sian's disappearance became apparent, she would
be dead, and Douglas MacGregor would find himself
facing Madame la Guillotine. Perhaps with his mistress
alongside him. One or both, she cared not. They would
be condemned by the hand of a dead woman, for Effie
did not intend the letter to arrive at the palace until
after her mistress's death.

# CHAPTER
# ELEVEN

'LE BLOND?' Peppito poked his head round the door at the top of the stairs and looked at the inert figure lying on the canopied bed. 'Are you awake?' It would be a wonder after consuming the contents of the bottle on the floor beside him, the dwarf thought, grinning as he advanced into the room. An unshaven face raised itself from the depths of the covers and stared at him.

'Go away! Take your miserable little body downstairs, and don't bother me again,' Douglas growled. His head felt as if it had a hundred bells inside it, all clanging at the same time. And all in an effort to blot one face from his mind. A useless attempt, as it happened. Her face had followed him into the realms of sleep, to plague his dreams and give him no peace. He did not deserve peace for what he had done. Hatred had consumed him like some carnivorous monster, which had eaten up his soul, his decency, every emotion. Because of Phillip Blakeney, he had destroyed an innocent woman with his hatred. He would never forget the terrible look of pain on her face as she learned who he was. She had not known before, of that he was certain. She knew only that he was a MacGregor, and so she sought to protect not only herself, but little Timothy from any repercussions that might arise from the past by remaining silent. He could not blame her for that.

But he had. He had blamed her for everything. It made it easier for him to turn his back and walk away from her . . . and the future she promised with her lips, her body, her love! He had chosen a coward's way. He had killed men for daring to whisper that name even in jest!

'Are you still here?' he snapped, looking daggers at the dwarf who stood silently by the bed.

'Are you interested to know of the stranger who was at Maurice's the day before yesterday?'

'No, why should I be?' Douglas returned ungraciously, and laid his throbbing head gently down on the pillow. He had no interest in anyone. Liar! But she was out of reach. Soon she would be on her way back to Scotland, to his home. How he ached to think of what he had lost! He would have given anything to be going with her. Even the sword-arm by which he had lived for so many years. His woman! He had called no other that in his life. Nor would he now. Such love would not come again. And he had placed his desire for revenge first—above the great miracle that had taken place and would have changed his whole life.

What a pair they would have made at Ard Choille. Robert would have approved of her, he thought, remembering with warmth the old retainer who had been instrumental in saving his life after he had been left for dead by Blakeney. If he still lived! So many had perished.

'You asked to be told of any strangers hereabouts,' Peppito said in a tone which conveyed great patience —as one speaking to a child who did not understand very well. 'Scotsmen like yourself. There was one at Maurice's, but he has gone now. Well, if it is of no importance . . .'

'Come back here,' came the order from the bed, and he turned back at the door, a cheeky grin on his face. 'Tell me about him.'

Already Douglas was struggling into his clothes, wincing as pain seared his head. If the room would remain still for just one moment, he would be able to pull on his boots. His injured arm felt as stiff as a board.

'What day is it?' He had lost all track of time.

'Really, Le Blond, Zara *has* been working her spell on you since you returned! Not able to tell the time of day!' Peppito broke off with a squeal and jumped back, barely managing to avoid the outflung arm meant to grab him by the shirt. 'Patience . . . I'll tell you. It's Thursday . . . morning.'

Thursday! He had been back and drunk for two days, and remembered none of it. Yet, in the back of his mind, was memory. Of calling her name as he tossed and turned in restless sleep, of someone coming to him, holding him, loving him. In his drunkenness he had thought it to be her. He had poured out his love, begging her to stay, not to hate him. She had stayed, and he had made love to her again and again, draining himself of all guilt as he did so, slipping into the sleep which claimed him at peace. And then in the morning he had awoken to find Zara sitting on the edge of the bed, staring at him, and he had turned away from her with a groan, knowing it had been she he had taken . . . she who had learned the secret in his heart and now stared down at him with something near to hatred flickering in the depths of her coal-black eyes. He had gone back to sleep not caring if she plunged a dagger into him then and there. Sian was lost to him. Nothing else mattered.

'So it's Thursday,' he grunted. 'Another day. So far, I have nothing to celebrate.'

'Maurice's guest was from Scotland, like yourself. Angus Campbell. A man of substance, from the way he had been spending.'

'The Campbells always did have a habit of lining their own pockets, yet without any inclination to spend any of it,' Douglas declared with a dry smile. 'Gone, you say? How long was he at Maurice's place?'

'Three days. Last night he paid his bill, hired a horse, and left. The Calais road, Jacques tells me.'

'Describe him.' Douglas sat frowning on the edge of the bed. Another Scot! It could have been purely coincidence—but coincidence at such a time smelt of trouble to him.

'Short, clean-shaven, well-dressed, quietly spoken. An accent, of course. Plenty of money. No visitors for the whole three days he was at Maurice's.'

'Damn,' Douglas said, and then saw the smile on Peppito's face. 'Well?'

'He had no visitors, I said, but he was seen to strike up an acquaintance with a pretty woman.'

'If he was far from home and lonely, I hardly blàme him.'

'Angus Campbell is not a stranger to these parts, although he was here before you, and so you would not know of him. He has a certain shall we say—penchant —for young boys? When he is in Paris on business he always comes to this quarter, where there are so many attractions to offer. He usually returns after his little amusing evenings to a house in the Avenue Noblesse, the house of the Comtesse de Saint-Rémy. Angus Campbell is steward of her estates in Scotland.'

'Not *her* estates,' Douglas breathed, eyes darkening suddenly. 'Those of Phillip Blakeney. Ard Choille. My home. The home he took from me . . .' He broke off. Never had he allowed himself to say so much—except to Sian! Now two people knew how vulnerable he really was!

'So that was the reason for your interest in her! Perhaps it explains Zara's interest in the man Campbell.' Peppito nodded slowly. 'She was the woman he met several nights ago. Directly afterwards, he left for the coast. There was some exchanging of money, and a package, but Jacques was not close enough to see what it looked like. Something small—jewels, perhaps? You said we were to watch her every move. We did!'

Douglas shook his head, mystified. This new turn of events had taken him completely by surprise, and the throbbing of his head did not help him to untangle the web of confused thoughts and suspicions flooding through him. Zara, who had betrayed him with her brother Simeon, had been instrumental in drugging Timothy Blakeney throughout his long days of captivity. Zara, who had lain with him and pretended to be another woman, made love to him while he believed her to be someone else . . . Zara—and Angus Campbell, Blakeney's steward. It could mean only one thing. Sian's life was in danger! She would soon be journeying along the Calais road. What would await her at the end of it?

'Have my horse saddled. I'll leave after I've talked with Zara. I want coffee, hot and black, and lots of it.'

'You go after your Comtesse, eh?' the dwarf asked with a grin. 'You will have to ride hard to catch her. She left Paris on Tuesday night, with the boy and all her luggage. I don't think she is coming back.'

'Someone means to make damned sure of it,' Douglas returned grimly. 'Where is Zara?' Tuesday evening! The day after he had left the house and probably lay in a drunken stupor on his bed! She could be dead by now, lying in some ditch with her throat cut . . . If she had been harmed, one hair of her head touched, he would never rest until those responsible had died by his sword!

'You love her as much as that?' Peppito was looking at him, his head on one side, brown, darting eyes alight with something Douglas could only take as excitement.

'Fool that I am, yes! Do you find it amusing?'

'My friend—and I call you that with true honesty, for you are one of the very few men who does not despise this shrunken body or this dim-witted mind. It hurts me to see you so sorely troubled.'

'You are one of the cleverest rogues it has ever been my pleasure to meet,' Douglas interrupted, and the dwarf beamed at him, tears appearing in his eyes.

'I shall miss you, Le Blond. You are one of us, and yet you never were. Never will be in your heart. Fate brought you here, and now she takes you away. I think she has something better in mind for you. I hope so. She was right for you, the little Comtesse. She had courage and such beauty. She was your woman? You did not lie?'

'No, Peppito. In truth she was my woman, and there will never be another to take her place. I pray to God I am not too late.'

'Zara is in her room. I trust her not. Be careful. Even now, when the vixen knows the huntsmen have gone, she is still dangerous. She could still turn on a friend.'

'That we never were, as you and I are.' Douglas's hand rested for a moment on Peppito's shoulder. Of all the people in this place, he would miss him the most.

'Zara did not only visit Maurice's,' Peppito added. 'She also went to the house of the little Comtesse on Tuesday.'

'To see Sian?' Douglas looked startled. 'Why should she do that? She hates her!'

'To gloat, perhaps. After all, you had returned to her. She was so crazy with jealousy that she would want to throw that tit-bit into her rival's face. Women are strange creatures, Le Blond.'

'Maybe more than that. I know Sian had no intention of leaving Paris until the end of the week. She was concerned for her brother's health. Yet suddenly she bundles him into a coach and they leave. None of this makes sense, Peppito. I only know she is in danger, and I must follow her. The coffee, man, quickly! I am no use to her or myself, feeling as I do now!'

Half an hour later he entered Zara's room so quietly that the woman lying across the narrow bed was not aware of his presence until she looked up and found him standing over her. One look into the cold eyes told her why he had come. For the first time in her life, Zara knew real fear. She cried out as his hands reached out to clasp her shoulders, but she was not quick enough to evade him . . .

. . . Peppito looked down at the leather pouch Douglas pressed into his hand when he came downstairs.

'What is this?'

'All the money I possess, except for a few coins to get me to Calais. Take it, old friend; it's yours. I wish I had more to give you. Take my hand, too. You have been a true friend to me. God knows, I've needed one these past years.'

They shook hands and then Douglas swung himself up on the back of the black stallion which was saddled and waiting as he had instructed, in the courtyard.

'If Sian is dead, I shall be back,' he said, looking up at the window of the room where Zara was. 'She betrayed us, Peppito. She has been working with them all along. She and that accursed brother . . . and she swore to me she had not seen him. The man she met at

Maurice's? He is the brother of Sian's maid. That one, too, is due for a reckoning when I catch up with her.' Grand-mère had been right in her reading of the Tarot. The danger was all round them, coming from all directions. Zara, Effie Campbell, her brother Simeon. Who else was involved in this treacherous scheme? Phillip Blakeney? Who else?

'The Comtesse is on her way to an inn called the Vache Noire, just outside Calais. Zara has given the maid poison. I am thinking Sian will never leave the place if I do not get there in time.'

'We lost three good men the night we rescued the boy, Le Blond,' the dwarf muttered. 'You need not return to take care of her. It will be done for you. She will pay the penalty for betraying her own. Go now. God speed. Find your little Comtesse alive and well.'

As Douglas reached the end of the street, a shrill scream cut through the air, bringing people's heads about as they sought to find whence it came, before shrugging their shoulders and continuing on their way. It was not wise to show curiosity in these parts. Douglas did not even look back as he urged his horse in the direction of the Pont-Neuf.

Sian stared open-mouthed at the man who stood in the doorway of the small, but clean, well-furnished room she had taken for the night at the Vache Noire. She had been all for going direct to the harbour and seeking a passage, but Effie had warned her against being too open and revealing herself when she arrived in Calais. What if Douglas or one of his men had arrived before them?

The newcomer was Angus Campbell, Phillip's Scottish steward. He was a man of medium height, bearing little resemblance to his sister, some four years his junior. His complexion was florid, his body corpulent. Too much ale and too little exercise, Sian always thought. He delegated far too much to others below him, preferring to swagger about the estate in Phillip's

wake, imitating him in both manner and habits, which
endeared him to neither her nor the villagers, who
detested both men with equal vehemence.

'Mr Campbell! Why, for a moment I thought my eyes
were deceiving me,' she exclaimed. 'What are you doing
in France? Is something wrong? Lord Phillip . . .?'

'Nothing is wrong, madam, but his lordship is very
worried.'

'Worried?' Again she had to drag herself back to the
present. 'Why? He knew we would be away for several
months.' Had word been carried to him of what had
happened? Only Douglas could have done that, but had
he? Had he thought that far ahead, and she not even in
her grave yet?

'He misses the lad. 'Tis only natural. He sent me to
ask you to return at once and bring your brother with
you. My lord thought—well, to tell you the truth, I
believe he's had time to think—while he's been alone.'
Sian doubted that. He would have found someone to
provide amusement in one form or another for him.
She prayed he had not taken another young girl from
the village.

'I think he wants to gather everyone at Ard Choille
and be done with old grievances. You've saved me a
journey, madam. There's no need for me to go on to
Paris now. I can book passages for us all on the ship
that leaves tomorrow morning. If you agree, of course.'

'As soon as possible,' Sian agreed. For once, she did
not mind the man's high-handedness. She could not
leave France quickly enough. How cruel Fate was to
drive her away from this country she loved!

'And your brother? You will send word to him to join
the master soon?'

'My brother Roland is dead. Murdered by an alley-rat
by the name of René three weeks ago. There is much
that has happened to us that you don't know, Mr
Campbell.'

Effie gave a sudden wail and burst into tears. She
flung herself into her brother's arms, sobbing against his
chest. Sian had never considered her to be an emotional

person. She was beginning to think how badly she had misjudged her.

'There, there, lass.' Angus looked embarrassed as he patted the dark curls. 'Don't greet. I always carry two loaded pistols when I travel, and you shall have one to keep by your side to protect your mistress. I shall keep the other by me at all times. No one will lay a finger on any of you, that I promise.'

'Thank you, Mr Campbell. I must admit I begin to feel safer now that we are in Calais, and the knowledge you are within call gives me hope that I shall see Ard Choille again. There was a time when I began to doubt it,' Sian said, forcing a smile to her tired features. 'There is a ship waiting to leave, you say? Whatever it costs, you must get us passages on it.'

'I shall. I see how important it is to you,' the man replied. 'I could hire some men, if you feel you are in danger. But from what, madam? Or should I say whom?'

'You will learn everything later. I want to rest now. Go with him, Effie. Tell him all he wants to know. I care not to discuss what has happened.'

'And leave you alone?' the maid protested.

'Timothy's room is only next door. I shall go and sit with him until you return. He is sleeping, poor love. He is still not fully recovered from that hideous drug. I hope he will not suffer from this journey.'

'We had to leave,' Effie said, moving towards the door and motioning her brother to follow. 'You would be dead if you had remained in Paris. *He* would have seen to that. I will have your meal brought up to you. You don't want to sit below with the others. I don't like the look of any of them.'

'Don't exaggerate, girl. You'll frighten madam even more than she has been already,' Angus reproved in a gruff tone. 'I'll be back shortly, when I have had a word with the landlord. A small payment will ensure he keeps his eyes and ears open until we return.'

Sian nodded gratefully. He was being unusually considerate. Perhaps in the past her attitude had been at fault—not his, not Effie's. Perhaps she had allowed her resentment of another woman taking her mother's place to blind her to the woman's true character. And Angus was being positively friendly! How she needed friends at this moment.

'You are sure she suspects nothing?' Angus demanded, drawing his sister away from the other guests clustered round the fire. She shook her head, pulling on her cloak. 'Good. This is a mad scheme, but it may work.'

'It will. Even if they suspect murder after we are gone, they can do nothing to find us. I gave false names. She doesn't know, and I've already told both the landlord, and the maid who looked after us when we arrived, that my mistress is ailing and doesn't have long to live. She is returning to Scotland to die . . .'

'You cold-hearted little bitch! I didn't realise the devil had spawned you,' her brother breathed. 'How will you handle *him* when he finds out?'

'Phillip? Don't worry, I can handle him!' From a pocket she took Sian's letter, and waved it beneath his nose, her eyes alight with a cruel gleam. 'I shall leave this beside the bed, in the book she is reading. It is addressed to Madame de Pompadour. In it she all but accuses MacGregor of being responsible for everything. Think what that woman will do to him when she learns her friend is dead! He will be lucky to live out the week.'

'We'd best be on our way to book these passages. The ship leaves on the high tide at eleven this evening.'

'Not tomorrow, as we told her? Tonight I shall give her some hot chocolate to calm her nerves and help her sleep. She will still be sleeping when we leave. She will never wake. I shall give the boy a little, too. He's too questioning these days. Do you know he actually took a liking to that pig of a MacGregor? His champion, he calls him. You should see her face when he rants on about him . . .'

'I don't understand your hatred,' Angus said, shaking his head. 'God help you if the master ever finds out! First his wife, now the daughter . . .'

'Quiet, you fool! You said you would never speak of that. Remember, there is much about you that I could tell.'

With a grimace, he turned and went out into the cold, grey November afternoon. Effie was smiling as she followed him, despite the unpleasant wind which chilled her to the bone. Soon she would be back at Ard Choille. Mistress of Ard Choille . . . Phillip's mistress. Beautiful dresses, a carriage and horses of her own. People would bow when she rode past, and speak to her with respect. She felt very pleased with herself.

The inn-keeper cursed whoever was knocking on his door at midnight. He had been sound asleep in his comfortable feather-bed for the past hour, and now he was dragged from it into the cold. And for what? Probably another drunken fool who had mistaken his inn for one of the many taverns which also lay on the outskirts of the town. He had threatened to move a dozen times. One day, he would.

The man who pushed past him, shaking the sleet from his thick cloak, was no drunkard. There was something very purposeful about the way his eyes scanned the room about him, swept towards the stairs and the landing where the guest-rooms were situated. He dwarfed the inn-keeper, who was barely five feet six, as he strode to the fire and thrust his hands out towards the flames. The man took one look at the scarred cheek, taut with cold, gazed into the cold eyes and knew chilling fear. He was going to be robbed! Murdered! Discarding his cloak, Douglas flung it across a wooden bench and found the inn-keeper's eyes riveted on his sword.

'You are in no danger from me. I want only information. Then I suggest you go back to bed and forget I am here. I seek a young woman. Black hair, grey eyes. The Comtesse de Saint-Rémy. She could have arrived yesterday, or even this morning. She has a young boy with her, and a maid,' Douglas said in curt, clipped tones, and waited impatiently for the man to gather his sleepy thoughts.

'Saint Rémy? No . . . No one by that name. There is a Madame Bellancourt here. There was a boy with her when she arrived, but he has gone now.'

'Gone? Where? When? Who took him? Quickly, man, every minute could be precious.'

'Where?' The man scratched his head. How was he supposed to think at midnight? And standing in a draughty room in only his underwear? 'Why—they took ship for Scotland, I believe. Not all. Only the man and the boy. The woman—the maid—was coming back because her mistress is ill. Pity, that . . . good-looking woman.' He cried out as Douglas leapt across the space between them and caught him by the front of his worn undershirt.

'Ill? Where is she? Which room?' Only with a supreme effort did he control the urge to shake the man until his teeth rattled. 'For the love of God, which room?'

'Third door on your left at the top of the stairs.' He was released so abruptly that he fell back on to Douglas's cloak. His startled gaze followed the tall figure as he took the stairs two at a time, and suddenly realised where he was going. 'Wait, come back! You can't go up there. Madame will be sleeping. Come back, I say!'

He was not to the top of the stairs when Douglas threw open the door of Sian's room. It was in darkness, but the light of the candle which came up behind him, held by a wheezing, blustering inn-keeper, illuminated the still figure on the bed.

'Light a lamp at once! That one by the bed,' he snapped, and the man had obeyed before realising how instinctive had been the reaction.

'You can't wake her . . .' he began, as Douglas bent over the woman who lay still and white, like a marble statue, beneath the bedclothes.

'Pray I can, my friend,' came the frightening reply. Douglas took Sian by the shoulders and shook her roughly. The man opened his mouth to protest, watched the woman's head loll limply back like one dead, and crossed himself, moving back from the bed.

'Stay where you are, I need you to get things for me.

Give me that candle.' He snatched the light and placed it against a book lying on the small table by the bed. Eyes narrowed to murderous slits as he saw the glass there, still containing remnants of chocolate. So that was how they had administered it! Effie Campbell and her murdering brother. They were well matched. Each a killer without mercy. Should Sian die by their hands, they would die by his . . . even if it meant returning to Scotland. Perhaps he had always been meant to return!

He thrust a hand inside the lawn nightgown against her breast. Beneath her fingers, the throb of life was still quite strong. They had not expected her to be found until morning, he realised.

'The woman said she was ailing, and soon to die,' the inn-keeper cried, not liking the way this man turned to stare at him. Those eyes . . . and that sword—and he wore a knife at his belt! He would never reach the stairs alive if he ran.

'You said they had left. When?'

'Madame retired about eight. The maid told me she would not be travelling to Scotland for another few days. She was going to accompany her brother to the boat, and then return. Well, I suppose she has. I didn't see her come in, but then I can't watch out for every-body! My orders were not to disturb madame before eleven tomorrow morning.'

'By then she would have been dead, and I think I might have been tempted to take your life in lieu,' Douglas replied, straightening. 'As it is, there is a chance to save her. Look in the maid's room and see if she is back, then bring me water—jugs of warm water and plenty of salt. And send someone for a doctor. I want one here within the hour.'

'You—you have money? You can pay?'

'I have more than enough. I also have a very sharp sword. Which would you prefer?'

The man fled from the room. Douglas kicked the door closed after him and took off his doublet. Discarding his sword, he laid it within easy reach and turned back towards the bed. His lips moved in a silent prayer as he lifted Sian from it and began to try to revive her. Praying to a God he had rejected in bitterness and anger ten long years ago!

# CHAPTER
# TWELVE

SHE WAS drowning, Sian thought, seized with panic as more salt water trickled down her throat. The ship was sinking! She struck out at whatever was holding her, and heard someone curse close by her ear. Drowning? How could she be—she had never set foot on the ship . . . Angus had booked the passages for all four of them, but she was still at the inn!

Her limbs felt like lead. She was sick and giddy.

'Go away, Effie. Let me sleep. I want to sleep until it's time to leave for the ship. Go away . . .' Her voice trailed off drowsily. She tried to open her eyes, but her lids were so heavy . . . She had felt like this once before, but when? Where?

She gasped, then coughed, as her head was forced back and more water flowed into her mouth. Salt again! She was going to be sick.

'Drink it!' That voice! 'Do you hear me, woman? Drink it. If you sleep now, you will not wake.'

Only one person had ever called her 'woman' in that mocking tone. She dragged her eyes open, blinked dazedly at the hard, brown face staring into hers and a hoarse scream escaped her lips.

'You! You followed me! You mean to kill me!' Effie was right . . . Zara had not lied! He had come to finish what he started. Where was Timothy? Where were her maid and Angus? 'What have you done with them? Have you killed them, too?' she cried in a trembling voice, and the hard eyes glittered angrily. Why did he look angry?

His arm tightened round her waist as she feebly struggled to free herself, tears beginning to stream down her ashen cheeks. Strands of loose hair clung to her wet skin as she realised how weak and helpless she was, and she collapsed against him, sobbing wildly.

'Walk!' he ordered, and dragged her across the room when her leaden feet refused to function. 'You must walk. You can't sleep!'

'Why not?' Her gaze fell on the still half-full glass of chocolate, and he nodded grimly. 'Drugged? Oh, no! Effie has betrayed me, too! Did you bribe her with money I gave you?' She gave a short laugh, and he heard a note of hysteria in it.

'I bribed no one, little fool! Effie and her brother are behind it all . . . carrying out Phillip Blakeney's orders, I've no doubt. Didn't I tell you what a swine he was? Why didn't you believe me?'

He raised a glass of water to her lips. Sian twisted her head away, but he forced it back ruthlessly and made her drink. For the next hour, while she called him every name she could think of, every impolite description she would never have dreamed of using in her life before, he forced her to walk. Backwards and forwards round the room. As the mists cleared from her eyes, and reality forced its way past the curtain of the dream world into which she had been slipping—which she had found so inviting, so peaceful—she saw he had moved all the furniture against the walls to give them free passage.

He sat on a chair, wrapped a cloak round her shoulders, brushing away her loose hair with a gentleness that made her remember other times when they had shared tender moments.

'What do you want with me?' she asked wearily. At that moment she did not care if she lived or died. Timothy! Another rush of tears began as she thought of him. If he was still in danger, what could she do to help him? She had tried so hard—and failed.

'I want you to do exactly as I say, and in doing so save your life,' Douglas returned, bending over her to take her hands in his. They were as cold as ice. She sat unbelievingly as he chafed them slowly, bringing warmth to the blue fingers. The eyes which looked up at her again contained no anger now. No hatred—no reproach.

'I don't understand! She said you were responsible . . .'

'Zara? I know. She lied. She gave Angus Campbell poison to kill you, on Effie's orders. It was Effie who killed Roland. Who else could have gone down to the cellar that night and come up so close behind him without his sensing the danger? She killed him, and freed René. He was meant to kill you. Then she would have taken Timothy back to Scotland—to her lover. Her very rich lover.'

'No! No!' Sian moaned. It was all too much for her confused mind to absorb. 'She could not hate us enough to kill us . . . We have never done anything to her. You lie! I have no reason to believe you. You hate Phillip; you would do anything to get back at him for the death of your mother and father!'

Douglas dragged her to her feet, curbing the impulse to slap her. He deserved her scorn, though it was hard to stand still and take it without retaliation. And he would not only tell her so, but show her, when she had recovered from this ordeal.

More walking, more salt water. She felt as if she would burst. Her vision was clearer now, but she was disoriented and could not stand by herself. Just when he thought his desperate remedy had had no effect, Sian gulped uneasily and pressed her hands over her mouth. Her stomach heaved. She retched . . . He spun her quickly round and held her over the basin he had put ready, and thanked God his prayers had been answered.

Sian was never aware of time when she opened her eyes. She alternated between periods of extreme cold —when she shivered in the bed and nothing could warm her—to growing uncomfortably warm, and perspiration would stream from her face, soak her loose hair and nightgown, and she would throw back the covers, gasping for air. They were always replaced and tucked firmly in as she tossed and turned in her fever.

The man bending over her, when she opened her

eyes with the realisation that she was feeling much
better and actually hungry—was not Douglas! He was
in his sixties, grey-haired, with a thin pointed face, but
kind eyes into which a smile came as she stared at him
apprehensively.

'At last you have returned to us, young woman.
About time! Quiet. No questions for the moment. Let
me finish my examination,' he said in an authoritative
tone as she opened her mouth to speak. She lay in
silence while he proceeded to take her pulse and listen
to her heart. 'It's good that you are strong and healthy,
or you would not have survived. You should thank
God for your good fortune, madame, and the timely
intervention of your husband.'

'Husband?' Sian echoed in a husky tone. Her throat
felt dry and sore.

The doctor turned and motioned to the small makeshift bed which stood against another wall. Outstretched
on it, his tall frame looking awkward and uncomfortable
on the spindly contraption at least a foot too short for
his height, lay Douglas. One arm was tucked beneath
his head. Instinctively she wondered if he had his dirk
beneath the pillow. His face was relaxed in sleep, wiping
away the hardness she was accustomed to seeing, the
lines of tension and mistrust so often there. Stray curls
of blond hair fell across his forehead, making him appear
unusually vulnerable.

'My—my husband,' she began, and the man at her
side smiled.

'Has known no sleep since he found you. But for
him, you would have slipped into unconsciousness long
before I arrived. Luckily he knew what to do. It saved
your life.'

'Yes,' Sian said with a nod, and relapsed into silence
again.

'I'll be back to see you tomorrow, madame. You must
remain in bed for at least three days, and take extreme
care with your health over the next few months. Drink
plenty of liquids, but no food until tomorrow. I will
have a few words with the inn-keeper when I leave, so

that he does not tempt your appetite with all the wrong things.'

'Thank you for all you have done, Dr . . .?'

'Talignac. Goodbye until tomorrow.' He took one slender hand in his and shook it slightly. 'And he is the one to thank, not me,' he added, looking once more at the sleeping figure behind him.

How do I do that? Sian wondered, as she lay back amid the pillows. She had accused him of the most dreadful things, threatened to have him killed! Even considered the ridiculous suggestion herself. And he was innocent! She raised a trembling hand to her aching eyes. She wanted to sleep again, but she could not.

There was a slight movement from the other bed. Douglas sat up, stretching cramped limbs, and it came into her mind that he had not been sound asleep, but listening to every word spoken, as he remarked,

'The doctor is pleased with you. Can you manage a little warm milk? Or thin soup? I expect the kitchen can provide something. The inn-keeper is terrified that something you ate here made you ill, and that I shall sue him if you die.'

'As my husband, it would be your right,' Sian answered quietly, and his lips twitched with the hint of a smile. He stood up and came to the bed and looked down at her. Instantly his gaze made her feel warm, whereas a moment ago she had shivered, realising she wore nothing beneath the bedclothes.

'It saved a great many questions. The authorities know the truth. I spoke with them yesterday and gave them all the facts. They will want to talk to you, probably tomorrow when you have rested. There is little they can do to lay their hands on Effie and her brother, but if they ever set foot in France again, they will be arrested at once. Blakeney, too. I found this in the book beside you.' Sian stared at the letter she had written to Jeanne, and raised astonished eyes to his face. What did she see there? Reproach, condemnation for what she had written—her fears that he was involved? If he had read that, he had also read where she had poured out her

heart to her friend, her confession of love . . . 'You will
have the devil's own job getting Timothy away from his
own father. You do realise that, don't you? Who is
going to believe he was behind everything so that his
son would inherit?'

Wordlessly Sian shook her head. Someone, somewhere, had to believe her story.

'I gave that letter to Effie in Paris.' At last she found
her voice. 'She said she had despatched it to Versailles
. . . the same afternoon Zara came to see me. I
thought . . .'

'To forestall me if I was planning to waylay your
coach?' Douglas demanded, a steely quality creeping
into his tone. 'Little fool! Do you think I would have
gone to all the trouble of riding the Calais road? I could
have had you taken from the house at any time I chose,
and your servants could not have stopped me. If I had
wanted you dead . . . If,' he emphasised harshly, 'as
revenge against Blakeney, your death would be at my
hands, do you hear? At no other's.'

His voice was so fierce that she flinched, and immediately he sat beside her, caught up her hands and held
them tightly between his. He could feel her trembling,
and an expletive escaped beneath his breath. 'Woman,
do I look as if I want to kill you? Far from it.'

She did not resist as he bent and sought her mouth,
forcing apart her stiff lips in a kiss that brought a low
moan of despair from deep in her throat. She had no
defence against him, and he knew it!

'Do you fear me, Sian? Do you?'

'No,' she answered truthfully and without hesitation.
'Not any more. You are right, I am a fool. How could
I have believed . . .'

He silenced her with his lips and she lay passive
against him, enjoying what he had to give her now,
longing for more, but content if he had nothing more
to offer. He had made no promises. She asked for none
—only to be with him and allow her to love him. She
said so when he released her and drew away, and a
strange light flickered in the depths of his eyes.

'I turned down your offer once before. I'll not do so again,' he said. His words raised fresh hope in her.

'Oh, Douglas, hold me,' she begged. 'Tell me the nightmare is over?'

She stretched out her arms to him, but he stood, and they fell back as she looked at him, not understanding.

'Do you realise how close I came to losing you?' he said, his voice unsteady. 'Another hour could have been too late. If you had finished that chocolate . . . If only I could get my hands on those two! I am going downstairs to fetch you something nourishing. You have been here for three days, do you know that? You are weak. You need to regain your strength again before we think of travelling.'

'Yes,' she murmured, not realising at that moment their plans of travel would take them in opposite directions and bring more pain. 'I shall do as you wish. I am in your hands.'

Sian managed to hold down two bowls of beef soup, after which she slept again. She slept most of the following day. Each time she awoke, she knew her strength was slowly returning. She should not make the sea-crossing for at least a week, she thought, but as the days passed and she grew stronger, she knew she could not wait so long. What if Douglas was wrong about one thing? What if Phillip was not the mind behind the whole thing? Did Effie's hatred of her mistress extend to little Timothy? Was he included in her list of death? Phillip then would inherit everything, and she would be there to share it. Only Sian could prevent that, and to do so, she had to return quickly to Scotland.

Douglas had told her of Peppito's help in proving Zara's complicity in the plot, but he gave few details of the time he had spent alone with his mistress before he left the Coq d'Or. And he made light of the wild ride to Calais, almost killing his horse in the process, he told her, with that half-smile that indicated he was not being as forthcoming as she would have liked. One day she would ask him again . . . when the memories were not so painful.

'I need to return to Scotland. I must go to the authorities and have Effie and Angus brought to trial for
Roland's murder and Timothy's abduction. I shall never
have a good night's sleep again if I do not.' Sian's lips
trembled as she spoke the words she knew would part
them yet again.

'Go back? To Ard Choille!' Douglas, who was sitting
on the edge of the bed, holding her hand and deep in
thought, looked astonished, then furious. 'For the love
of heaven, woman, you will be signing your own death-
warrant if you set foot there again—as I would.' He
sprang to his feet, eyes blazing. 'You are not serious? I
will not allow it.'

'Yes, I am serious. You cannot stop me, Douglas. I
must go.'

'You make no mention of Phillip Blakeney. Is he to
go free?'

'If Timothy is alive and well, I shall know he was
involved. If—if anything has happened to him, or I
suspect his life is in danger, then I shall be certain that
Effie and her brother were behind everything. Phillip
loves his son in his own strange way. I do not believe
he would allow him to be harmed. He plans to mould
him in his own image.'

'Poor mite,' Douglas growled dryly, and she felt him
beginning to slip away from her.

'I want you to book me a passage on the first ship
going to Scotland. I have lingered too long as it is,' she
insisted.

'You had damned little choice,' he snapped, and she
winced.

'I have now. The doctor said a week, but I cannot
stay as long as that. Timothy's life could be in danger.
I am not strong yet, I know, but I will shut myself in
the cabin for the whole trip and rest. Then, when I
arrive, I shall go direct to the Procurator-fiscal in Inverness and tell him everything. I shall ask him to send
someone back to the house with me to confront the
others. You see, I have thought it all out. I shall not be
in danger.'

'And what am I supposed to do?' Douglas demanded ungraciously. He could not believe she was serious. Could not believe she was willing to risk her life again, throw away this chance for them both to seize a little happiness . . .

'Will you go to the château and wait for me?' she asked, an expression of pleading in her eyes.

He turned to her, caught her by the shoulders as if he were about to shake her—but he did not.

'You little fool! Little fool!' he repeated softly, and his voice broke. At the same time tears came into Sian's eyes. Never had she thought to see him bordering on losing control. He did care! He could not find the words, but he cared!

Her fingers traced the line of his mouth, caressed the scarred cheek. He turned his mouth against the palm and kissed it tenderly.

'I deserve your anger . . .' she began.

He stopped her mouth with his own, and neither spoke for a long while.

'There is nothing I can do to prevent you, I know it . . . short of using force, and that I cannot do, even though it is the only answer,' Douglas said at length.

Tears welled up in her eyes. If he had hit her, she would not have reproached him. The pain in his expression cut her like a knife-blade.

'Go to the château . . . wait for me. I shall come to you as soon as I can.' He did not answer, and her heart almost stopped beating in fear. 'Do you believe I love you? I will come back, I swear it.'

'If you are alive, perhaps you will,' came the quiet answer.

'Douglas . . .' He turned away, and alarm flashed through her as she watched him slide the scabbard containing the broadsword over his shoulder. Securing his cloak, he turned back and she sat up, knowing this was their moment of parting. Was he not going to stay with her until she went on board? Yet perhaps that, for either of them, would have been too cruel.

'I'll make arrangements for you to sail on the first

available ship.' His voice was without emotion, his
features grey and drawn in the dullness of the room.
'I'll send back details by your coachman.'

'Do we have to part in this way?' Sian said tremulously. He was letting her go, without lifting a finger to
stop her. To do so would mean either tying her to a
horse and dragging her back to Paris, where he had no
doubt he could keep her adequately amused until such
time as she gave up all plans to return to Ard Choille.

Or he could go with her, and that would mean certain
death. She knew it—which was why she had not enlisted
his help on this final foolish venture, he realised, and
again, his heart momentarily warmed towards her. Little
fool!

'You will go back?' she pleaded.

'Yes,' Douglas said, with a sigh, and watched her
relax in relief. 'I am going back. I shall wait for you.'

As the door closed behind him, she sank back on
the pillows, overcome with tears. She had not meant to
cry, she could not afford any show of weakness any
more, but suddenly she came to realise how alone she
was . . .

Word of a passage late that afternoon was brought to
her by the coachman who had accompanied Douglas to
the shipping office. Douglas stood out of sight by one
of the wharves as she alighted from the coach and
went on board, waited until the servant had taken her
luggage, and then went to stand beside the coach for
the man's return.

'She is settled?' he asked, and the coachman nodded.
Douglas pointed to the black horse whose reins were
tied to the back of the carriage. 'Take him back with
you. God willing, I shall ride him again one day.'

'Good luck, monsieur. Take care of the Comtesse.'
The man asked no questions; it was not his place, even
though he had been overcome with curiosity ever since
he first realised Douglas, too, was sailing for Scotland.
A curious match, he had always thought. The gentle
Comtesse and this rough mercenary. But he had saved

her life and he must care for her, or why else would he
be risking his neck returning home?

Douglas's mouth deepened into a smile. He adjusted
his cloak the better to conceal the sword at his back,
and pulled his hat down over his features. Without a
word he turned and walked slowly up the gangplank.
He had booked his own passage in the name of Roland
Saint-Rémy. If anyone thought it necessary to ask if
there was a connection between himself and the woman
in another cabin who bore the same name, he intended
to say that she was his wife. For personal reasons they
wished to be regarded as travelling separately. They
could think what they liked, he cared not one iota. Sian
would remain resting in her cabin, of that he was sure,
so he was in no danger. Not until he set foot on the soil
of Scotland again. The hard, brown earth of his beloved
Rannoch . . . Why did he feel no fear?

Sian stayed in her cabin for most of the tedious journey
to Leith, venturing out only in the evenings after dinner
for air, and then she remained on the cold, dark deck
for no more than a few minutes. Arrival in Leith found
her dull-eyed, with shadows of tiredness standing out
against ashen cheeks, yet somehow she had the strength
to dress and drag herself from the ship. She found herself
standing at the bottom of the gangplank, surrounded by
her baggage, not knowing where to go or what to do
next. She had never had to fend for herself like this
before. Journeys were always well planned in advance,
usually by Roland, or by the servants acting on her
instructions. Now, here she was alone in a strange town,
feeling stupid and helpless. It was because she felt so
ill, she thought, sitting down on the largest trunk behind
her. She was a sensible, level-headed person, and
extremely independent. At least she thought so. She
wondered what Douglas would have said about that?
She had been neither sensible nor level-headed since
the day she first saw him.

By now he would be back at the château. She had
given her coachman the letter that Effie had delayed,

with orders to deliver it into the hands of Madame de Pompadour personally. To it she had added another page, relating how Douglas had followed her to Calais and again saved her life, and that she was now in no doubt as to his innocence. He was safe, and would be so until she returned. She shivered and drew her cloak more firmly about her, telling herself firmly it was on account of the cold, and not fear.

The ship was being made ready to return to France. People milled around her almost knocking her over as they made for the gangplank, carrying trunks and kegs and luggage of various shapes and sizes. How she wished she could be on it . . . She had to hire a carriage to take her to Inverness. Pull yourself together, she reproved sharply. Sitting here, with people smirking at you, will not get you back to Douglas. And that was what she wanted with all her heart.

As she rose to her feet, a wave of giddiness washed over her and she swayed unsteadily. A well-dressed man in a dark suit turned and steadied her.

'Are you not well, miss?' he inquired politely.

'Can you help me? I need to hire a carriage.'

'Surely you are more in need of a doctor? My carriage is across the street. Let me take you to one. Surely your business cannot be so pressing as to endanger your health,' the man murmured, but she stubbornly shook her head.

'A carriage, if you please. That is all I want. I must get to Inverness as soon as possible.'

'There are many people going aboard ships here, so there may be a carriage for hire. Wait a moment, and I'll see what I can do.'

'Thank you,' Sian murmured gratefully and resumed her seat on the trunk. He returned in less than ten minutes, smiling as he came to a halt before her.

'You are in luck! I have found a driver who is willing to take you where you want to go. Leave your baggage; he will fetch it in a moment.'

In her relief, Sian failed to notice many things. The fact that her companion was English, not a Scot, and that his clothes, though well pressed and neat, showed signs of wear and were certainly not the clothes of a gentleman . . . and in Scotland, in those days of poverty and hardship for all, only the rich or the English gentry who had come to take over prime Scottish land possessed carriages.

A hand solicitously beneath her arm, he escorted her away from the quay, to where a carriage with four snorting, impatient horses waited. Sian could have cried with relief at the sight of it. The journey to Inverness would tax her strength to its ultimate, but once there she could rest after telling her gruesome tale to the Procurator-fiscal . . . rest before she set out for Ard Choille and the task of facing Effie and Angus with their crimes. They could suspect nothing. They thought her dead! The sight of her alive and well might just be the inducement needed to break one of them into confessing. And then she would go home to Douglas, to the arms which would be waiting, the peace, the knowledge she need no longer be afraid.

'Here we are, miss. Let me help you inside.' The carriage door opened as they drew near. Something inside her cried out a warning—why, she did not know —and she tried to hang back, but it was too late. Her companion lifted her bodily from the ground and thrust her inside. Another man caught her arm, dragging her down beside him.

'Don't scream, my dear, or Johnson will be forced to silence you, and he can be very rough and unpleasant when he chooses!' Phillip smiled into her horrified face as she choked back a cry and sank, half-fainting, in her seat. The man who had helped her climbed in and closed the door, and Phillip called up to the coachman to move off. *She* was being abducted!

It could not be! How was he here? She tried to speak, but no words came. She stared at the figure beside her as if he were some frightful apparition of death come to claim her for the hereafter. If Douglas's suspicions were right, he was!?

'Here am I, preparing to embark for the shores of

France to find out what has happened to you, and you
reappear before me like someone back from the dead,'
Phillip murmured, reaching out a hand to push away
the hood from her face. 'Dear me, you look like a ghost.
Effie always was heavy-handed in everything she did.'

Sian looked into the glittering eyes, and knew terror.
'You know she tried to kill me?' she whispered. She
was seized with the idea of flinging open the door and
jumping out, but she doubted if her fingers would ever
have reached the catch. Johnson was watching her con-
stantly. He looked a cold, ruthless man, the sort Phillip
had always liked to have about him. Men who obeyed
his orders without question so long as he paid them.
'He was right! You were behind it all . . . Roland . . .'

'But of course, my dear, although Effie had to persuade me that getting rid of you would be worth while.
It would have been, though, don't you agree, so that
Timothy inherited everything? But she blundered. And
as for that brother of hers . . .' His lips drew back over
his teeth in a wolfish smile which made the cruel features
look even more menacing. 'Johnson has taken his place.
And my son is safe at home, in his father's loving care.'

Sian knew instinctively that Angus had gone the same
way as René and Roland. She fought to keep control
of her senses, knowing tears were of little use against
this inhuman monster who took life without a qualm.
She had to stay in control, to fight him with every
weapon at her disposal—but she had none! He would
kill her, too. She would never see Douglas again! He
would think, in time, that she had abandoned him. No,
he could never do that! He would realise that she, too,
had fallen victim to his arch enemy, but there would be
nothing he could do. To return to these shores meant
certain death. At least in France he was safe!

Phillip Blakeney was in his late forties. As Laird of
Ard Choille, he knew he was hated, and cared not one
jot. He had few diversions these days. Girls from the
village came and went from his bed and left no
impression on him. Few women did, except those whose
appetites were as depraved as his own. His own wife

had hated him and made it necessary to dispose of her. And then there was Effie. Solace for a while, but he wearied of her and her incessant demands that she become first lady of Ard Choille. A whore, mistress of his home!

Now, if it was Sian! She had always remained aloof from him, rebuffing his advances. He looked at the figure cringing from him in one corner. She was his, now, and this time her cold looks and scornful remarks would not deter him from taking what he wanted.

'Why do you look at me like that?' Sian cried, catching her breath. His gaze stripped her, and he cared not that she saw it and understood his intentions. 'What are you going to do with me?'

'Your taste in men leaves much to be desired,' Phillip said harshly. 'I thought I'd killed him. No matter! He had a little fun with you, I believe, by way of revenge against me. How futile. I shall do my best to assuage your wounded pride. You will not find me as uncouth as your Scotsman.'

'I will—die before I let myself be pawed by you,' Sian sobbed, open fear registering on her face. She could no longer hide it.

'No, you will not, my dear. Not until I have finished with you—and I think that will be a very long time.'

# CHAPTER
# THIRTEEN

FOR ONE whole day Sian remained locked in her rooms, seeing no one except the timid little maid who brought her food and was too frightened of the threats she had received to speak a single word. Then Phillip came unannounced into her sitting-room on the morning of the second day. She turned from the window, where she had been sitting when he returned from hunting, and faced him calmly. There was no trace of fear on her lovely face as she demanded,

'How long am I to be kept a prisoner in my own home?'

'That depends on you, my dear Sian.' He ran his eyes over her slender figure. Her deep burgundy woollen gown flattered her colouring, despite the paleness of her cheeks and the grey shadows lingering under her eyes. He suspected she had not slept since she had been brought back. Her choice! When he chose to take her, nothing would stop him, not even a pretended show of illness. 'You are at liberty to come downstairs at any time, providing you give me your word, here and now, not to give any hint of what you know to Timothy. You really should think of being sensible, you know. The boy is most upset for you. I have had to reprimand him this morning, and confined him to his room. His rudeness was intolerable. His months in France have not taught him manners, as I had hoped. His sole conversation is of you and MacGregor. He seems to have formed some childish attachment for the man.'

'That is not surprising! He saved his life,' Sian returned coldly. 'You should be grateful to him—if you know what gratitude is, and I doubt that.'

'My, what a sharp tongue we have these days! Did

your mercenary friend teach you how to handle yourself out of bed as well as in? I look forward to seeing if you heeded well his experienced lessons,' Phillip chuckled. The prospect excited him. She was young and fresh, although well used, he had no doubt, by the MacGregor he had failed to kill ten years before. It mattered not. She would amuse him for a time.

Sian blenched at his mocking taunt. Of course Effie had told him everything, but she still believed Douglas had deserted her. She did not know he had followed her to the inn. Sian had told them she awoke and was violently sick in the night, which the doctor, when he came to attend her, said had saved her life. She made no mention of him. If Phillip had sent his assassins across the Channel to kill her and Roland, he might do the same for Douglas. She would not be the cause of his death!

Phillip frowned at the faint smile which lit up her features. 'Why do you smile? Does the prospect of coming to my bed no longer frighten you?'

'It never frightened me! It nauseated me, and it still does,' she returned with a sudden show of spirit that told him their first encounter would be a stormy one. It excited him even more.

Sian watched him ride away from the house early that afternoon, so she was not afraid of her privacy being invaded for several hours at least. Even so, her nerves felt as taut as bowstrings. She sat for hours by the window, looking out across the rainswept landscape, wishing herself back at the château and knowing she would never see it again. Ard Choille was high above Rannoch Forest, beside a small tributary of Loch Ericht. The view from her window was breathtakingly beautiful, even on a dull day.

She could see Sgór Gaibhe, some three thousand feet high, close to the mountain where Charles Stuart was rumoured to have hidden from the English, safe and snug in a cave on Ben Alder called 'Cluny's Cage', until a boat had come to take him to France and permanent exile. A romantic figure, she had always felt somewhat

sorry for the unfortunate Prince and the followers destined for death and hardship, deportation, the destruction of their way of life. More so now that she had met
Douglas and knew what he personally had suffered.
And, for their part in it all, men like Phillip had been
rewarded with lands and fine houses and titles. It was
unjust!

She had tried many times to draw out Robert Mac-
Nish, the oldest retainer in the house, on the subject of
those who had lived in Ard Choille before her, but he
had only given her a solemn look and said they were
dead and gone and could not be helped with talk. She
knew now that Phillip had warned him and all the other
servants of the consequences of relating any part of his
involvement in the taking of Ard Choille before it
became his property by an act of the Crown.

His property, she thought, stretching out on the bed
and staring up at the muralled ceiling. It never belonged
to him. It was Douglas's still—and she was here,
beneath his roof! Which had been his room? she wondered. There were so many in the house. She had one
of the larger ones on the first floor, above what had
once been a magnificent ballroom. It was never used
these days, except when Phillip gathered all his cronies
and their women and tried to recapture those by-gone
days. She realised now how badly he had failed. Ard
Choille, from the way Douglas had spoken of his
parents, must have been a gay place, the village bustling
with activity.

Without wanting to, she slept, still fully dressed,
across the four-poster bed. She was roused by a strange
grating sound that brought her up on one elbow in
alarm. The room was in darkness. She had been sleeping
for hours, exhausted, and incapable of staving it off at
long last. Where was the candle? What was it—a rat?
No, more like the sound of a key being turned cautiously
in a lock. Her heart rose in her mouth. She pressed a
hand across her lips to choke back a scream. Phillip!
He had returned early and come to her!

Hardly daring to breathe, she recoiled against the

back of the bed until she could go no further. The creak of a door . . . not the bedroom door, for that opened on well-oiled hinges . . . a beam of light. Dear God, she was going to faint! Was she imagining things? There was only one door in her room. From the depths of the shadows someone began to whistle softly . . . It came out of the darkness to her like a peal of golden bells. She gasped—choking back another cry, this time of disbelief . . . joy!

The grinning features behind the candlelight swam before her vision. Douglas gave an oath as her eyes closed, and thrust the candle into Robert's hand.

'Take this, man. We've frightened her half to death,' he muttered, striding to the bed.

'Not us, master. He! You don't know the things he's been saying to the poor wee thing,' the old man said in a fierce whisper, and Douglas's face became grim as he gathered Sian into his arms.

'I saw him hit her; that was enough to set my blood boiling.'

'You heard,' Sian said faintly. She could not believe it was his voice, his arms that held her against his chest, and then his mouth was on hers and she knew without a doubt that it was no dream, but wonderful reality. For a moment she lost herself in the ecstasy of his kiss, his touch, holding him as though he might suddenly vanish from her sight. He groaned as he ran his hands over her body, and she knew somehow he was aware of the days of agony she had been forced to endure.

'You fool!' she gasped, and thrust him away. 'Are you mad? You are risking your life in coming here. Oh, Douglas, you are in such grave danger!'

'I've lived with danger all my life, woman,' came the low reply. 'I'm not afraid of it.'

'I'm afraid—for you! If you are caught, you will be hanged. Why?'

'I came for you,' he said, reading the unspoken question in her eyes. 'But I won't leave—if I leave at all—without settling with him. There's more now . . . for you.'

He touched her cheek with gentle fingers, wiped away a trace of tears. She looked exhausted, frightened, helpless. He had never seen her quite so lost before. Sian laid her head against his shoulder and began to cry. He looked up at the silent manservant at the bedside, and said urgently, 'Bring the whisky, man, she's in dire need of it.'

He hugged Sian in his arms, rocking her gently like a baby, soothing her, his lips against her hair. She felt him remove the pins and loosen it about her shoulders, turned her face up to his, hoping he would kiss her, comfort her in the way she knew they both needed, but he only laid his lips against her cheek, and said softly, 'Don't greet, lass.' It was an old word his nanny had always used. He could only ever remember saying it to his mother. 'Don't cry, I can't bear to see it. Blakeney won't lay a finger on you, I swear it. I've come to get you safely away, and then I'll settle with him. It's the only way.'

'That's why you really came, isn't it?' she said dully. Robert put a bottle of whisky on the table, and a glass. Douglas nodded, and he filled it. She turned her head away as a strong smell invaded her nostrils. 'I don't want any.'

'It's *usquebaugh*—the best. I should know! It's been hidden in the cellars for years, thanks to Robert here. He's been quite a little squirrel in his way; haven't you, you old rogue?'

To Sian's surprise, the old man's leathery face split into a wide grin. She could not recall ever seeing him smile like this. He was always polite—servile, even. Never jolly, never friendly.

'This and that, master Douglas. Things I knew you would want when you returned. I knew you would come back, you see.'

'You knew more than I did,' Douglas said, putting the glass to Sian's lips and making her drink. It went down her throat like nectar and reached her stomach like the fires of hell. She gasped and choked and pressed her face into his doublet. 'Good stuff, eh?' He downed the rest and gave an appreciative nod. 'That's all I've had for the past two days to keep me company.'

'Two days?' She looked at him, startled. 'But how?'

'Despite your nasty suspicions, woman, I came only for you. I know Blakeney, remember? I was on the same ship. I saw you taken on the quayside, and glimpsed his face as the carriage drove off, so it was easy to guess what had happened and where he would bring you. He has plans for you, I believe?'

Sian shuddered, drawing back from him. Despite her loathing of the *usquebaugh*, she had to admit it had warmed her. He had never intended her to face Phillip alone, despite the danger to himself!

'I don't want to talk about him—it's you I'm concerned for. How do you mean to take me away? Where? You cannot roam the countryside. If your identity becomes known . . .'

'I shall swing at the end of a rope. I have accepted that. It will be worth it, if he is dead and you are mistress here. I should like that.'

'Douglas!' she gasped, horrified, knowing he was serious.

'You don't think I'm going to turn about and walk away from here and let him live, do you? Even for love of you, woman!'

She stiffened, and it came to him what he had said. He nodded slowly.

'Ay, I love you. The only woman in my whole life I have ever said that to.'

'Then let us not talk of hanging,' she pleaded. 'We can send someone for the Procurator-fiscal, and charge Phillip with murder . . .'

'On your word alone? You have no proof. Dead men tell no tales,' he snapped, angry she would not accept what must be done. 'On mine? As you say, I shall hang by name alone . . . let alone the carrying of weapons with which I shall despatch an English butcher to his maker the devil.'

'If you love me, you will not speak of death; of killing Phillip. The authorities will listen to us—they have to

—and when they have heard what happened here ten years ago, how the villagers are treated, how my brother was murdered . . . they must act. Perhaps they will not be harsh with you.'

'A prison sentence? Woman, that's death to me! Cage me?'

Douglas's eyes blazed in the flickering candlelight, and she knew she had lost her battle. He would not heed the words. He would kill Phillip, and hang for it. Or he would be killed, and she would become the mistress of a man she detested with all her heart and soul. No, she would fight on!

'If you stay, then I stay too. I am not going to let you throw your life away if I can stop you,' she said in an equally fierce tone, and he swore at her. 'Nor will that do any good! I have shared too much with you to lose you now, Douglas MacGregor. I, too, am a fighter.'

'Damn you!' Douglas exclaimed, and pulled her into his arms, silencing her with his mouth. He covered her face and lips with burning kisses, pausing for a brief moment only to say, 'We must go soon.'

'Where?'

'I know a place where you will be safe. You will stay there until I come for you. It is a cave high on Ben Alder. You tread in famous footsteps. The Prince once hid there from English soldiers. Phillip will never find it, and I shall have a guard of two loyal villagers to make sure.'

'They hate me as they do Phillip. They care not what happens to me.'

'I have told them you are my woman. If anything happens to me, they will turn to you for their orders. I leave them in good hands, I know.'

'Tell me of Ard Choille,' she breathed. 'I live here, yet I do not know it.'

'Ard Choille came about when the MacGregors were driven from their rightful lands nearly one hundred and fifty years ago. The English king, James, ordered "all of that race" to be exterminated. We were a lawless lot even then, and bowed to no man save our chieftains.

Six or seven score of desperate men were besieged at
Loch Katrine on Eliean Mharnoch, but the MacGregors
were by no means beaten, even though the odds were
overwhelming. They scattered, eastwards to Comrie
and Fortingall. Westwards to Loch Awe. They lived
in caves until a house could be built. Came out for
Montrose, and had it burned to the ground for their
trouble. Rebuilt it and called it "Ard Choille"—"High
Wood". It is the war-cry of my clan.'

So that was the strange cry he had uttered that night
he had killed Simeon! At last she was beginning to know
him.

'Ours is a history of fighting, of pain and loss—but
of survival,' Douglas said, a smile touching his lips as
memories crowded in on him. 'Of life and death, and
much in between which is never regretted. My people
took another motto in those turbulent days: "E'en do
and spare not". Blakeney will discover I still live by
those words. Come, woman, 'tis time to go. Much as I
would like to linger here with you. If I had my way . . .'

Sian laid a finger against his lips. 'You will have your
way, MacGregor of Ard Choille. And afterwards, I
shall have mine.'

He laughed softly and kissed her for a last time,
already preparing himself for what lay ahead. It was a
long, lingering kiss which drew from them more than
either had intended to give in those precious moments.

Had they not been so engrossed in each other, either
or both might have noticed that the bedroom door had
been unlocked and swung open. Sian was the first to
become aware of shadowy figures standing on the
threshold, and pushed Douglas away from her with a
warning scream. He wheeled towards his escape route,
his fingers tugging at the wrought-iron torch-holder
on the wall which, when pulled sharply downwards,
released the catch to the secret door.

As men launched themselves across the room, he
caught Sian's arm and pulled her quickly out of reach,
swung her about and thrust her through the half-open
door. As she fell to her knees on the dirt floor beyond,

she heard a cry of pain and wheeled about in time to
see one of Phillip's men sink to his knees, his hands
pressed against the wound Douglas had inflicted. He
almost tripped over her as he squeezed through the
door, barely open enough for him to get his tall frame
through, and began to close it again. Another scream
of pain as he wielded his *sgian dubh* mercilessly on a
hand that appeared round the panels.

Sian scrambled to her feet and threw all her weight
behind his, and could have cried with relief as the door
slowly began to close. Then there were others in the
passageway behind her. Someone pulled her away so
that two heavy men could take her place. As the door
sank into place, a heavy iron bar was wedged beneath
the torch-holder and levered upwards until it broke. No
one would follow them through that door tonight.

'Douglas!' She caught her breath as he turned, and
for the first time she saw blood on his shirt. It was
Robert who came forward to help her to support the
reeling figure. 'Can you walk? Is there somewhere you
can hide?'

It was an effort to hold back the tears, but she did
so. Such pride rose inside her as he lifted a shaking
hand and laid it against a pale cheek. The ghost of a
smile touched the suddenly ashen features. And such
pride in his eyes for her courage. His woman!

'How I wish I had had you by my side ten years ago!'
he murmured.

She blinked back a tear. No show of weakness now.
It was not expected and would not be welcomed. She
had to be strong for them both.

She turned and stared into the solemn faces behind
her, many she recognised as belonging to the village.
Douglas had said that, if anything happened to him,
they would take orders from her. Would they? Some
carried pieces of stick, others gleaning-knives for the
corn. One or two had rusty old dirks, but deadly nevertheless. Only one carried a sword. An army of desperate
men who had been driven to the limit of their endurance.
Douglas's return had brought them together in one

defiant attempt to be rid of Phillip. Had any of them counted the cost, she wondered—and knew they had. Each one, including the man she loved, was willing to give up his life to see Phillip Blakeney dead.

'Come, there is a place prepared,' Robert said urgently. 'He had it made so for the two of you if he could not get you to Ben Alder.'

The house was a maze of passages and secret entrances, Sian discovered within the next harrowing minutes. She could hear the sound of voices raised in anger, the sound of blows, of cursing, as she and Robert helped Douglas along the darkened ways. There was no light, and they dared not show one. When her strength began to fail, someone took her place beside Douglas, leaving her to feel her way along grimy walls, centuries old, past rooms she had lived in for years, past Phillip's room, where he ranted and raved at the escape of his enemy and cursed the incompetence of his men.

And then they came to a long, narrow passage that led into a bare room, containing only a trestle bed and a wooden table. Wall torches, burning with a fierce light from the turpentine in them, illuminated the starkness of it.

Douglas groaned as he was lowered to the bed. Quickly she grabbed up the single rough blanket there and covered him with it. Robert turned and left them again, and she felt as if everyone, including herself, was waiting with bated breath for his return. Looking round, Sian saw no fear on the faces with her. Nor was she regarded with suspicion and mistrust any longer. They watched her kneel and lay her head against Douglas's chest . . . watched his hand slowly caress the long dark hair which fell across a bloody arm . . . and she felt they wept inside with her . . .

Robert came back with a bowl of water, towels, and a sheet that he began to tear into strips with which to bind his master's wounds. Sian stared up at the watching faces, and knew there was only one thing she could do.

'Robert, can these people return to the village unseen?' she asked.

'Yes, mistress, but they won't. They will stay with the
master until this business is finished. They know what
will happen if they fail.'

'Then they must return to their homes. Whatever
happens here now must bring them harm. It is between
Phillip Blakeney and us.'

'No, my lady. We share it all. We have waited a long
time to have our due. Ten long years. You do not
know,' a man said, and she looked into the blazing eyes
and saw the past, and nodded. She knew she did not
have the right to deprive them of their revenge.

'I know. I want only to save you from what is to come.
Have you not suffered enough?' She tried, however,
knowing the answer before it came.

'Woman, these are Highland men,' Douglas said
weakly, and grasped her by the wrist. 'My men. My
father's men. They look to me to do what has to be
done, and I shall do it. Afterwards . . . perhaps they
will be in your hands.' Painfully he eased himself into
a sitting position, despite her fierce protests. 'Ach, I've
suffered worse at the hands of the English! Bind my
sword-arm, I shall have need of it soon.'

His gaze met hers, held it, challenged her to refuse
him this demand. And demand it was, she knew. Before
the watching men, it could be no other. In silence she
did as he bid her.

'Would I could have put a ring on your finger,
woman,' he teased.

Briefly she laid her lips against his . . . without
passion.

He set her away from him and lay back with a heavy
sigh. No one spoke or moved as his eyes closed and he
drifted into a restless sleep. They could only wait until
he chose the time and place for the final encounter
that would avenge the lost souls of Rannoch who had
perished in the defence of Ard Choille and their own
homes, their loved ones and their way of life—those
ten, long, years ago.

# CHAPTER
# FOURTEEN

IT WAS impossible to keep track of time in the tiny room.
Only Robert, when he came, or one of the servant-girls,
was able to do that. Phillip was searching the house and
grounds in a mad rage, threatening to fire the crofts in
the village if someone did not reveal Douglas's hiding-
place to him, but no one came forward.

He had at least a dozen men at his command. Men
who would do anything if he paid them or threatened
them enough. She looked at the set faces around her.
Here there were seven able-bodied, vengeful men and
four of the women from the household. The desire for
revenge was written on every expression. Most of them
had had a father or mother, a son or daughter, some
relative that had died at Phillip's hands ten years ago or
fallen foul of his wrath in the years since.

Occasionally someone looked her way and she
glimpsed compassion, if not pity, in their eyes. Not
animosity, as she had been used to. Here she was with
her man, prepared to die beside him. Now she was no
different from any of them.

She knew she must not dwell on the future. If he did
not have one, then she would not. But how her mind
repeatedly returned to the happy days at the château
with Roland. She and Douglas would have been safe
there from the world, protected by the powerful name
of the King's mistress, Madame de Pompadour. The
old house would lie empty now . . . she might never see
it again. One day Timothy would inherit it. He would
like that; he had always preferred France to Scotland.
What a pity it might not be possible for Douglas to show
the boy his Scotland . . . the beauty of the countryside,
the loyalty of the people.

She slept with her head resting on Douglas's uninjured shoulder, and the villagers of Ard Choille kept vigil over their Laird and his lady, as their fathers and forefathers had done in times of old.

She awoke to find that someone had covered her with a shawl. Douglas was talking in low tones to the men, and instantly she was afraid. As his eyes met hers, she saw they burned with anger. He took her hand and slowly touched her fingers to his lips. A gesture of farewell?

'I must leave you, woman. Don't try to stop me. I have to do things my way now. I can wait no longer,' he said in a fierce whisper.

'Wait? For what? I don't understand,' Sian said, clinging to him.

'I've placed myself in the hands of the English soldiers.' He gave a short, mirthless laugh. 'They may get to hang me yet, but they will have to hurry. Blakeney is insisting he has the first attempt at taking my life. Before I came to you last night, I had Robert send a lad we could trust to Fort William. He has to tell the officer in charge that Douglas MacGregor had returned to Ard Choille, and that there would be murder done if help did not arrive. I told him to make it sound as lurid as he could, to bring them in haste.'

'Oh, Douglas,' she said weakly. 'Why? If—if Phillip was dead, we could have fled to France. No one would dare try to touch us there. We would be under the protection of Jeanne.' He had deliberately placed his life in danger!

'If anything happens to me, I have to be sure that you are safe and no longer in danger. The butcher and I have fought before. I was not wounded then, and still he bested me. He left me for dead ten years ago. Tonight he wants to finish what he failed to do then, and with this shoulder . . .' He shrugged, and slight though the movement was, it brought a grimace of pain to his lips. 'The boy should have been back by now. Perhaps they didn't believe him—or his horse went lame. It is a hundred and twenty miles to the fort. Anything could have happened.'

'Then we must wait,' she cried, and several men near by nodded agreement.

'No, I cannot. Blakeney has threatened to kill Timothy if I do not surrender myself to him within the hour. I have but a few minutes left before I face him and finish this.'

'His own son!' Sian was aghast. 'He could not harm his own flesh and blood!'

'Who would there be to accuse him of murder if you and I were dead? These people? They are loyal, and would die for me if I asked it of them, but I will not. Some of us have to live on, Sian. They—and you.'

'And you!'

'We shall see.' He straightened with a grin that touched her heartstrings with its wickedness. 'Either way I'm between the devil and the deep blue sea! If Blakeney doesn't get me, the English will. I'll have added the murder of an English gentleman to all my other crimes. But he won't get you, my love, and that's all I care about now. Come, kiss me and let me go.'

'No! You fool, you are too weak to fight him!' She was beside herself with fear and anger. He was throwing his life away!

'Would you save my life at the expense of your brother's?' he asked quietly, and bright tears started to her eyes. 'He is only seven, Sian. He has all his life ahead of him. As you have.'

And to save him from certain death, she had to relinquish the love and happiness which had been with her such a short time. She laid her head against his shoulder, gaining strength from the touch of his lips against her cheek. He tilted back her head and kissed her, and for the duration of that single, burning kiss, they were alone in the tiny room.

She sprang away from him as Phillip's distorted voice floated to her from the other side of the thick wooden panels.

'Where is he?' she breathed, and Douglas motioned to the wall behind her.

'In the Great Hall. It is time.' He held out his hand, and Robert placed in it the broadsword. The blade gleamed in the torchlight. It had been polished with loving care, she saw, and knew it was the final service the old retainer thought he would ever do for his young master.

'You are not to interfere,' he ordered Sian. 'If—if I am killed, you will be taken to safety until the soldiers come. You and Timothy. Watch my back for me, woman. Treachery comes in many ways.'

He meant Effie, Sian realised, and nodded, wishing she could appear as prepared as he did, but she could not. Nothing could ever prepare her to lose him! Robert deliberately stepped in front of her, barring the way as Douglas reached up and touched a hidden mechanism. A section of the wall began to open. She tried to pass, but another man came up beside her, and she knew that if she attempted to follow, she would be stopped.

'I have no intention of allowing him to sacrifice his life,' she said in a low tone. 'Stand aside, both of you.'

Her tone was suddenly commanding. It was an order, not a request, but for a moment she thought she would not be obeyed as Robert's gaze challenged hers. Then he gave a slight nod, and both men moved from her path.

'Where is Effie?' she asked. 'She must be found and held until the soldiers come. She can prove that everything Douglas and I tell them is the truth. She has killed without mercy, but I do not think she is a brave woman. If her own neck is at risk, she will speak.'

'With your step-father, mistress. The moment master Douglas escaped, he ordered her to bring young Timothy downstairs to the great Hall. He has men—only three I grant you—but well armed, guarding the main entrance and the stairs,' Robert told her. 'The rest are outside the house.'

'Is there no way you can come behind them, from upstairs? Are there no more passages like the one leading to my room? If we could lay our hands on a pistol.'

'You shall have your pistol, lady.' A smooth-cheeked lad of about eighteen pushed his way to her side. 'If we don't make a stand now, we're as good as dead anyway. If Blakeney lives, he'll have us killed for our part in this —our families put out of their homes. That's the very least he will do. Have you all forgotten the special pleasure he gets from inflicting great pain on a man's body—and a woman's, come to that? I haven't! He took my sister for himself last year, and she died in childbirth, carrying his bastard . . . I swore he would die then. If the Laird fails, I won't. And I'll tell him my name before I kill him. Jamie MacGregor—and proud of it!'

'Send someone with him,' Sian ordered Robert quietly as the boy spun on his heel and disappeared into the passage. 'See he does nothing foolish. Too much blood has been spilled already.'

Picking up her skirts, she bent her head low beneath the opening and stepped through—and caught her breath. To one side of her a fire blazed in the enormous hearth. Directly in front of her was the main door, brass-studded and hinged. And barred, she noticed, with a sinking feeling in her stomach. Phillip was taking no chances of anyone leaving. One of his men stood before it, a dirk in his belt, pistol in his hand. Another was positioned at the bottom of the staircase. A third, by one of the latticed windows. This also was shuttered and barred, she saw. The house had been shut up tighter than a fortress. Even if the soldiers did arrive, they could not gain entry and offer assistance.

At one end of the long oak table sat Phillip. Facing him, Douglas was like a man carved of stone in the flickering light of the fire and the wall-torches which played across his features. Before him, within reach of his fingertips, the broadsword lay, hilt towards him. But before he could grasp it, a bullet would end his life, Sian thought, looking to each of the three sentries in turn. All held pistols aimed in his direction. Was it

Phillip's intention to shoot him down in cold blood? No, she decided, he would get no satisfaction from that.

Perched on the edge of a chair, tightly gripping Timothy's hand, sat Effie. The woman's face bore a smile as she stared at the tall Highlander. Her gaze switched to where Sian stood beside the hearth, Robert at her back, and her smile grew.

'Have you come to watch your lover die?' she asked. Timothy struggled in her grasp, and she roughly slapped him. 'Be still, you little brat! You are as expendable at the rest of them.'

'As you are,' Douglas drawled. How calm he sounded. Unafraid. Sian prayed she could contain her composure throughout, whatever was to come. 'You don't imagine you will be welcome here any longer? You are an embarrassment. Don't you believe me? Look at Blakeney's face. His eyes are not for you any longer, but for another. It's her he wants in his bed, and will have if I die. A real woman—a lady, not a slut! Perhaps he will give you to one of his men . . .'

'Or kill you as he did Angus,' Sian broke in, and Effie's eyes dilated as she looked across to the chair where Phillip lounged.

'You said you had sent him to Inverness on business. Dead? You have killed my brother?' she demanded, her voice quivering.

'He was a fool. And you are a whore. I have no time for either,' came the chilling reply. Douglas's eyes gleamed as she screamed out an oath and sprang to her feet, releasing her hold on the boy.

Timothy ran to Sian, buried his face against her skirt, crying, trembling. This was the second time he had been a witness to violence and bloodshed, she thought worriedly as she gathered him up in her arms. He would be lucky if it did not affect his mind.

'I hate them! I hate all of them,' he sobbed, and she held him tight, trying to soothe him in his anguish. 'I don't want to live here—I want to go back to France with you. Take me back, Sian. I want to live with you and . . .' Eyes brimming with tears peered back at the man standing beside the table. 'Him! He's nice to me. I hate my father . . . He doesn't love me, does he?'

'Hold your tongue, boy, and come here to me,' Phillip ordered, and at the sound of his voice, Timothy gave a wail and hid himself behind her.

'Take him away from here, Robert,' Sian ordered quietly. 'He must not see what is to happen.'

'Let him stay, to see me kill his champion,' Phillip thundered, climbing slowly to his feet. Douglas stepped back warily as he reached for the sword at his side. 'It will be a lesson he will never forget. Ten long years this man has waited to kill me . . . Tonight I shall give him peace.'

A faint movement came from the landing above them, a shadow creeping from the minstrels' gallery. Sian's eyes tried to pierce the gloom, but she could distinguish no clear figure. Had she been mistaken? Quickly she averted her gaze, lest Phillip became suspicious. She felt Timothy's fingers, gently but firmly prised from her skirt, and looked round to see Robert pushing him through the secret door into the arms of someone beyond. Safe! Out of reach of the father who would have taken his life! The knowledge still sickened her! If Douglas died here in this place, she thought, touching the cold blade in her pocket, she would kill Phillip. The consequences of the act did not enter into her head. She alone, with Douglas gone, would be left to avenge the deaths of his parents—of Roland—of him. She would fail none of them, she resolved.

'You will die slowly, MacGregor. Very, very slowly,' Phillip chuckled as he came from the table towards his opponent. 'When I have finished with you, she will share your grave. Is that not considerate of me?'

'You are deranged,' Sian breathed. His threat did not frighten her. She was prepared for death in her bid to keep the man she loved alive—and free.

'Quite mad,' Douglas said, grasping his broadsword. The effort to lift it, let alone use it to defend himself, would cost him dear. It was no weapon for a wounded man to wield, but if he was to save Sian and himself,

he could use no other. 'You English have never known
how to treat a woman. And you call us animals! Man,
we are saints compared to you. You laid your filthy
hands on my mother, do you remember? Now, for that,
and for my woman, I am going to kill you.'

'I hope she is worth dying for!' Phillip said, lunging
suddenly towards him, but Douglas was not to be taken
unawares. He sidestepped, the huge sword coming up
in a wide arc and narrowly missing his enemy's throat.
'A good try, but you are no match for me. Now, your
mother . . . It took me a week to break her.'

Phillip laughed as Douglas swore at him and attacked
wildly, driving him back across the floor towards the
stairs, the polished blade of the broadsword gleaming
in the torchlight. Phillip gave a howl of pain as it slashed
across his arm and wheeled away, thrusting the sentry
behind him into the path of the oncoming man whose
face was contorted with rage. The latter died without
being able to defend himself, so unexpected was the
treacherous move.

The staircase was undefended, Sian saw, and her
hopes mounted. Again a hint of a movement in the
gallery, any sound lost as a chair crashed to the ground,
swept aside by Douglas's determined onslaught. Blood
was pouring from the wound in Phillip's arm. So, too,
from the one in Douglas's shoulder. The weight of the
weapon he held was beginning to take its toll of his
limited strength. Phillip saw it, and renewed his own
attack. Douglas slipped and fell, rolled over with an
agility that made her gasp and came up on his feet again,
still holding his weapon. But she saw how grey his face
had become. How tightly his lips were clamped together
in pain and concentration. He was weakening fast . . .

She looked towards the stairs, risked a tentative step,
and saw the man at the window switch his attention
from the fight to menace her with his pistol. If she could
only distract him . . . A silent message passed between
her and Robert, who laid a warning hand on her arm.

'Wait,' he whispered. 'Jamie is above. I sent him to
Blakeney's room to fetch his duelling pistols. Do

nothing yet, mistress. We must use the small advantage he will give us well. I doubt if the poor lad could hit a barn-door, let alone a man, down here in such shadowy light.'

It was at that moment that Sian saw Effie moving surreptitiously away from the table where she had been standing and watching, saying nothing. Her hand was clenched against her breast as she stared at the two figures coming towards her. Phillip, his back towards her, was upon her before he realised her presence so close at hand. He cursed her, and swung an arm out to push her aside. She caught at it, screaming at him.

'You killed my brother! You swine! After everything he has done for you. He killed for you, as I have . . .'

'Shut your mouth, you stupid bitch, and get away from me.' A look of surprise turned to rage as she continued to hang on to his arm. Douglas fell back, afraid to use his sword for fear of striking her, but he hesitated for a moment only, remembering it was she who had administered the poison to Sian in Calais. She was as guilty as Phillip. Neither deserved to live . . .

'You won't have her. I won't let you!' Her hair became free of its combs and fell about her face and shoulders. No matter how Phillip struggled, she clung stubbornly to his arm, her nails raking at his cheeks. 'I killed her mother for you—and her brother! Doesn't that matter to you?'

Sian gave a low moan and sagged back against the wall. Her mother, too!

'You swore I would share everything with you once you were rich . . .' Effie was sobbing now.

'You shall have more than I promised you,' Phillip said in a strange tone, and she stopped her attack on him. Hope sprang to her eyes, and greed, as she considered the full extent of Sian's wealth. She died instantly as Phillip's sword entered her body. Contemptuously he flung her from him.

Douglas was caught off balance as Effie's lifeless form crashed backwards into him. As he twisted to be free of her, Phillip lunged at him, and Sian screamed as blood appeared from a fresh wound in his side.

'He cannot go on,' she breathed. 'He cannot! Robert, we must act.'

'Yes, mistress, now is the time,' came the quiet answer, so full of confidence that she turned and looked into the lined face in surprise. He motioned with a nod of his head to the figures on the stairs. She swayed unsteadily, caught his arm, and fought to control her reeling senses. Uniforms! Soldiers! English soldiers from Fort William! But how had they gained entrance? How long had they been upstairs, waiting, listening? Dear God, they had heard everything, she realised, sudden joy sweeping over her. There was no need for Douglas to kill Phillip.

An animal snarl broke from Phillip's lips as he, too, caught sight of the scarlet coats advancing down the stairs, fanning out to surround him and the reeling, bloody figure, barely able to stand, yet reeling forward for another attack. If he did not end it now? He saw his men throw down their weapons in surrender, and shouted curses at them for their cowardice. Phillip had never known loyalty for loyalty's sake. He paid men to work for him or frightened them into his service, rewarding them with blows and rudeness and often death. Sudden, violent death as had come to Angus Campbell; payment from a grateful master! And now, in this moment of his greatest need, he found himself alone—abandoned.

Something snapped inside his brain. The room spun. Douglas's face blurred and receded, then returned, staring at him with death in the steely eyes.

Douglas gave a groan as Phillip threw himself forward, sword and dirk raised for the kill. He stumbled back, warding off first one blow, then another, but without warning, blackness began to descend upon him. He could not lift his injured arm, and the pain in his side was agonising. He knew he was fast losing blood. Too fast . . . too much . . . A shot rang out as, with a supreme effort, he swung the broadsword high in the air, a bloodcurdling cry ripping from his lips. The Great

Hall rang and echoed with the MacGregor war-cry as he pitched forward, his weapon slipping from numb, useless fingers to lie beside Phillip's inert body. As his senses dimmed and began to fade, he saw the bullet-hole just above the right eye. What strange quirk of fate had deprived him of his revenge? The last thing he remembered was Sian throwing herself down at his side, cradling him against her breast, regardless of his blood soaking the stark whiteness of her blouse. Tears were streaming over her face, and her lips moved, but he could not hear what she was saying.

Faith, did she not find it funny too? An English soldier had avenged the death of his mother and father . . .

'When will he be ready to be moved? Tomorrow?'

Sian had just come out of the room where Douglas still lay unconscious. She stared into the face of the English captain, who had introduced himself as Steadman—John Steadman—and her eyes were cold and unfriendly. She felt like hitting him. His soldiers had rounded up the last of the men sympathetic to Phillip: another four had been found skulking in the village, and they had imprisoned them in one of the barns until they were taken to Fort William.

'Moved?' she echoed, and the young man was left in no doubt that she thought he was out of his mind. 'Douglas MacGregor cannot be moved, Captain, and even if he could, I would not let you or anyone take him from this house.'

Robert came out on to the landing behind her. He held one of Phillip's duelling pistols. On either side of her were other men, not so well armed, but with weapons of a kind. They had been prepared to fight and die on her behalf against Phillip. They had voiced their intention to back her against the soldiers in defence of their Laird.

'Young woman, you are not to use that name unless you yourself want to end up in prison . . .'

'You will not address me in that tone, Captain! I am not one of your doxies—or a frightened village woman who has been on the end of your justice once too often to retaliate,' Sian snapped, and the boyish face before her flushed uncomfortably. He had not long been promoted to his new rank, she suspected, and thought to browbeat everyone he met in order to impress others and instil confidence in himself. He would not do so with her. 'My father was Richard Blakeney, a brave officer who died at Culloden. My mother was the Comtesse de Saint-Rémy. I advise you not to provoke me too far. My mother was killed by that man below'—she stared down at the figure still lying in the Hall covered by a sheet—'my brother, too. He almost had me killed. Would have, in the near future, once he had raped me and satisfied the lust that has been eating at him for years. Douglas MacGregor,' she said the name with fierce pride, 'saved my life and that of my younger brother . . . and I love him. I shall protect him with my last breath, as will these people round me. Tread carefully, Captain. I will not allow you to take him from here, to hang like a common criminal. He set foot on these shores again only to ensure that I was not murdered by Phillip Blakeney, as his parents were when the English took this house and despoiled the women here, burned the village, killed and plundered like wild animals. I am ashamed to have the same blood in me. Scotland needs men like Douglas MacGregor—proud men, not afraid to fight for what they believe in . . . I will not let him die,' she repeated resolutely.

'Bravo, my dear young lady! Forgive me . . . Comtesse!' Below, in the Great Hall, a thin, angular-faced man with grey hair, solemnly clapped his approval of her words. She stared down at him in a shocked silence. Who was he? Where had he come from? She had been in a daze since one of the soldiers had killed Phillip. She had held fast to Douglas's hand as he was borne gently to her bedroom by some of the villagers. She brushed aside the soldiers who attempted to bar her path, and threatened those who followed with the dirk taken from her pocket until Captain Steadman had given orders to allow her to pass unmolested.

He had followed at a distance and stood in the doorway watching as she feverishly tore strips of sheet into
rough bandages and tried to stem the fast flow of blood
from Douglas's wounds. Seeing the extent of his injur-
ies, he had come forward and helped her, raising the
inert form of the man she loved so that she could
complete the task quickly and efficiently. Sian realised
she had not even thanked him for his kind gesture—
somehow the words would not come.

And now, with Douglas still unconscious, barely
breathing, this man dared to speak of moving him! It
would be to his death!

'Oh, God help me . . .' The captain looked decidedly
uncomfortable. 'Mr Murcheson, sir, forgive me. In all
the confusion, and with this woman . . . I forgot you
were outside. You should not have come in, sir. Please
return to the carriage and I shall join you in a few
minutes.'

'I sincerely advise you not to refer to the Comtesse
in those terms again. I think she is going to hit you,' the
man chuckled, not showing the least inclination to obey.
'I shall not wait outside, Captain. I am cold and wet. I
am sure the Comtesse could afford me a little of the
Highland hospitality which I have found so stimulating
these past few days, and find something warming to
take the chill out of these old bones. Do come down,
both of you. You are making my neck ache, craning it
at this awkward angle.' When Sian hesitated—not so
the young officer who was half-way down the stairs
before the man had finished speaking—he added, 'I
think you and I should have a talk. It may be to your
advantage.'

'I think I already have the advantage,' she said stiffly,
eyeing the men about her who were moving closer,
protectingly.

'Advantageous to the man you love, then. At least,
do not risk that pretty little neck before you hear me
out.'

'Who are you?'

'My name is Murcheson, Comtesse. I am a member

of His Majesty's Government. Only a very insignificant
member, I assure you, but I may be able to help you to
save that life that is so precious to you. Is it not worth
a moment of your time?'

'I would dance with the devil if it kept him alive,' Sian
returned. 'You may have your moment, Mr Murcheson.
Robert, find a bottle of the master's *usquebaugh*. Let us
show a minister of the Crown what Highland gentlemen
drink to keep out the cold. I'll warrant he'll not touch
French brandy again.'

Henry Murcheson resided at Ard Choille for three days,
much to the chagrin of the young officer, who headed
his escort back into the Lowlands and safety from the
Scottish rabble he had been expecting to fall on the party
and cut their throats throughout the whole hazardous
undertaking. Sian spent little time with him the first
day, as she waited in an agony of suspense for Douglas to
recover consciousness. When he did, it was an additional
blow that he did not know her. He was conscious for a
brief five minutes only.

Almost immediately he relapsed into a feverish state,
which worsened as the days passed. She rode with the
English minister through the village and showed him
the deplorable conditions in which Phillip's tenants had
lived. He made endless notes and asked many questions,
but said little to give her hope.

She had told him her story from the very beginning,
from the first day she set foot in the Highlands a week
after her mother remarried. Of her hopes for the people
who relied on Ard Choille for their livelihood, of the
dream that, some day, peace and tranquillity might
return to this beautiful place. That she would be allowed
to find it, to share it with the injured man tossing and
turning in her bed. With Robert's help—for he was
the only one of the household who could write—she
collected testimony after testimony to the wanton
cruelty and destruction that had been perpetrated after
the rebellion—and in the years that followed.

She unburdened her soul to a man who sat opposite

her, and spoke little as he listened to her revelations. When she had told everything, he said he would present the many testimonies and her petition that Douglas be allowed to remain at Ard Choille, his rightful home, to his minister-in-chief, Lord Chesterfield. He gave her no hope, only a faint flicker of light in the darkness, for he had listened and not denied her request to be heard outright. If one man listened, surely another might. Was it possible it could reach the ears of the King? Here was the opportunity to right a great wrong, she insisted. Return an exile to his home, where he would work for the rest of his days, caring and protecting those less fortunate than himself.

She described her plan for the village women to weave the famous Highland cloth to send abroad. If the idea appealed to him—or if he thought it ridiculous—he gave no sign. He was the most exasperating man she had ever encountered, she thought, dragging herself into bed in the early hours of the morning. Yet she would not give up hope . . . Douglas was to remain at Ard Choille. Murcheson had allowed her that in return for her given word that she would not permit him to leave, or lay his hands on a sword. She promised. She would have promised anything to keep him at her side! Yet, in the grey light of dawn, she wondered what Douglas's reaction would be? Somehow she knew he would not thank her for rendering him helpless in the face of his enemy!

The fever increased to danger point as she sat in a chair by his side, hour after hour, refusing to leave. And then, a week later, he opened his eyes on to the pale, drawn face of the woman who sat sewing in the fading light by the window. His restless movements and oaths as he struggled to sit up, and found himself too weak to do so, brought Sian to his side, restraining hands on his shoulders. His skin was cool to the touch, and she dropped on to the bed with a soft cry of relief.

'My sword, woman. Where is it? I'll not be taken without a weapon in my hands,' Douglas muttered, his gaze sweeping the room.

'The soldiers have gone, my love. Days ago—nearly
a week. You have been out of your head with fever.'
Of course, she realised, the last time he had had a
conscious thought, it was that he was surrounded by
English soldiers! She lightly touched his unshaven cheek
with fingers that trembled. 'You look like a Viking
warrior with a beard.'

'Then look to yourself when I am stronger,' came
the quick reply, and a brief flash of his old mockery
registered on the gaunt face. He had lost a great deal
of weight, she thought, drawing the sheets about his
shoulders. He tried to move again, winced, and swore
so violently that she drew back. 'Why? Why am I not
in some stinking prison cell?'

He ran a hand over his bearded chin and grimaced at
what he found there. Exploring fingers discovered that
his side and one shoulder were swathed in bandages.
He was stiff, and every muscle was taut. A week!
Suddenly it dawned on him what she had said. A week!
He caught her hand and held it fast for a moment,
before drawing it to his lips.

'Forgive me. I am out of my head for a week, and
the first thing I do is bite your head off. Come here, let
me show you how glad I am to see your face.'

'No,' Sian replied firmly, and he stared at her in
surprise. 'I have not spent sleepless nights watching over
you to have you open those wounds with—with such
foolishness. You are far from well, Douglas. You have
to rest.'

'Rest, be damned,' he cried. 'I want to kiss you,
woman! I need to kiss you, don't you understand that?
To tell me this is real.'

Against her will, Sian allowed him to draw her down
and kiss her on the mouth. It was a kiss more eloquent
than a thousand flowery adjectives, and she completely
forgot her determination not to allow him to rouse her.

'If you do not behave yourself, I will have someone
else sit with you,' she threatened. 'Oh, Douglas—my
love! I thought I would lose you.'

'You may still,' Douglas returned, averting his gaze

from the happiness in her eyes. 'I am due for the hangman's noose, remember? Accept it now. It will make the parting less difficult.'

She opened her mouth to tell him of Mr Murcheson, but decided against it. Her own hopes were rising daily. Three weeks, she had been told. Four, perhaps, before she heard if anyone else would even listen to her petitions. After that, time was on their side. So long as Douglas remained at Ard Choille and behaved himself, no soldiers would show their faces to aggravate an already volatile situation.

'I have given my word you will not leave here, or take up arms again while in this house,' she said quietly. She could tell him that much, at least.

'You took too much upon yourself, woman,' he said harshly, and she watched the lean, brown hands bunch into tight fists upon the coverlet.

'It is because I am your woman that I thought I had the right to do what was best for my man. I am sorry if you do not agree. You can leave here as soon as you feel strong enough. You will be hunted down in the heather, as your ancestors were before you. You will die with a sword in your hand, cursing the English. Do you really want to waste your life? Is your hatred so deep, still, that you would abandon me and all that we have here? Perhaps it is only for a short while, but then there was a time when I did not expect you to remain with me more than a day—a few hours! I was prepared to let you go then, my wild Viking, as I am now. If you so desire it.' Stiffly she rose to her feet and turned towards the door, tears blinding her vision.

'Come back, Sian. Ach! I'm a brute,' Douglas exclaimed, and she looked back at him, smiling through a mist of tears.

'You are . . . But even brutes must eat. I shall bring you something.'

'You will come back?' Once it had been she who had been so afraid he would disappear from her life. Now . . . He sank on to the pillows, his cheeks chalk-white. He was as weak as a kitten and totally in her power—

as she had once been in his. Fate always had a way of evening the score!

'Yes. And I shall stay if you wish,' Sian answered softly. In this time, when every moment was so precious, she would deny him nothing!

In a few short days, Sian felt as if she were experiencing a whole lifetime. Every moment she could spare—and now she was mistress of Ard Choille she came to realise the enormity of what she had undertaken, with or without Douglas at her side—she spent with him. His return to health took her aback. He refused to stay in his bed once he knew the soldiers were not lingering below. He told her stories of his childhood and of the bloody war that had sent him across the Channel to wander as a mercenary in strange lands, without hope of ever being able to return to his beloved Scotland. After the expulsion of Charles Stuart from France, he went to Spain and then Italy, returning to France after several years to offer his sword again to the highest bidder. Embittered, hardened beyond recognition, vengeful still, he had been on his way to the estates of the Duc de Bouillon when he had discovered a wrecked coach and three dead men—and Sian.

And so it had begun, Sian thought, watching the grim features slowly soften as she smiled at him and he allowed painful memories to recede into the depths of his mind. Far away, in exile in France, they had come together. It would end here—one way or the other—in the land he loved.

The soldiers came without warning. She was in the library, going over the estate ledgers, when Robert, grave-faced, came in to tell her that Murcheson had returned—and with him an escort of soldiers. They had come to take him away, she thought, springing to her feet. She had no time to warn him—to return the broadsword she had hidden beneath his bed. Despite her promise, she would never have allowed him to be taken without a fight!

Six long weeks of waiting were at an end. But how
would they end? When she emerged from the room
some fifteen minutes later, the servants clustered
anxiously in the Hall turned and looked at one another
in dismay. As white as a ghost—and trembling. All
these weeks she had kept their spirits high with her
cheerful manner—yet now . . .

From the landing above them, Douglas watched them
emerge. He was fully dressed, a dirk beneath the ruffles
of his sleeve. As he started slowly down the stairs, two
uniformed soldiers went to meet him, and Sian wheeled
about with a cry.

'He is unarmed!' The sudden gleam that showed in
his eyes told her otherwise, but she did not retract the
statement. Whatever happened now, it was up to him—
and him alone. She could do no more. Thank goodness
Timothy had gone riding with one of the young grooms.
As long as she lived, she would not allow him to witness
more violence. His nightmares were terrible, and only
the arrival of the red colt purchased from Inverness had
shaken him from an attitude which had begun to worry
her to distraction. After days, weeks, of sitting alone in
his room, refusing to participate in any games, refusing
to set foot outside, even when his 'champion' offered
to walk with him, the sight of the tiny pony with a
gleaming red coat had succeeded in rousing him. Within
an hour, he was riding it about the courtyard. The
following day he took it out on the moor, and had done
so every day since.

'Will you not come down and join us, Mr Mac-
Gregor?' Mr Murcheson asked, turning to gaze at the
tall man descending towards them. Sian caught her
breath. The MacGregor name was proscribed, yet he
used it without hesitation. She saw that it took Douglas
aback. He came to a halt. 'Your good lady here has
been most eloquent on your behalf . . . I think we
should talk.'

'Man, you make her sound like an old spinster.'
Suddenly Douglas gave a dry chuckle, and took another
step. His eyes swept the Great Hall, as if seeking an

avenue of escape. There was none, he saw. Uniforms
guarded the entrance; through the windows he could
see more beside their horses. Two waited for him at the
bottom of the stairs. His eyes met and held Sian's, the
devil's laughter in them—and an acceptance of his fate,
she realised. Only she knew the tumult of emotions
coursing through him. The desire to run—the desire to
stay . . . 'That she is not!'

She felt her cheeks flame; saw Henry Murcheson
smile slightly.

'I shall leave the two of you alone.' Douglas gave her
a quizzical look, but she pretended not to see it and
turned quickly away. As the two men went into the
library and the door closed behind them, her footsteps
quickened in the direction of the front door. No one
attempted to detain her as she left the house and made
her way down the narrow path that led from the house
to the edge of the small loch she could see from her
windows.

She shivered in the keen, frosty air, drawing her shawl
round her shoulders. If Douglas rejected the terms
offered to him . . . she did not want to consider that he
might. How grey the sky looked. Perhaps it would snow
later. Tonight the fires would be built high, scented with
dried rosemary. She would send a sheep down to the
village from Douglas. They would eat as she did from
now on. If life improved for her, so would it for them.

Ard Choille! High Wood! She could see for miles
from this vantage-point. How long should she linger?
A few minutes—half an hour? She sat by the loch and
stared into the green-grey depths, her head in her hands.
If she lost him, she would die. No, she would go on—
to do all the things he would have done. But—oh! The
loneliness after his love . . .

The surface of the water rippled, and then her image
vanished as another stone bounced across the loch in
front of her. She choked back a cry as she sprang to her
feet, her eyes scanning the trees. No one, yet . . . from
out of the denseness came a low familiar refrain that set
her heart racing. Douglas stepped into view, a heavy

jacket thrown about his shoulders. He stood looking at her, hands on his hips. He demanded in a grim tone,

'Were you not expecting to see me, woman?'

'I—you . . .' she could find no words. She sank on to the stone seat, her hands against her mouth.

He came striding over the hard brown earth to snatch her up in his arms, tilt back her head to stare down into her white face with steely eyes.

'The things some women will do to get a man to marry them!' he said. 'I am ordered to marry you within the week, do you know that?'

He gave her no chance to answer, for his mouth sought hers, taking it by storm. Sian sagged weakly in his arms, too frightened to accept that her wildest hopes had been realised. Her fingers touched his sleeve, and felt the hardness of the dirk still there.

'It is only a small knife,' Douglas mocked. 'I'll not go naked, even for you. Woman—woman, what am I to do with you? No one has ever cared enough for me to do what you have done. I shall have to marry you, won't I, and repay you?'

'No,' she gasped, trying to pull free of him. 'I don't want you like that! What I did was out of love . . . I told him I would go away if—if you hated me for it . . . I will . . . I won't have you stay out of pity?'

'Then I would have to follow you again!' Douglas held her close against him, and she felt a warmth begin to steal through her body as he caressed her cheek, her throat, the uplifted breast pressed against his chest. She wanted to tell him to stop and let her know what had been said, but his kisses wiped all thought, save the pleasure she gained from his touch, from her mind for a long while.

Besides the many testimonies she had given Mr Murcheson, the sworn statements from the villagers and her own witnessed account of Phillip's plan to inherit the Saint-Rémy wealth, she had promised to invest half of her fortune in the restoration of Ard Choille to its former glory and, in doing so, bring a new prosperity to the villagers. She had offered everything she thought might be an inducement for the English Government to grant clemency to the man she loved. A pardon, so that he could live in peace. And forget the past!

She knew it would mean his taking an oath of allegiance to King George, and that worried her more than anything. Also a promise never to take up arms again against his King. He, who had sworn never to be without his broadsword! Even now, she could feel the hardness of a dirk pressing into her breast.

'Douglas, please, tell me . . . I cannot bear it,' she pleaded, and he lifted his head with a slow smile.

'He has had his oath. I have promised to be good. Though I'll not live on your money.'

'If we are to be married, there is little you can do about it, and if you will not spend it making life better not only for us, but for the wonderful people who have stood beside you in this, then I will,' she flung back stubbornly, and he laughed and kissed her again with a rough passion that betrayed to her the depths of his emotions.

'Woman! The Tarot was right. One day I will take you to have your—no, our—fortunes told again by Grand-mère . . . and we shall stay at the château and it will be a happy place again.'

He lost himself in the exploration of her mouth, her body. Two figures merged into one on the bare landscape . . . It took Sian some while to realise they were no longer alone. Only feet away, astride his new pony, Timothy sat watching them, a grinning stable-lad beside him.

'We must go back and bid farewell to our guest,' Douglas murmured, his eyes brimming with laughter at her scarlet cheeks. 'Then, woman, you and I have plans to make . . .'

'Are you leaving? I saw more soldiers.' Timothy's mouth drooped in a gesture of disappointment that Sian had become accustomed to over the past weeks. She shook her head, too overcome with emotion to speak, as Douglas tucked her arm beneath his, and took the reins of the colt in one hand and turned it about.

'Nay, lad, I'm staying. I have promised the soldiers I
will behave myself from now on. It will be a hard
promise to keep . . . but I'll manage it somehow, if you
help me.'

The boy's mouth dropped even more. These days
Sian found it difficult to determine what was in his mind.
His eyes were angry.

'Will you not have your sword to fight with? How will
you defend me?' he demanded in a small, petulant
voice, and Douglas grinned up at him and patted one
thin leg.

'I have no need to fight any more. I have come home.'
He lifted his head for a moment, staring out over the
thick forest below. As if listening. 'Can you not hear
them? My ancestors are welcoming me home, too. Now
they can rest in peace . . .'

'What was that tune you were whistling? Will you
teach me?' Timothy had not spoken of his father since
that day. Sian, when she thought the time was right,
had told him simply that Phillip had died like a brave
soldier, and that his son should be proud of him. Looking at him as he leaned towards Douglas, intent on his
every word, she wondered if his 'champion' might not
soon take the place of the father who sought only to
use him for his own aims. She hoped so.

'Where to begin,' Douglas murmured. 'Let's see,
now. The tune is a lament of my clan, the MacGregors.
We are called "Children of the Mist"—we come and
go as elusively, as stealthily as the mists that come down
about the mountains on a cold winter's evening . . .' He
looked up into Sian's shining eyes, drew her closer as
they started up the path towards the house. 'I have
come home,' he said again in a quiet tone meant only
for her ears, and bent to kiss her quivering lips—while
Timothy waited impatiently for his story to
continue . . .